Praise for

THIRTEEN DOORWAYS,
WOLVES BEHIND THEM ALL

———

National Book Award Finalist

Amazon Best Young Adult Books

BookPage Best Young Adult Books

New York Times Best Children's Books

NPR Best Books

SLJ Best Young Adult Books

Shelf Awareness Best Children's & Teen Books

Today Show Best Kids' Books

"Haunting and hopeful in equal measure."
—*New York Times Book Review*

"Ruby's delicate, powerful storytelling reveals profound,
bewitching truths about the vast, sometimes cruel, sometimes
loving, possibilities of human nature. Subtle and stunning."
—ALA *Booklist* (starred review)

"A beautiful and lyrical read that pushes against the
boundaries of what we often think a young adult novel can
contain."—*BookPage*

"A layered, empathetic examination of the ghosts inside all
girls' lives, full of historical realism and timeless feeling."
—*Kirkus Reviews*

Praise for

Bone Gap

—⊶⊷—

Michael L. Printz Medal Winner
National Book Award Finalist
ALA Best Fiction for Young Adults
ALA *Booklist* Editor's Choice
SLJ Best Books of the Year
Publishers Weekly Best Books of the Year

"Ruby's novel deserves to be read and reread.
It is powerful, beautiful, extraordinary."—*SLJ*

"Ruby raises incisive questions about feminine beauty, identity,
and power in a story full of subtle magic that is not compelled
to provide concrete explanations. A haunting and inventive
work that subverts expectations at every turn."
—*Publishers Weekly* (starred review)

"Ruby weaves powerful themes throughout her stunning
novel: beauty as both a gift and a burden; the difference
between love and possession; the tensions between what lies
on the surface and what moves beneath; the rumbling threat
of sexual violence; the brutal reality of small-town cruelties.
Wonder, beauty, imperfection, cruelty, love, and pain are all
inextricably linked but bewitchingly so."
—ALA *Booklist* (starred review)

—⊶⊷—

THIRTEEN DOORWAYS,
WOLVES BEHIND THEM ALL

THIRTEEN DOORWAYS,

WOLVES BEHIND THEM ALL

LAURA RUBY

Balzer + Bray
An Imprint of HarperCollins *Publishers*

Balzer + Bray is an imprint of HarperCollins Publishers.

Thirteen Doorways, Wolves Behind Them All
Copyright © 2019 by Laura Ruby

ISBN 978-0-06-231765-0

Typography by Molly Fehr
21 22 23 24 25   PC/LSCH   10 9 8 7 6 5 4 3 2 1
❖
First paperback edition, 2021

For the original Frankie,

FRANCES PONZO METRO
1927–2018

"The golden moments in the stream of life rush past us and we see nothing but sand; the angels come to visit us, and we only know them when they are gone."
—George Eliot, *Janet's Repentance*

"Sweet Dreams Though the Guns Are Booming."
—Erich Maria Remarque, *All Quiet on the Western Front*

CONTENTS

Spring, 1946 — The Sleep of the Dead
1

1941 — THE GUARDIANS

Our Lady of Perpetual Sorrow
7

Angels of Blood and Stone
22

On the Coast of the Moon
31

Haunts of the Haunt
42

Drowning
56

The Crow Prince
57

1942 — FAIRY TALES

Weak Hearts
73

Mermaids of Chicago
84

What Didn't Burn in the Fire
99

Fairy Tales
111

What Frankie Didn't Confess
117

Golden Arm
130

No and Yes
143

1943 — WOLVES

The Song of Solomon
157

The Three Spindles
170

Light, More Light
185

Little Red Riding Hood
195

What Are You Doing, What Have You Done?
204

Three Letters
208

1944 — JEZEBELS

The Boys of War
221

Bambi
232

Bombardment
241

For I Have Sinned
253

The Jezebel
266

The Churning Furnace
275

The Dragon King
289

The Magic Words
298

Tooth and Claw
306

1945 — DOORWAYS

The Queen in the Tower
309

Hunger
324

Bless Me
325

Mercy
333

No Memories but One
345

Witness
350

Doorways
351

Author's Note
359

Acknowledgments
363

THIRTEEN DOORWAYS,
WOLVES BEHIND THEM ALL

THE SLEEP OF THE DEAD

LISTEN:

The first time they took Frankie to the orphanage, she couldn't speak English. Only Italian. "Voglio mio padre! Voglio mio padre!" That's what she said, over and over and over.

At least, that's what the nuns told her she said. She couldn't remember any of it.

The second time they took her to the orphanage, the last time, she didn't say anything at all. Not one word. For months.

She didn't remember that either.

What she did remember: her father's shoe shop on Irving Park Road. The scent of calfskin and polish. The cramped apartment behind the shop. The metal tub sitting in the middle of the kitchen. Cold bathwater wrinkling her little toes. The rough scrape of Aunt Marion's brush on her back.

And then the shot from her parents' bedroom—so sharp, so loud, so wrong. The thud of Aunt Marion's footsteps as she ran from the kitchen. The screams. So much screaming.

Frankie remembered climbing from the tub, falling to the floor, hitting her elbow so hard the bones sang all the way up to her skull. Crawling, hot tears on her face. Pushing at the bedroom door to see the body slumped on the bed, smoke and copper in the air. Crossing the threshold from one world to another.

Most of all, she remembered the door itself. The rusted hinges. The gouges and nicks. The pencil smell of the wood, and then all the other smells that had seeped into it—leather, garlic, salt, blood. How Aunt Marion turned, scooped her up, and slammed that door behind them.

Frankie wouldn't always let herself remember these things. Most of the time, she didn't think about them at all. Yet she had her quiet days, her pensive ones, those days when she dug through her memories, trying to find the truth at the bottom of them. As if the truth were a jewel you could unearth and hold in your hand, as if the truth wasn't more like something you'd find under a rock, gray and faceless and squirming away from the light.

But Frankie hadn't done any kind of digging on this particular night in the spring of 1946, unless you counted picking through a garbage pail to find a dime tip she'd accidentally tossed away with a customer's half-eaten sandwich. After working a double shift, she'd gotten home at midnight and collapsed fully clothed onto her bed, not even bothering to take off a mustard-stained apron that stank of onions. And though the air wafting through the cracked window held the sweet promise of spring, though all her wars were over, though she should have felt safe, finally safe, after all this time, Frankie woke up

2

hours later in a prickling sweat, tangled and feverish, certain her mother had been whispering in her ear.

She sat up, clutching at her throat. "Mama?" she said. But her room was still and silent, the moon cutting a wide silver swath out of the dark. Her mother wasn't there. Would never be there. It was impossible. Frankie remembered that now, just when she didn't want to.

Then she called again. Not to her mother, but to someone else. Someone she'd only glimpsed once, another person she wouldn't allow herself to think about.

"Hello? Is that . . . you?"

No answer.

Frankie smiled a grim little smile at her own foolishness, rubbed her eyes to get the sting out. With the moonlight slicing through the room, she could see everything inside it, though there wasn't much to see. A chair with a pile of dresses draped over the back, a bureau with a hot plate and a dusty trumpet, two twin beds and a nightstand between, a seashell the size and shape of a child's ear resting in an ashtray on top. Frankie's younger sister, Toni, was a motionless lump in the other bed; Toni hadn't heard Frankie come in or cry out, which wasn't surprising. The nuns used to say that she and Toni both slept like the dead. Once, Frankie had believed that only people whose hearts were true could sleep so soundly, but that was a long time ago.

The wind stiffened outside, whistling through the leaky window, blasting Frankie out of bed. She stood just long enough to strip off her apron and uniform. She was being silly and sappy and she couldn't afford it. Didn't she have more than sixteen dollars to add to the wad tucked under her mattress? Hadn't she made the rent for seven months straight, all on her own? She was just nineteen, but she'd weathered worse nights, far more pained and feverish than this. The silver swath of moonlight was beautiful, beautiful, she told herself, as she yanked a nightgown over her head. The whole damned room was beautiful because it was *her* room, hers and her sister's. That was something she could hold on to, even when so much else had been lost.

The moonlight caught in the cup of abalone on the nightstand, winking pink and blue, drawing her attention. Frankie traced the pearlescent edge of the shell with her finger. This delicate shell had come so far, had come through so much, and still wasn't broken.

Neither was she.

Frankie punched the pillow as if her restlessness were all its fault and fell back onto the bed, fell asleep. The shadows lengthened, shifted, creeping over the floors, the furniture. Mice scratched in the walls. A fox cried in the distance, or maybe it was a wolf. In and out, the sisters breathed in unison, agreeing for once. And yet the papery whispers wafted through Frankie's dreams. Sono qui. Io sono qui per te, Francesca. *I am here. I am here for you.*

Of course, it wasn't her mother's voice she heard. It was mine. Because the dead never sleep, you see.

We have so many other things to do.

4

1941
THE GUARDIANS

OUR LADY OF PERPETUAL SORROW

A WASH OF SLEET FELL on the buildings of the Guardian Angels Orphanage, blurring their outlines, making the place look hazy and gaslit, like the cover of some cheap gothic novel: *A Dram of Poison. Secrets Can't Be Kept.* I passed by the larger building that housed the older children and went right for the baby house, the way I always did. In the baby house, the cribs were lined up in tidy rows, like gravestones. Maybe that's why I was so drawn to them, little cradles of life. The babies—chubby baby faces peeking out from the blankets, new baby eyes screwed up tight—slept like kittens, all shivers and fits. They cycled their legs and gnawed on their fists as if their hands had been smeared in honey. I visited each crib in turn. Hello, you baby, I said. Good morning, cupcake! Like everyone else, sometimes they heard me, sometimes they didn't. When they heard me, their tiny bud lips opened and closed and opened again, as if to tell me how hungry they were. And though I didn't get hungry in the way they did, I knew hunger. I knew how it hurt. Soon, I told them. Soon the nuns will come, and they will feed you, and you won't be hungry anymore.

7

Perhaps it was mean to lie. But they were only babies. They would discover the churning furnace of this world soon enough.

After I made the rounds of the baby house, I moved on to the other cottages, which was what the sisters called the dormitories where the children slept. They kept the boys and girls separate, so I visited the girls. The six-year-olds, sweaty hair pasted to sticky foreheads, the ten-year-olds, knotted up in their sheets like third-rate Houdinis, then the girls in their teens, heads studded with rag curlers, faces slack with dreams. I talked to them too, I told them that their hair was going to look lovely once they'd brushed it out, that one day, sooner than they could ever believe possible, someone would run their fingers through that hair and they'd wish it would never stop, never stop, don't stop. As with the babies, sometimes they heard me, but mostly they didn't. Every once in a while, a girl would wake up and stare right at me and I would think just for a second that she saw me, that I was *there*, solid and real as anyone. Then the girl's eyes would flutter, she would frown in confusion. Maybe she'd rub her temples or laugh at herself. Later, she would tell the other girls that she heard somebody muttering during the night in a voice that hissed and clicked like a radiator.

I was thrilled when they heard me. I would talk to that same girl the next night, and the next. I would pluck at her sheets, run a chill finger down her arm, poke at her feet. The nuns would want to know why she kept kicking off her covers, it was cold, did she want to get sick? And the girl would swear she wasn't kicking anything anywhere, that somebody wouldn't stop mumbling and poking, that the place was haunted. The nuns would cluck their tongues and proclaim that there were no ghosts but the Holy Ghost, only stories made up to scare harebrained children.

If anyone in the orphanage had woken up right then and seen what was huddled in the corner of the cottage, they'd have offered up a whole different sort of prayer, a back-of-the-hand-pressed-to-the-lips sort—*Sweet Mary, Mother of . . .*

It was a girl, like me, one I hadn't seen before, slumped against the wall, rocking and moaning, hair ropy with blood. Who knew where she came from? Maybe she'd wandered in from the streets outside. Maybe she'd wandered up from the catacombs beneath the orphanage, a place even I was scared to go. I would have asked her, but most of us were stuck in our last horrible moments, unable to communicate anything but our pain or our fear, and even the ones who could speak gave vague, cryptic answers that satisfied no one, themselves least of all. This one keened at nobody in particular, left cheek and eye socket shattered, jaw unhinged and hanging at a disconcerting angle, making it seem as if she were about to swallow something very large and awkward. Like a car.

I'd seen worse.

I turned my attention back to the living, who were starting to climb from their beds one by one. None of them heard the moaning from the corner, none of them noticed the rocking or unhinging. Certainly not Frankie, who was still fast asleep—not the sleep of the dead as much as the sleep of the half starved, half loved. As the sky outside brightened, as the other girls yawned and stretched, I stood at the end of Frankie's bed, the sixth one in the row by the door, and waited.

The door creaked open, and Sister George stalked in. Sister wouldn't wait a minute past five, Sister never did. She kicked over the mattress, taking Frankie right with it.

Frankie sat there in a puddle of blankets, sleepy gaze sharpening to a glare.

That was new. That glare.

Sister took two steps toward Frankie, her black habit making her look like a vampire out of a horror picture. One of the other sisters would have made a joke: "Oh, Frankie! Did I wake you?" Or "So nice of you to join us this beautiful morning!" Or "Jesus says rise and shine!" But not Sister George. Sister George never joked, Sister George never smiled.

The order of nuns that ran the orphanage was called the Sisters of Our Lady of Perpetual Sorrow, but some sisters served Our Lady of Perpetual Sorrow, and others simply caused perpetual sorrow for everyone else.

Sister growled, "Did you have something you wanted to say, Francesca?"

Frankie's eyes spoke for her—the glare hot, so hot. But Frankie shook her head.

"I thought not." Sister George marched away, looking for the next sleeping girl to dump from her bed. Sister would never admit it, not even in confession, but kicking over mattresses before Sunday mass was the most fun she'd ever had.

Frankie shoved the mattress back onto its frame, the fire in her gaze cooling a bit. At least Sister was in one of her good moods. Her bad ones were rather spectacular. Frankie tugged at her hair, a knuckle's worth of fuzz around her head.

"Pulling at it ain't gonna make it grow back any faster," Stella Zaffaro said from the next bed over.

Frankie didn't even glance at Stella. "Shut it, chooch."

"*Shut it, chooch,*" Stella mimicked. Stella flipped her own hair, shiny and blond as any movie star's. Stella never let the other girls forget that hair, never let them forget that her name meant "star" in Italian. Frankie liked her own dark hair just fine—at least, when she'd had some—and didn't care what Stella's name meant in Italian. Stella wouldn't know a meatball from a baseball.

As soon as Frankie thought the word "meatball," her mouth started to water. Meatballs were what Sundays were for. Visiting Sundays, anyway. You might think that the orphans at Guardian Angels had no parents, no family at all, but that wasn't always true. More than a decade after the stock market crash of 1929, too many people were still reeling—out of work, homeless. Rather than watching their children go hungry, they gave the kids over to the care of the nuns. A few beatings and a whole lot of church seemed a small price to pay for food and shelter—at least, that was what the parents told themselves. Some of these parents would visit their "half orphans" every other Sunday. Frankie's father never missed one. And the things he brought made Frankie feel rich, feel like a daughter, at least for a few hours. Meatball sandwiches, with thick red tomato sauce soaking the bread. Spaghetti slippery with butter, just as good cold as it was hot. Shiny, crunchy apples. Sometimes he brought presents, like a pair of shoes he'd just made, the leather so clean and new that it didn't seem right to wrap your feet in it—too special to touch the ground. And sometimes her father filled his pockets with rock candy or even a few wrapped chocolates. He would hide them behind his back so that Frankie, her sister, Toni, and her older brother, Vito, would fight over them, but only Toni was young enough for that. Frankie could almost taste the chocolate melting on her tongue.

I could almost taste it.

"What are you grinning about?" Stella said to Frankie.

"Are you still here? I thought you would have run off to Hollywood by now." Frankie elbowed past her and followed the other girls to the washroom.

The washroom was a whole lot of room to wash, with six flush toilets, eight sinks, showers, a tub no one used, and cubbies for their "private belongings." Funny, because none of them had many belongings and nothing was private. But they should have been grateful to have the bathrooms because there were still people with outdoor privies. Frankie liked the indoor plumbing, but she didn't like having to clean it. Her knees were always sore where the little bits of dirt cut into the skin when they scrubbed the floor, and her hands were raw and cracked because of the strong brown soap they used.

Once Frankie had begged her father to bring some hand

cream on visiting day and he had, the fancy sort that smelled like roses and came in a heavy jar. The whole cottage teased her, said she was putting on airs, acting as if she was one of the swells. "Aw, look at Frankie," they said. "Where are your silk stockings, Frankie? Where's your gown?" Stella had the most to say. So Frankie sneaked the hand cream to supper and put a fat white ball of it on top of some cake. Told Stella that her father had brought it to her. Stella was so hungry that she ate two huge bites before she realized what Frankie had done.

I'd been coming to the orphanage for as long as I could remember, but when I saw Frankie scoop that hand cream on top of that cake and offer it to Stella, I started watching Frankie, really watching her. I liked to think that what she did, that trick—not humiliating enough to be truly cruel, but just cruel enough to be funny—was something that I would have done when I was still real enough to fight, a little harmless rebellion.

But, as my mother had often reminded me, I only looked harmless. That's the problem with girls, she said. They trick you every time.

At that moment, Frankie *was* harmless. She wasn't concerned about Stella's name or her blond hair. She wasn't thinking about her own hair, either, or the fact that her tan skin made some of the nuns mutter about her mother's blood, or why nobody warned her to stay out of the sun the way they did Stella. She wasn't even thinking about the orphanage, about how so many people thought it was so sad and so terrible to live here, while Frankie understood that though things could be better, they could also be worse.

Instead, Frankie jostled with the other girls at the sink, trying to get a little room to splash water on her face. She toweled off, wondering what her father was going to say this afternoon. He had something important to tell Frankie and her brother and sister, the nuns had informed her. Something that could change their lives. Frankie doubted it. Along with his flair for meatballs, Frankie's father had a flair for drama. He'd once announced a move to a new apartment as if he were taking up residence in a French castle.

(What he had not needed to announce: that the new apartment had had no room for his children. That they shouldn't ask if it did.)

Frankie didn't expect much from her father; in her experience, fathers weren't particularly reliable. All Frankie could hope was that her father wouldn't bring what's-her-name with him again. Visiting Sundays weren't the same when *she* came along. When she showed up, her father never had shoes, he never had chocolate. She made him cheap. She turned him into a whole different man.

Frankie brushed her teeth hard enough to hurt. Who wanted to think about her? Nobody. Not even her own kids probably, who were here at the orphanage too, somewhere in the other cottages. Frankie didn't know their names, she didn't know what they looked like, and she hoped she never would.

"Snickers," hissed the girls in the hall. And then, all through the cottage, the girls passed it down the line: "Snickers, snick-ers, snickers." *Nuns coming back, shut it, move it.*

Frankie pulled on her Sunday dress and her coat just in time for Sister George to wave them out the door. The cot-tage wasn't really a cottage, just a big room that opened out onto a bigger corridor. The girls from other cottages marched in line down the hall, their footsteps echoing so loudly that it was almost like there were more girls marching on the ceiling above. There were boys at the orphanage too, but their cottages were in another building. They'd see one another across the aisle in church. Shorn as a sheep, Frankie would have been hap-pier not to see any boys, unless it was her older brother, Vito. She barely saw him as it was. Even brothers and sisters were separate at the orphanage.

Up at the front of the line, Sister George opened the door to the outside. The girls kept their heads down and their traps shut as they stepped outside and trudged toward the church. It was sleeting hard, and the girls tried to cover their hair. For a minute, Frankie was happy she didn't have any. And then she saw the boys walking toward the church too, a few of them laughing and pointing at her, and was sorry again. Frankie was fourteen in October of 1941, which might sound young to some, but wasn't, not for a nation on the cusp of another war, not for an orphan, not for Frankie. She was just three years younger than I was. Am. Was. A—

Anyway, it was no fun having boys laugh at you for some-thing you couldn't help, laugh at you for something that had been done to you. Especially if none of the boys were your brother and some of the boys were filled out just enough to be called handsome.

They reached the church and filed inside, sitting in their regular pews. The whole orphanage wasn't there yet, only the cottages with Sunday confession day. One at a time, they marched into the confessional. Most of the orphans were out almost as fast as they went in, mumbling Hail Marys and Our Fathers to repent for whatever sins of deed or thought. A few kids took longer.

Poor Father, Frankie thought. She hoped he'd had his coffee this morning.

Frankie and the other girls hadn't had anything. They wouldn't have breakfast till after morning mass, and that meant another hour and a half at least. Frankie clamped a hand over her rumbling stomach as she walked to the confessional. She sat in the booth and pulled the curtain closed behind her.

"Bless me, Father, for I have sinned. It's been a week since my last confession."

She couldn't see him very well through the mesh, but she could hear the rustling of the pages in his Bible. Father Paul said, "How blessed is anyone who rejects the advice of the wicked and does not take a stand in the path that sinners tread, nor a seat in company with cynics." Frankie didn't know what a cynic was, but it didn't sound so bad in Father's Irish accent.

He said, "Do you have something to confess?"

Frankie's tongue was salty with hunger. She wanted to turn the question around—"Do *you* have anything to confess,

Father?" But she was too obedient for that, and also too jaded. She thought about telling him about taking the Lord's name in vain or thinking vicious things about her younger sister. Things he expected to hear. Instead she said, "Sister George has a face like the Mummy. Only not as cute."

From my perch on the ceiling, I smiled. Frankie winced. First because she thought it was a childish thing, a sinful thing to say out loud. Second because she'd probably get about a thousand Hail Marys.

But Father Paul didn't say anything about any Hail Marys. He started laughing, a barking laugh that sounded a lot like a cough.

Frankie leaned closer to the screen. "Are you okay, Father?"

"Just a tickle in my throat. You were saying?"

"She dumped me out of my bed this morning. She's always dumping me out of my bed." Frankie tugged at her hair and then stopped when she realized she was doing it.

"Was it time to get up?" asked Father.

"Well," Frankie said.

"There you go. Do you think you're showing Christlike respect for Sister George by calling her, uh, what was it?"

"The Mummy. Only not as—"

"Cute," he said. "I think I've got it now." More coughing. "And are you truly sorry?"

Frankie didn't know if she was. Maybe she was. Maybe if she didn't *say* bad things about Sister, Sister wouldn't *do* bad things to her. It wasn't true, but who could blame her for thinking this way? She had no idea that Sister George disliked Father simply because he was from Ireland. Frankie had no idea that too many people believed you could be from a right place or a wrong one.

The orphanage was German Catholic, and Sister George was more German than German. In Frankie's language class, they'd learned that the German word for "squirrel" could be literally translated as "oak croissant."

That was what Sister's face looked like. A croissant.

"Yes," Frankie was saying, "I'm truly sorry."

"Well, then. Anything else?"

"I've been thinking mean thoughts about *her*, too."

"Her?" said Father Paul. "Who's her?"

Frankie blushed and was glad for the screen. "My father's . . . his . . . friend."

Frankie didn't have to explain. There might be nine hundred orphans at Guardian Angels, but Father Paul seemed to know the lives of every single one of them. "What kinds of thoughts?"

"I want her to move to the North Pole. Or the South Pole. Whichever's colder. And where there are bears. Starving ones. With big teeth."

Father cleared his throat. "She might be your stepmother one day. Some young ladies would be grateful to have a stepmother who cares about them."

"She hates me worse than Sister George."

"I'm sure that's not true," he said. "From what I hear, she and your dad visit all the time."

Frankie said nothing.

"And bring you all sorts of nice things. Things the other girls never get. You must learn to appreciate the gifts that God has given you. A father who loves you. A new mother."

Sharp now, like the sting of a strap: "My mother is *dead*."

"Your mother is with God. In a better place."

I hoped Frankie's mother was with God. I really did. I hoped she and God were sharing a coffee cake. Once I'd confessed to my own mother that I thought God was a woman, because who but a woman would care so much about the oceans and the plants and the animals, who but a woman could build a whole world in seven days? My mother slapped me so hard my ears rang like church bells for hours after.

More things Frankie wasn't thinking about: coffee cake, because she'd never had it, which should have been some kind of sin but wasn't. Church bells, or the time it took to conjure all those mountains and trees, sharks and whales, bears and wolves. No, Frankie was too busy imagining how lonely her mother must have been when she stepped off that boat from Sicily, about what made her mother get on that boat in the first place, the kind of courage it took to sail across the ocean all by yourself. What had her mother hated so much about her home, and what had she missed once she'd left?

Frankie put her hand to her middle again. I remembered doing that, remembered when the feelings were so strong they turned your insides to a frothing stew. Frankie's mother had been just sixteen when she came to America to build her own new world, and had died for it.

But Frankie only smoothed the fabric of her dress. "Do you think there are meatball sandwiches in heaven, Father?"

Coffee cake, I said, still floating against the ceiling. With lots of brown sugar.

Father said, "I always imagined there'd be corned beef. But I suppose there could be meatballs too. Ten Hail Marys. Give thanks to the Lord, for He is good."

"For His mercy endures forever," Frankie said.

When Frankie finally threw herself back on the pew next to Stella, Stella said, "What took *you* so long?"

Frankie said, "I was telling him about all your impure ways."

"What?"

Sister George gave them one of her don't-make-me-come-over-there looks. Frankie slapped her hands together and prayed, but she was praying that Sister wouldn't drag them out of church by their necks. It had happened before.

Sister must have been too tired from kicking over mattresses to drag people out of church, because confession ended without anyone losing any more hair. The rest of the boys and girls filled the church pews all around them, going silent as dolls when the nuns gave them what Frankie called the stink eye. Frankie tried to focus on Father Paul. Father was always different during mass than he was in confession, facing away from the congregation, droning on and on in Latin about hell and fire and brimstone, infernos and abysses and sinners. His lilting, musical accent made the Latin words sound less frightening, but it wasn't supposed to. Everyone in the whole place was certain they were going to burn for something. There was no need to keep bringing it up.

Frankie believed there was nothing that any father could say that would surprise her.

She was wrong.

In my best Irish accent, I bellowed, Hill! Fyre! Breemston! right in Frankie's ear. She didn't even turn her head.

I got bored with the sermon, so I drifted back out of the church and into the courtyard, standing in the curtain of sleet that couldn't touch me, couldn't chill or soak me. Across the courtyard, on the upper floors of the dormitories, a shadow darted from window to window. That shadow traveled from left to right until the ghost girl with the broken face burst through a pane without shattering the glass. She plummeted to the ground, screaming, No, please, wait! the whole way down.

See?

Hell is never what you think it's going to be.

ANGELS OF BLOOD AND STONE

I LEFT EVERYONE TO THEIR various hells and went to visit the angel in the middle of the courtyard. Carved from white marble, with her huge wings reaching into the air, she stood on top of three tiers of stone like the decoration on a wedding cake. The angel held the hand of a little girl, while a boy sat beside her, reading a book. The nuns told the orphans that she was there to watch over them, keep them safe. In good weather, the children gathered around her, perching on the edge of the stone like so many birds flocking. But with the orphans in church and the sleet falling in a silvery curtain, I had her all to myself.

I sat on the stone at her feet, and I told her what I had seen that morning, from the hungry babies to Frankie kicked out of bed to the girl with the shattered face. The angel was my confessor; even if I could have, I wouldn't have told Father Paul anything. I had seen Father Paul in his striped pajamas, curled up in his bed like a child. Once you've seen someone in their striped pajamas curled up like a child, eyes shifting under thin lids, it's hard to think of him as a person you should trust with your deepest secrets, your greatest sins, a person who could offer you absolution. But perhaps it was a sin to judge a priest's pajamas, so I confessed these things as well. And then I told the angel what I always did, that I loved her wings, that I wanted to know how to get my own.

How do you become an angel? I asked her. How do you leave this place? Why am I here? Haven't I paid enough? I would wait for her to answer, as foolish and impossible as that was. But then the whole world seemed foolish and impossible to me; how much more impossible would it be for the angel to offer a little advice? I didn't think it was too much to ask. *That's your problem, you never think anything is too much to ask,* a voice said. Not the angel's. That voice was in my head; my mother's voice, yammering on as if both of us were still alive. *You never think of anyone but yourself, you never think.* I ignored the voice and told the angel about meatball sandwiches and corned beef and coffee cake in heaven. More impossible things. The angel didn't judge.

After the angel had tired of me and I of her, when her beatific smile started to look more like a smirk, I left the courtyard. When I was a little girl, I'd heard about ghosts, or rather, the places they haunted—old houses, cemeteries, dark roads at night. The girls in Frankie's cottage still whispered about Resurrection Mary, a beautiful girl in white who was killed by a hit-and-run driver while walking home from the Willowbrook Ballroom in the suburbs of Chicago. Apparently she walks northeast on Archer Avenue until some unsuspecting young man picks her up in his car. She's quiet during the ride, and when the driver nears Resurrection Cemetery, she disappears.

And yet, unlike so many others, I didn't skulk around graveyards. All right, I didn't *only* skulk around graveyards. I'd boated down the Chicago River, I'd ridden the train all around the Loop downtown, I'd motored through every inch of the city and beyond, I'd gone wherever and whenever I wanted to go. But I had my favorite haunts, so to speak. So while I did walk through the St. Henry Cemetery—Hello, ladies, hello, gentlemen, I said to the gravestones—I kept going, moving through the wrought-iron fence and out onto the street. I passed the orphanage greenhouse and the Angel Flower Shop, where the orphan boys grew the blooms, cut and arranged and delivered them. And then there was the butcher shop, the hardware store on the corner. Because it was Sunday, the streets were filled with people wearing their coats over their best church clothes, clutching their collars and hats and wincing at the sleet. They ignored two men, faces creased with wrinkles and grime, sharing a bottle on a stoop, laughing through broken teeth. A big-domed car rumbled by, splashing a well-dressed man as he hustled down the sidewalk. The man shook his fist, but the car didn't slow, not for the man shaking his fist, nor for the woman lying battered in the middle of the street, limbs shattered into a dozen extra joints. I wondered how many times she'd died. Two? Two hundred? After a few moments, the woman peeled herself off the pavement and crabbed past me, fast, a giant pink spider scuttling across the sidewalk.

I left the spider woman to her spinning and continued on my way, sometimes walking, sometimes floating, the streets a blur of shops and apartment buildings and bars locked up tight.

I skirted along sidewalks and swam down streets till I reached the shores of Lake Michigan, one of my very favorite places. The lake was so beautiful, especially when shrouded in a glistening veil of sleet—the water, even the air, full of mysteries. I sat in the sand and watched for the slap of mermaid tails in the gentle surf. My mother's voice intruded again: *There is no such thing as mermaids! Stop with this fairy-story nonsense.* But I put my fingers in my ears and sang to myself the way I imagined mermaids would sing, a wordless hum that vibrated in the chest, powerful enough to stir the currents. And though I could not feel the sand under me, nor the vibrations, I imagined my mermaid song luring unsuspecting boys into the water, desperate boys chasing their happily-ever-afters, their delicious dooms.

That's it, I'm putting these obscene books in the fire. You will marry Charles Kent and you will be grateful, do you hear me? Are you listening? Listen—

You listen, I said to the sleet, to the sand, to the water.

Listen.

Listen.

Listen.

By the time I returned to the orphanage, mass was over and Frankie and the rest of the girls were at the slop house, though the nuns called it the dining room. The girls each got a cup of Postum and a slice of bread with lard. As hungry as she was, Frankie still had a hard time eating that bread, that lard. The bread was chewy, the lard thick and sticky. And the other girls wouldn't stop talking about the new girl who had thrown herself—or was chased? But who would have chased her?—from one of the second-story windows and come to a bad end in the courtyard the week before. (None of the girls knew that that same poor soul was now standing right next to the table, tearing at her bloody hair.) Frankie gave her bread to another girl, a strange one named Loretta who'd eat anything. Loretta wrapped it in a napkin and slipped it into her pocket. Later, in the yard, she would pull it out and nibble at it when the nuns weren't looking.

And that was what Loretta was doing, gnawing on that sticky, lardy piece of bread, when the other girls tried to get Frankie to play ball outside. Frankie could throw straight and far and she was faster than a cat on fire, but she wasn't in the mood to play, even though it had finally stopped sleeting. Instead, she climbed to the top of the slide to get a look over the fence. The yard was split in two, boys on one side, girls on the other. Besides visiting days and maybe church, the only time Frankie saw her brother was when she sat at the top of that slide. And even though she'd see him later this afternoon, she wanted to get a look at him now. He was growing so fast and changing so much that sometimes, when he first walked into the visiting room, she didn't recognize him. It scared her in a way she couldn't even explain to herself.

But there he was, huddled in a pack of boys, all of them scratching like dogs at their woollies, the itchy pants they wore. If Vito saw Frankie, he knew better than to wave. One of the other boys didn't. As soon as he lifted his hand, a nun was on him, giving him such a smack Frankie was surprised his eye-balls didn't pop out onto the blacktop. She didn't want other boys waving at her, not until her hair grew back, and she didn't want to get anyone else in trouble. She turned to climb down, but someone was standing on the ladder. Toni.

Though Toni was not even a year younger than Frankie, they didn't see each other much because Toni was in a different cottage. That suited Frankie just fine. Her sister was almost as full of herself as Stella Zaffaro. And Toni didn't care about getting anyone in trouble. She waved at the boys as if she were signaling for planes.

Frankie elbowed her in the kneecap. "Stop it!"

Toni's hand dropped. "Take my leg off, why don't you?"

"I'd like to take your head off."

Toni knelt down behind Frankie, her bony knees digging into Frankie's back. "You're just mad 'cause I have a fella."

"That boy?" Frankie said. "He's just a kid. You both are."

"Say, you *are* jealous."

"Say, you *are* dumb. I'm not mad 'cause you *think* you have a fella, I'm mad because every time you're in Dutch with the nuns, I am too."

Toni was decent enough to turn red. "That's not my fault."

"Sure it is," Frankie said. Nobody knew how Toni had managed it, but one afternoon she'd snuck off with one of the boys; Father found the two of them at the candy shop across the street, drinking one soda with two straws. Even though Father and the nuns never found out what, exactly, Toni and that boy had done, Toni was strapped something fierce. Then

Sister George made *Frankie* clean out all the sinks in the washroom even though she hadn't done anything with any boy. Yet.

And not long after, Sister had caught Frankie making a face behind her back, shaking her finger like Sister George did when she was angry about something. It was nighttime, and Frankie had her hair all rolled up in rag curlers. Sister George cut off every single one of those curlers. She dropped them in the wash bucket one at a time, where they floated like the mice they sometimes found drowned in the toilets.

"Did the nuns tell Daddy about your so-called fella?" Frankie said.

Toni stopped smirking. "Do you think they will?"

"Yeah. But if they don't, I will."

"If you want me to keep *my* mouth shut when *you* get a fella, you'll zip your lips," said Toni.

Frankie figured that, when she had a fella, she would never be stupid enough to sit in the candy shop window where everyone could see her. "Come on," Frankie said. "It's almost visiting time."

"I wonder what Daddy wants to tell us," Toni said. "Do you think he got a bigger place?"

"No," said Frankie, and shoved at her sister's knees to get her moving. They climbed back down the ladder. Some of the orphans would go to the visiting room to meet with their fathers or mothers or aunts or whatever distant cousin took pity. The rest would play cards or listen to the radio. They never looked too happy, those kids who had no one to visit them, or no one who wanted to. Frankie decided not to be so mad at Toni.

At least not today.

———⊗⊗⊗———

While they waited for their father in the visiting room, Toni could barely sit still. Frankie had to press her hand on Toni's knee to keep her from bouncing them both off the bench. But as much as she tried not to, Frankie's knee also had a hopeful twitch. In her pocket was a new a sketch that she thought was better than almost anything she'd done before. And even though she didn't allow herself to hope for much, she wanted to show her father. She wanted him to see how good it was. She wanted him to say it.

A few minutes later, Vito came through the door, his cap rolled up in his hand, his fingers still plucking at the itchy woollies. "Hey, girls," he said, sitting next to Frankie. And then he went quiet. He never used to be so quiet. Lately he acted as if he was a million miles away, far too grown up for his sisters. And then Frankie was angry all over again.

"Why didn't you wave to me before?"

Vito grunted. "You want me to get beat too? Or maybe you just want me to get a haircut like yours?"

He didn't say this in a cruel way. "It would look better on you," Frankie muttered, tugging at it. Again.

Vito smiled then. "Well, you don't look half as bad as you should."

"No. She looks twice as bad," Toni said. And then she

clapped her hands like a little one in the baby house. She yelled, "Daddy!"

There he was, striding across the enormous room. He wore a black suit and a long wool overcoat that sailed out behind him like some kind of cape. With his hat tilted at an angle and his tan skin and dark eyes, he looked like one of the movie stars Stella Zaffaro was always going on about, Tyrone Power maybe. He had to pass through the crowd of kids waiting to see their own relatives, and Frankie noticed some of the older girls watching him, tugging on their skirts like they could get him to notice them if only their hems were straight. She wanted to remember their faces so that she could short-sheet their beds later. But she couldn't be bothered, not really, not with the smell of meatballs and fresh bread in her nose. Not with her father heading straight for them, his huge bag full of food putting everyone in the room to shame.

"Hello! Hello!" their father called. Dangling from his free hand were the most beautiful green shoes, perfect shoes, *women's shoes*, with a good heel. They were for Frankie, she was sure they were. *Maybe you should listen to what Father Paul says*, she told herself. Maybe you should be more grateful for the things you've been given.

That was when Frankie noticed what was behind her father. *Who* was behind her father. Hanging on to him like she owned him. And Frankie couldn't see what she'd been given anymore. All she could see were the things that could be taken away.

ON THE COAST OF THE MOON

WHAT I KNEW ABOUT MY mother: Her skin was creamy white. She had perfect posture. Her hair went silver by the time she was twenty-five. When she was angry, her lips pulled tight like a row of sutures. Her most prized possession: the set of pearl-and-diamond wedding rings she wore on her left hand. I often begged her to let me try them on. She said that the day my father slipped those rings on her finger was the happiest of her life, and she would never take them off.

"Not even when you're dead?" I'd asked.

Her face was a thundercloud. "There's something wrong with you."

What Frankie knew about her mother: Her name was Caterina Costa. She came to America on a boat from Sicily in 1918. She didn't know a word of English, she didn't know a soul except a second cousin who would be taking her in till she got a job. But she met Frankie's father the shoemaker instead, and she married him. They lived in an apartment behind the shoe shop. She had three children, Vittorio, Francesca, and Antonina. They made her so happy. That was why everyone was shocked when Frankie's mother took the gun from the drawer in the shoe shop, the gun their father kept in case someone tried to rob them. Shocked that she shot up the room where she and Frankie's father slept, accidentally wounding Frankie's father. But she only wanted to see what it felt like to pull the trigger, that was what she told Frankie's father, what Frankie's father told Aunt Marion, what Aunt Marion told Vito, and what Vito told Frankie. Frankie's mother would never try to hurt anyone, she would never commit such a sin. Frankie's father threw out the gun and placed the children in Guardian Angels so their mother could rest. After a while, she was okay again. Everyone came out of the orphanage. She and Frankie's father tried to have another baby, but Frankie's mother died, and so did the baby.

When Frankie was little, she asked Vito about this so many times he got sick of it. "She's gone," he said. "Dad has to work, and Aunt Marion does too. We live in the orphanage now. I don't want to talk about Mom anymore." But Frankie still wanted to talk about it. So she told Toni the story, adding details to make it better. She told Toni that she'd seen pictures of their mother. She was beautiful, with long, dark curling hair. Big chocolate eyes. Sun-kissed skin. A laugh that sounded like the chimes in Christmas carols they played on the radio. Delicate hands that fluttered like butterflies when she talked. Frankie said that their mother loved them more than anything. And even when she held the gun just to see what it felt like, she wanted her children to be happy. That was all she ever wanted.

Now, in a crowded visiting room filled with forced cheer, the sallow woman who was not Frankie's mother was holding out a hand that didn't flutter at all. No pearls and diamonds here, but a thin silver band on the fourth finger.

Frankie knew what it was. Of course she knew what it was.

Frankie folded her arms across her chest. "What's that?"

The woman looked at Frankie as if she were as dumb as a plant. "A wedding ring, Francesca." The woman waited, maybe thinking one of them would say something smarter. Wow. Bully for you. Swell ring.

But they didn't. The three of them stood there, staring at their father. He'd put the brown bag on the table and was unpacking it. Meatball sandwiches wrapped in newspaper, apples, some homemade peanut candy, hard and sharp enough to scour the roofs of their mouths raw but so good they ate it anyway. Other families gaped at all the wonderful food, their tongues practically flapping to the ground.

Frankie's own tongue felt like a scrap of leather. The tongue of a shoe.

Finally Vito said to the woman, "Congratulations." He leaned in and gave her a peck on the cheek.

"Thank you, Vito," she said.

He *had* gotten too grown up for the likes of his sisters. Frankie pulled her arms in tighter, like she would never let herself go. No way was Frankie kissing that woman. No way. Her lips would shrivel and fall off, and there she'd be, no hair, no mouth, nobody.

Speaking of hair. "Francesca, did you have lice?" the woman asked her.

"No," Frankie said.

33

The woman arched one eyebrow the way Stella did when she was practicing her actress face in the mirror. The blood burned in Frankie's cheeks. "I just wanted it short."

"Oh," the woman said. "Well. It's . . ."

"Horrible," said Toni. "She looks like a ringy."

"A . . . what?" She—Ada, their new stepmother's name was Ada—never seemed to understand them when they talked. Or pretended she didn't.

"A kid with ringworm," Toni said. "Only if she was a ringy, she'd be wearing a sock on her head too, to hold in the medicine for the worms. Are we going to eat now?"

Ada's mouth curled like wet paper. "I don't know if I'm hungry anymore."

Their father smiled, big and bright, as if nothing was going on, as if nothing was different. He ignored Frankie's folded arms and pulled her into a hug. He curved his rough hand around the back of her nearly bald head. "Bella!" he said. "Bella!" Frankie used to know Italian, the language she spoke till was three. She only remembered a few words, but she knew that one. It made her want to cry.

He hugged Toni and gave Vito a clap on the back. "Wedding is good news, eh? Everybody happy?"

Toni didn't care about anybody's happiness but her own. "Are those my shoes, Daddy?"

"For Francesca. Something else for you." Daddy dug around in his bag. He gave Toni a paper-doll book, an ice skater on the cover.

Toni squealed like someone just poked her with a fork.

"Sonja Henie! Thanks, Daddy!"

Frankie wished she had a fork, Toni was so dumb and mixed-up and everywhere at once. Running off with boys! Playing with paper dolls! Toni couldn't decide if she was eighteen or eight. Frankie nudged her, but Toni nudged Frankie right back.

Daddy pushed the shoes at Frankie. "You try," he said.

Frankie didn't want to, not in front of *her*, but she kicked off her old shoes and slipped into the new ones. Unlike the other orphans, who had to wear scuffed and donated shoes molded to other people's feet, Frankie and her brother and sister had new shoes their father had made just for them. As always, these shoes were perfect—more than perfect, delicate and ladylike— which just made Frankie feel worse. She walked back and forth to show him, the shoes heavy as bricks on her feet.

"Daddy," Toni whined, already sick of poor Sonja Henie. "I'm hungry."

Their father broke off pieces of the peanut candy and gave one to each of them. Then he took off his raincoat and laid it over the back of a chair. He pulled a knife from the bag and started slicing the sandwiches.

Frankie popped the candy into her mouth, where it sat like a rock. Toni wolfed hers, bits of sugar and nuts spraying everywhere. Vito took his piece and frowned at it, as if he didn't know what it was.

Toni reached for it. "If you ain't gonna eat that—"

Vito's dark eyes flashed as he whipped the candy away from Toni. "Cool it."

"No fighting," said their father, though with his accent

it sounded like he was saying "No-a, fighting-a." "Plenty for everybody." Frankie's father smoothed the newspaper flat and placed the sliced sandwiches on top. He motioned for them to sit at the table. They all took a slice and started to eat. Nobody said much. The tomato sauce dripped off Toni's chin as if she were bleeding. She didn't notice. The meatballs were delicious, as usual, but Frankie's gut was locked down tight as a submarine. She gave up. She peeled away a part of the newspaper and wrapped her sandwich in it.

"I hope you're not going to throw that over the fence," Ada said. A long time before, Vito used to spit out the terrible orphanage food into his handkerchief, knot it, bring it out to the yard after supper, and throw the handkerchief over the fence. Until someone noticed a strange pile of handkerchiefs on the girls' side of the yard. One brave nun untied one to find Vito's name and cottage number written into the fabric. After the nuns got through with him, Vito couldn't sit down for weeks. He said they used a belt with a heavy buckle. Then the nuns told their father, who just used his hand. Vito said it hurt a lot worse than anything the nuns could do.

Frankie pulled the sandwich closer. "I'm going to eat this later."

Toni wiped her chin with the back of her wrist. "I'll eat it now."

Ada's lips twitched. "You don't worry about your figure much, do you, Antonina?"

A shadow passed over Toni's face.

Frankie clenched her jaw so hard that her teeth ached.

"Here," she said, placing her sandwich in front of her sister. "You can have it, Toni."

But Toni had figured out what Ada meant. She pushed it back to Frankie. "That's okay."

"No, take it."

"I don't want it."

"Come on," Frankie said.

Toni fluffed her curls, pretending she didn't care. "You have it. You're way too skinny anyway."

"Girls, girls," their father said. "Everybody just right, eh?"

Behind their father, a few tables away, a woman was crying. Her hair was dripping wet. I'd seen her before. Frankie had too. Once every few months she showed up, always wearing the same grubby coat, big and long enough for a man. Sometimes she sang, sometimes she talked to herself, sometimes she sobbed. Today, the only thing she had on underneath the coat was a dirty green blouse, loose and watery white flesh hanging from her bones. A girl tried to get her to button the coat, get her to cover up, but the woman slapped the girl's hands away. The girl was Loretta, the one Frankie had given her breakfast to, the only one who liked sticky, lardy bread. The woman looked straight at us, at *me*, and wailed even louder, her shriek like a siren, and a couple of nuns came to steer her away. Loretta glanced down at herself, now wet as the madwoman had been.

"We need some pictures," Frankie's father was saying. Though Ada was shaking her head, though she had just shamed Toni, though Frankie didn't like her and hadn't liked her from the first minute she saw her, she wondered if maybe it wouldn't be so bad, them being married. Maybe the new apartment they'd get would have a room she and Toni could share. Maybe she'd even get her own.

The voice in my head said, *You will be grateful.*

Pictures done, Frankie's father picked up Frankie's hand and patted it. "So grown-up. Is good. You take care of your little sister."

She always did. "Okay."

"The nuns don't want Vito no more. Too many kerchiefs over the fence," he said, smiling. "And work for me not so good, here. So I think we move. I think maybe Colorado is nice. Fresh air."

"Colorado?" said Frankie, the word rolling around like marbles in her mouth. He might as well have said, "I think maybe Neverland is nice. I think maybe the coast of the moon."

"Not so easy to visit," he said. "I write letters. One a week."

"What?" She didn't understand. The shoes, the food, and Ada with her ring—what was happening? Frankie looked at Vito. His eyes were wide. He didn't know either. Their father cleaned up the table, tucking the knife under his coat, like a person who thought he might get jumped.

Ada excused herself and disappeared into the sea of people. On most visiting Sundays, they didn't see Ada at all. She took her own kids out for walks around the grounds. But today was different. She left, but she didn't stay gone. Just a few minutes later, Ada was back at the end of their table. Five kids, two girls and three boys, most of them as big as Frankie and Vito, were gathered around Ada like a bunch of crows. They each had a beat-up suitcase with them. The younger ones seemed confused. The oldest boy, taller than Vito, was smirking like he was thinking of a joke. He waved at Frankie, waggling his fingers. His oily gaze slid down her body.

Toni, who'd been tearing out Sonja Henie's outfits from the book, too impatient to wait for scissors, stopped. She folded her hands on the table. She said, "When are you going?"

"Soon," Daddy said. He held out an apple to Toni and another to Frankie.

Frankie took the apple, feeling her throat closing up as fast as her stomach had. "You're going to Colorado? With Ada?"

Their father nodded.

Frankie pointed at the kids surrounding Ada, kids she'd never seen before, kids she'd never wanted to see. "And they're going with you?"

He nodded again. "Vito too."

Vito's mouth dropped open, but nothing came out. Frankie didn't want to say it, she wasn't supposed to say it, but she couldn't help it. "What about us? What about Toni and me?"

Her father stood and pulled on his coat. "I send for you."

"When?"

"I make new shop in Colorado. Hard work. Not for girls."

Again Frankie pointed at Ada. "She has girls."

He didn't answer, but he didn't have to. They were Ada's girls. Frankie and Toni were some other woman's girls. A dead woman's girls. They were nobody to Ada.

A sister arrived to drop a bag at Vito's feet, an old bag Frankie didn't remember. It had his name on it. The nuns had packed up his things. Good riddance to the boy with the handkerchiefs. Frankie stared at Vito and he stared back. He knew it was unfair, he knew she hated him for it. She wanted to be a boy. She wanted to be someone somebody wanted.

Frankie thought she'd been prepared for anything, but who is? She sat stunned as the rest chattered about Colorado for another half hour. She made herself kiss her father good-bye when he left, and she made him promise to write. She hugged Vito as hard as she hated him, and then squeezed him even harder to show him one day she might not mean it. Then she and her little sister Toni watched them—their father, their brother, Ada and her terrible kids—walk away, fading into the bobbing sea of heads and faces, just a few more ghosts.

Frankie sat back down at the table where they'd eaten. Toni had the paper dolls in her hands again, but now she was ripping off Sonja Henie's arms. Frankie still had the sketch in her pocket; she'd never shown it to her father. She pulled it out and opened it. It was a drawing of her mother, just the way Frankie had always imagined she looked. It *was* good, the best she'd ever done. She crumpled it in her fist.

She didn't need anyone thundering at her in church. The ground had already opened up and swallowed her whole.

Next to Frankie, Toni tore off Sonja's head. Bye, Sonja. Nice knowing you. Loretta was still slumped on the bench where the crying lady had been. Her hands went from the table to her face, back to the table. Loretta didn't know what to do with her hands, she didn't know what to do next. The nuns had forgotten about Frankie and Toni, and they had forgotten about Loretta.

And that seemed to be the worst thing of all. That the nuns could forget too.

"Hey!" Frankie said. "Loretta!"

Loretta turned. Frankie pointed at the seat across from her. Loretta came over, but she didn't sit.

"Was that lady your mother?" Frankie said. "The one who was crying?"

Loretta nodded slowly, as if she didn't want to admit it. Frankie didn't blame her. She pushed the wrapped sandwich across the table. Loretta frowned as if she was afraid Frankie was trying to pull a fast one, but she let out a little "Oh!" when she saw what was in there. "Are you sure?"

Frankie's turn to nod. Loretta picked up the sandwich and took a bite, her eyes closing as she chewed. She swallowed hard, then opened her eyes again, strange eyes, like new pennies. "I never had anything so good."

Loretta took another bite, and another. Frankie watched that odd girl eat the last sandwich her father would ever give her right down to the crumbs on the greasy paper. One of the stains on that paper looked like Jesus in profile. I waited for Frankie and Loretta to notice, but they didn't.

Loretta folded up the greasy paper with its picture of Jesus and sighed in contentment.

Well, I said. At least someone is grateful.

HAUNTS OF THE HAUNT

I WASN'T CONTENT, I wasn't grateful.

After her father swept out of the orphanage bound for the coast of the moon, Frankie went hard and quiet. For weeks, her quiet was a wall that no one could get through, not even Toni, who raged and cried and trashed what was left of her paper dolls as if all her dreams had been dashed, because they had. But Frankie drew the quiet deep down inside herself, honing her bones against it, her eyes flinty with a resigned sort of wisdom. I followed her around the orphanage yelling, Hello, you baby, good morning, cupcake! But if the living couldn't get through to her, what hope did I have?

I wandered Chicago, antsy and ghostful. Before 1871, the city was made of wood: the buildings, the homes, even the sidewalks. And then came the Great Chicago Fire that killed three hundred people, destroyed eighteen thousand buildings, and left a third of the city's residents homeless. After that, Chicago remade itself into a city of brick and stone. It was hard to find a frame house among all that masonry, but there were some. My favorite was a tiny blue house in a sea of brick, the paint peeling, the windows smudged.

That was what first drew me to it—the wood it was made of, how different it was from the other buildings that surrounded it, how easily it could catch fire, how quickly it would be consumed. What kind of people lived in such a house? What kind of people welcomed that kind of danger? I thought they'd be kindred spirits . . . so to speak.

They were, but not in the way I thought.

Now, as always, I could have walked straight into the house, through the door or the wall, but I didn't. I might have been a revenant, but I wasn't a creep. I floated around the back of the house and peeked inside. A pale young woman, fine boned and lovely, dressed only in a slip, stood in front of a mirror. She smoothed her waterfall of glossy black hair, rubbed her berry lips, pinched at her high cheekbones to pinken them. She slid one strap of the slip from her shoulder and turned left and right, posing like a starlet. A noise behind her startled her, and she pulled the strap up and jumped back into the rumpled bed. She closed her eyes and pretended to be asleep when the bedroom door opened, and a young man limped in bearing a tray. Despite the limp, the young man had a boxer's broad shoulders, and light brown hair brushed from a clear, fair brow. He was already dressed for the day, his loose white shirt clean but worn at the cuffs and collar, gray trousers thin at the knees. They didn't have much, it was clear. But they did have a tray with eggs, toast, and coffee, sleepy morning smiles, each other.

Berry pretended to wake, murmuring something I'd have to burst through the wall to hear. I could have done that, burst through the wall, I could have listened in on her thoughts, or his.

But I stayed on the outside where I belonged. The dark-haired, berry-lipped girl sat up in bed, and the young man arranged the tray on her lap. He pulled a napkin from the tray, flicked it open, and laid it across her chest. She laughed. Shyly, she pulled him down for a kiss, a kiss that started out soft, then lingered, and deepened. I closed my eyes, closed whatever sense allowed me to perceive this impossible world and all the impossible people in it.

I might be doomed to watch, but I could choose what to witness.

I turned from the window. In the scruff of trees surrounding the tiny, weed-choked garden, a red fox sat, staring. I glanced all around, but I was the only one in the yard.

What are you gaping at? I said.

The fox kept staring. Many animals could see what people could not. Cats could, dogs, birds, squirrels—those oak croissants—and foxes, I supposed. I wished, just for a second, it was a wolf pup. I would have liked to meet a wolf pup.

What? I said to the fox. What do you want?

The fox panted. It was probably hungry. Everybody and everything was hungry.

You never think anything is too much to ask, you never think of anyone but yourself.

If I'd had a body—skin that could flush, muscles that could tense, a jaw that could ache—I would have flushed, tensed, ached. I told that fox: Do I look like I have food? Because I don't. I have nothing for you, do you understand?

The fox suddenly turned to go. Maybe it wanted to choose what it witnessed as well, and I was embarrassing both of us.

Right, I said. Go back to the woods. You're going to get yourself shot if you lurk around backyards.

The fox smiled at me, a knowing smile that said I had no secrets from it, it knew why I was here, it knew why I'd come back, it knew me better than I knew myself. Which it didn't. It didn't.

But before I could yell again, it vanished in the brush.

Dear Frankie,

Hello to you out in Chicago! I bet it's cold. But I bet it's even colder here. And a whole lot quieter. It's the snow. I know you think Chicago gets plenty, but usually not in November! Denver has so much snow already you wouldn't believe it. It looks like God threw a big white blanket over the whole world just to tidy up his view, or shut everyone up. Sometimes I stand outside and listen to the quiet. It's a little hard to get used to, but I expect I will, eventually.

You might be surprised to hear that I haven't been doing much to help Dad open the new shoe shop. He says that he's got enough help with Ada's boys, and that they need more looking after than I do. But I guess the orphanage was good for something, because I was able to get a job working at a print shop on account of the training I got at the Guardians. The pay's okay, even though I have to give most of it to Dad. I do have a little bit left over for some smokes and a show every once in a while, so it works out. I'm at work six days a week and sometimes Sundays, but I try to get out to the shows as much as I can. It's not so quiet in the apartment. It's not quiet at all. Too crowded with Dad and Ada and all Ada's kids. The girls don't bother me much, they're just sort of spoiled. (Hard to imagine them in the orphanage. I don't know how they lived without new hats every week!) But Thomas and Dale, the oldest boys, are pretty bad, the way they carry on; and Dewey's the worst. Dad's always trying to get them in line and prove to them he means business. But I really don't want to write about them, and you sure don't want to hear about it.

I got your last letter, and I'm glad they finally moved you to the senior girls' cottage. Took them long enough! That Sister Bert sounds nice (as sisters go). So do your friends—Loretta, and that other one with the funny nickname. Huckle, was it? Strange name for a gal, if you ask me, but what do I know? Oh, and you can't forget that Stella, either. She sounds like a pistol. Tell her that she can write me whenever she wants to. (Just kidding.)

I'm glad too that you'll be working in the kitchen soon. It will take your mind off things, keep you from getting too gloomy. And maybe you'll be able to get some better food than what they serve in the slop house. You have to be thankful for whatever you can get. (I try to remember that when Dale steals the loose change from my coat pockets or eats the last meatball in the pot.)

Toni never answered my last letter. Have you seen her? I hope she hasn't run off to any more soda shops. Tell her I said hello, and tell her I said to stay put. She's already gotten herself *in enough trouble for two little sisters.*

Dad says to tell you that he misses you both, and that he's sorry he's not so good at writing letters. He asked me to write to Aunt Marion, which I did. She wrote back and said she's going to come see you and Toni on the next visiting day. Or maybe the one after that, she wasn't sure. Maybe she'll remember to bring you something special.

Anyway, it snowed again and I have to get out and shovel the walk in front of the shop. I don't like shoveling, but at least I can look at the mountains while I do it. There's no place like Chicago, but the mountains here are all right. You can see them from almost anywhere. Sometimes I think about trying to climb one. Can you imagine that? A city boy on a mountaintop? Maybe I should take up yodeling.

> *Your crazy brother,*
> *Vito*

Frankie sat at a table in the slop house with Loretta and another girl named Huckle. The other girls had their forks hanging in the air, waiting for Frankie's report, as if Vito wasn't just Frankie's brother but somebody famous and important. A bandleader. A general in the war everyone was preparing for, or avoiding.

Frankie folded the letter into neat squares and placed it next to her bowl. The stony quiet that had kept her walled off for weeks had broken like a spell. She'd emerged both more careful and more reckless. The kind of girl who would fold a letter into neat squares. The kind of girl who refused to be surprised again by anyone else, the kind of girl who would only surprise herself.

"So what's it say?" Loretta asked.

"Nothing much."

"Oh, come on," said Huckle. Her real name was Dolores Huckleberry.

"He said there's lots of snow in Denver. He said that you can see the mountains from everywhere, and that he thinks about climbing them."

"Wow," said Huckle. She'd never seen Frankie's brother before, never heard of him before she met Frankie, but she acted as if she was half in love with him. And she couldn't hear enough about Denver. To Huckle, Denver might as well be Paris.

"Vito won't be climbing any mountains," Frankie said. "He works seven days a week."

"Well, what else is he going to do?" said Loretta. "I'd work seven days a week too, if I had to live with my wicked stepmother."

"He never says anything bad about her."

"Just because he doesn't say anything bad doesn't mean there's isn't anything bad to say," said Loretta.

"What could be bad about getting out of this hole and living in Denver?" said Huckle.

Loretta whacked Huckle's arm. The spoonful of porridge flipped from the spoon and hit Huckle in the face. "Hey! What did you do that for?" Huckle said, wiping at it.

Frankie poked at her porridge. It lurched in the bowl as if it were alive. Ever since her father had left and taken her brother with him, she tried to eat what she could of the lumpy puddings, squashy parsnips, and half-cooked stews, even though it was so much harder without the visiting day treats to look forward to. Today, with Toni snickering with Stella Zaffaro at the next table as if she didn't have a care in the world, with Vito's letter sitting like an open mouth on the table, ready to go on and on about the snow and the quiet and the mountains, Frankie couldn't do it.

Huckle scooped another spoonful from the bowl. "When you start working in the kitchen, Frankie, why don't you make sure they give us better food than this, okay?"

Every girl placed in the senior girls' cottage got a job somewhere in the orphanage. Most of them were looking forward to it. But it was hard for Frankie to look forward to anything now.

"What's wrong with the food?" said Loretta. "I thought it was all right."

"You'd eat the bottom of a shoe," Frankie said.

"When you're hungry, you do what you have to," Loretta said. "If you don't want it, I'll take it."

Frankie pushed the bowl over to her.

Huckle said, "Ain't you gonna need your strength?"

"It tastes like warm spit."

Loretta had been spooning up the porridge as fast as she could, but now she dropped her spoon. "Thanks a lot for that."

"Well, it does," Frankie said.

"Warm spit or not, *I'm* going to need my strength," said Huckle.

"For the sewing room?" said Loretta. "You think the spools of thread are going to be too heavy for you?"

"I don't know what you're griping about, Huckle," Frankie said. "You love to sew."

"Sheets and pillowcases, that's all they do over there," Huckle said. "Nobody loves to sew sheets and pillowcases!"

"How do you know that?" Loretta asked her. "You haven't even started your job yet. Besides, how would you like to work in the laundry with me? Remember that girl a couple of years ago who got her arm caught in the mangle?"

Huckle shuddered. "I heard it split like a sausage."

"Well then. Stop complaining. Worst that could happen to you is that you prick yourself with a pin. Frankie here could cut off her whole hand with a cleaver!"

"Thanks for that," Frankie said.

Loretta held up the bowl of warm-spit porridge, as if she were some rich lady making a toast. "You're welcome."

Loretta wasn't wrong. The kitchen was huge and packed with cleavers the size of axes. The pots were like bathtubs and the iceboxes like cottages, as if the place had been built for a family of very hungry giants. About a dozen girls scrubbed pans, chopped vegetables, peeled potatoes, and stirred stews. There was even a bakery crowded with enormous barrels of flour, sugar, and pudding powders, and racks for breads and cakes. Just thinking about the racks packed with freshly baked cakes made Frankie's mouth water.

The whole place, explained the roly-poly nun in charge, was separated into sections: babies' section, nuns' section, boys' section, and girls' section. "Because of dietary restrictions and recommendations, each section prepares and serves different foods," Sister Vincenze said, her soft chins squishing out of her wimple like rising bread dough as she talked.

Sister paired Frankie up with an older girl she called Rosalie. Rosalie was the perfect girl to work in the kitchen, because she was nearly as huge as everything in it. Her face was wide and pink, her hands were the size of hams, and she was a head taller than everyone else in the room, including Sister Vincenze. She was as big and beautiful as one of those goddesses you see in paintings, Frankie thought, except Rosalie had all her clothes on.

"Folks call me Choppy," Rosalie said, after Sister walked away.

"What for?" Frankie asked.

Rosalie/Choppy held up her left hand; her middle finger was shorter than the rest by a knuckle. "Chopped it clean off," she said. "Blood all over the meat I was cutting."

"I guess they had to throw the meat out."

"Are you nuts? Rinsed it off, good as new." She grinned. "They never did find the tip of my finger, though. I expect it ended up in the stew."

"So that's why it tastes so terrible," Frankie said. "Too many fingers."

Choppy smacked Frankie upside the head in a friendly sort of way. "You're all right, *Fran-ces-ca*."

"Frankie," said Frankie, but Choppy was already walking toward the pantry.

"Here, let me show you where we keep the rice and stuff."

Soon Frankie found out what Sister Vincenze meant by those "dietary restrictions." Babies got good food because they were babies, nuns got good food because they were nuns, and everyone else got slop.

"So okay, Fran-ces-ca. Hey, you listening? So this is what we're gonna do. We're gonna make some rice, okay? You take one of these big pots," Choppy said, grabbing an enormous black pot by the handle and swinging it up underneath one of the spigots to fill it with water. "Here, feel how heavy it is."

Frankie tried to lift the pot herself, and almost dropped it to the floor.

Choppy laughed. "It's okay. You'll get used to it. Soon you'll be big as me."

"I don't think so," Frankie said. "You're bigger than my father." Frankie hoped she hadn't insulted the other girl, but Choppy was hard to insult. She just laughed again.

"Drag that bag of rice over here, little Fran-ces-ca," she said.

Frankie grabbed both corners of the bag of rice and dragged it across the kitchen floor. "Why do you keep calling me Fran-cesca?"

"Why not?" Choppy said. "So take this knife, see, and rip open the top of the bag, like this."

"Make sure you watch your fingers," said Frankie.

Choppy snickered again. "You're a funny thing," she said. "Okay. So when the water's boiling, you use this measuring cup and scoop out some of the rice and dump it in the water. Then you cover it, wait forty-five minutes, and you got your rice. You got it?"

"Sure," Frankie said.

"Then go to it."

While Choppy watched, Frankie pulled open the bag and shoved the measuring cup into the bag. As she scooped the rice, Frankie noticed something funny. Some of the rice grains were squirming.

"Uh, Choppy?"

"Yeah, Fran-ces-ca?"

"This rice isn't any good."

"What do you mean?"

"Well, look at it. I don't think it's supposed to move around by itself, you know?"

Choppy squinted at the rice. "You got a few bugs, is all. Just those little white ones."

"So I guess I get another bag of rice?"

"What?" Choppy laughed again, as if Frankie had made the funniest joke she ever heard. "No, you don't get another bag of rice! This bag was donated by . . . uh . . . I don't know who it was donated by, and we don't got any more. This is it. Just go ahead and use it. The bugs will float up to the top. You just skim them off, okay?"

Frankie stared at her, and once more, Choppy laughed.

Frankie had never seen a person who laughed so much, especially about such things as chopped fingers and wormy rice. Choppy took the cup of rice out of Frankie's hand and dumped it into the water. "Bye-bye, little buggies!" she said, in a singsongy sort of voice. She stirred the bug soup with a long wooden ladle. "See?" she said, pointing. "Already they're floating up to the top. Those guys can't last long in the hot water."

Frankie spent the next fifteen minutes skimming the bugs out of the pot, wondering how she was ever going to eat again. Then Choppy showed her how to make beef stew. The meat was glistening with knobs of fat, the potatoes like the dark rocks the kids kicked around the yard. They put up some Postum—no real coffee was served to the kids. Finally Frankie couldn't take it.

"How can they feed us this trash?" she said. "The stuff we pick out of the garbage looks better than this!"

Choppy looked over her shoulder to see where Sister Vincenze had got herself to, but Sister was busy yelling at one of the other girls for spilling some sugar on the floor. Didn't they know it was donated and they had not a grain to spare? Choppy motioned for Frankie to follow her to another section of the kitchen, the nuns' section. "Take a gander," she said, lifting the lid off a large pot. Some sort of rich brown meat simmered in its own juices, the smell of it enough to make Frankie woozy. Another pot held whipped potatoes. Beans as green as grass filled another. Choppy smiled a wicked smile that made her look like a carved pumpkin and picked up a spoon. "Of course, we gotta taste the food to make sure it's cooked right, don't we? Wouldn't want nobody to eat food that's turned." She spooned up a fat cloud of potato and held it out to Frankie.

Just as Frankie was putting that spoonful in her mouth, just as the taste of butter and salt exploded on her tongue, she heard a noise in the hallway right outside the kitchen. There was a yelp and a thud as a dark-haired boy was shoved through the door so hard he slid across the floor and ended up at her feet. When he turned his brown eyes up from under the brim of his cap, when he smiled—lips full, cheeks flushed—she felt like a mermaid spat onto shore, half naked, tail thrashing.

Frankie sucked in a breath and inhaled the potatoes. She coughed and coughed, wondering how she'd ever be able to breathe again.

DROWNING

ONCE, I'D KNOWN A BOY like that.

I haven't taken a breath since.

THE CROW PRINCE

MY BOY WAS NAMED BENNO. The first syllable a kiss before the lips parted, pouted, and the second syllable fell like fruit. When I couldn't sleep, I would say his name over and over again just to feel it in my mouth.

Frankie's boy was named Sam. Not that he had the time to introduce himself. There she was coughing up a storm, Choppy pounding on her back, while Sister Vincenze chased the boy around the kitchen, slapping him with a pot holder. He ran out the door, the hooligans who had pushed him laughing and whooping.

"Are you all right?" Choppy asked Frankie, after they were gone and the coughing had died down.

"Who was that?" Frankie said.

"The boy? I think his name's Sam. Why?"

Frankie shrugged, and coughed some more. "No reason."

Choppy smiled a long, slow smile. "He is a pretty one."

"Pretty is for girls," Frankie said, though she was wrong.

"Handsome, then."

"Maybe," Frankie said. Frankie didn't know boys could be

pretty or handsome or any of it. It didn't seem possible, with
their woolly pants, dirty faces, and big clown feet. She coughed
some more, trying to hide her own face, which was damp and
hot, as if she were hanging over a pot of lumpy stew.

"Uh-oh," said Choppy. "Looks like somebody's going to
have lots to say at confession this week."

"What do you mean? I didn't do anything."

"Yet," said Choppy.

Frankie thought about the word "yet" as she hurried down the
hall toward the infirmary a few weeks later. For such a small
word, it felt a lot bigger. A lot heavier. It echoed in her ears and
pulsed through her veins as she ran—*yet, yet, yet*. She ran so
hard that she almost lost the package of food under her sweater.
She tucked it in tighter, hoping no nuns would notice the bulge
or hear the crinkle of the butcher paper. And she'd nearly made
it to the infirmary, too, when she heard the voice.

"Francesca Mazza!"

She turned, gripping both her elbows around her stomach
as if she were cold or maybe even had a bellyache. Sister George
lurked in the dark hallway like a giant bat. She was holding
something. A breadboard. Frankie didn't want to know why.

Sister rubbed her knuckles against the board. "What do you
think you're doing?"

"I'm visiting Loretta in the infirmary. She has chicken pox.
I won't catch them because I already had them. I wanted to
cheer her up."

"Who gave you permission to visit the infirmary at this hour?"

"Sister Bert," Frankie said.

"Sister Ber*tina*," she corrected.

"Sister Ber*tina*," Frankie said, exactly the same way Sister had.

Sister squinted at Frankie, trying to figure out if Frankie was making a fool of her, which she wasn't; anyone could see Frankie just wanted to get away and see Loretta. I could see it. Sister Bert said she could, and besides, it was a cold afternoon, just after supper, and what else did she have to do?

"If Sister Bertina gave you permission, then I suppose I'll let you go." Sister stepped forward, her eyes like coals. "But don't you think for a minute that I won't ask her to make sure that you're not sneaking around on your own."

Frankie stepped back, wishing she could be brave enough to stand her ground. "Yes, Sister."

"If I find out that you were lying to me, you're going to wish that you never met me," Sister said, which was a stupid thing to say, because Frankie didn't know a single orphan who didn't wish that they hadn't met Sister George.

"Yes, Sister."

Sister George held Frankie's stare for a moment or two, then swept off down the hallway like some kind of queen or something. Frankie felt a headache brewing over her eyebrows. When she was a grown woman with a house of her own, she swore to herself, she would come back here wearing a beautiful suit and matching hat and shoes. White gloves, too. She would find Sister George and tell her exactly what she thought of her, which was that Sister was just a bully, no better than the boys who roamed the streets stealing little kids' candy, and Frankie wouldn't care if she had to say a million Hail Marys every confession for the rest of her life.

"What took you so long?" Loretta said when Frankie finally made it to the infirmary. "I finished my book this morning and I've been bored out of my skull all day." She scratched at the red scabs dotting her face.

"They wouldn't let me visit till now," Frankie said. "And then, on my way up, I got caught by you-know-who."

"She has to be the worst nun in this whole place," said Loretta.

"That's saying something." Frankie glanced around to see if anyone was looking, and pulled the package out from under her shirt. "Here. I brought you this."

Loretta took the package and fingered the wrapping. Frankie had drawn a bunch of different kids with chicken pox all over it.

"I love your drawings," she said. "I bet one day they'll be hanging up in museums."

Frankie didn't know how a bunch of faces with chicken pox was going to end up in a museum. "Are you gonna open it or what?"

"Keep your shirt on," she said, unwrapping the paper, careful not to rip it. She gasped when she saw what was inside. "Oh, Frankie! How'd you get it?"

"I have my ways," Frankie said.

"I could eat this in one whole bite," Loretta said, "but I don't want anyone to see me." She looked over my shoulder to where Nurse Frieda and her aide, Beatriz, were taking the temperature of some other sick kids.

Frankie moved closer to Loretta, blocking her from the nurse's view. "How's that?"

"Perfect!" she said. She lifted the roast-beef sandwich from the package and bit down into it, her eyes nearly rolling back in her head. Frankie would have gotten her some cake, but Loretta wasn't one for sweets as much as meat. Frankie wished she'd been able to get her some meatballs, but they didn't cook things like that at the orphanage, not even for the nuns. But thinking of meatballs made her think of her father, of him moving away and leaving her and Toni. She pushed those thoughts right out of her mind. She thought about the boy instead. *Sam.* She wondered if she would ever get a chance to talk to him. And then she wondered what she would say. And *then* she wondered if she would be able to catch her breath long enough to say anything.

She wondered about the word "yet."

"Frankie? Hello?"

"What?" Frankie said.

"You were staring off into space. You looked like Sister Bert, the way she gets when she's reading one of her books. I think she reads more than I do."

"Not possible," Frankie said. "What's the book you finished this morning?"

"Anne of Green Gables."

Frankie had no idea what a gable was, but she wasn't going to ask. "What's it about?"

"An orphan."

"Why would you want to read about an orphan when you've got so many orphans right in front of you?" Frankie said.

"She's a different kind of orphan. She gets a home with some nice people, and . . ." She stopped talking and shook her head, as if she'd just said something she'd have to confess to. She had juice dripping down her chin. She wiped it off with her fingers, then licked them. "Delicious!"

"I'm glad you like it, 'cause I'm probably gonna have to say a lot of Our Fathers."

Loretta smiled and took Frankie's hand. "You're the best."

Frankie looked down at their clasped hands. "What are you, my fella or something?"

Loretta blushed, the rest of her skin reddening to match the chicken pox. She let go of Frankie's hand and picked up the butcher paper like someone admiring a nice photograph. "Maybe you can get a job working for the pictures. You know, painting all those movie sets."

"Right," Frankie said. "Maybe I'll work for Mr. Walt Disney."

"Well, why not?"

That seemed like a silly question to Frankie. More nuts than reading about some made-up orphan. "Because I'm a Guardians girl, that's why."

"So? Why can't a Guardians girl get a job working for Mr.

Disney? What does he care where you been, as long as you can do what he wants?"

"Why don't I run for president while I'm at it?"

Loretta raised an eyebrow. "I'm the one who's sick and still I'm not so cranky as you are. Why are you so cranky?"

Frankie couldn't explain it. "I don't know. Sorry."

"You're cranky, I'm hot. I didn't think I could be so hot in December, but I feel like I'm burning up. I keep trying to open this window. Help me, okay?"

The two of them stood and pushed up on the sash, and the huge window squeaked open. Frankie had to hold on to the back of Loretta's nightgown so that she didn't fall out.

Nurse Frieda didn't notice, but Beatriz, her aide, barely older than Frankie and Loretta, hurried over to them. "What are you doing?" Beatriz said, voice low. With her dark eyes and skin, everyone thought Beatriz was Sicilian, like Frankie, something that Beatriz, whose family was from Mexico, didn't bother to correct. She was also thick and lush everywhere— hair, lips, body. Frankie had seen plenty of senior boys gawking at her, wishing they were sick and that she'd be the girl to take care of them.

Beatriz eased the window shut. After laying the back of her hand on top of Loretta's forehead, she clucked her tongue. "You're still warm, and you need rest. I think it's about time for your friend to leave."

"Does she have to?"

"I'm afraid so."

63

"I'll be back to visit you," Frankie said.

"You promise?"

"Yeah. Hey, next time I'll bring Stella with me. She can sing you a song and tell you about how wonderful she is."

"You mean her head's gotten bigger?" said Loretta.

Beatriz huffed, put her hands on her hips. "You two are going to get me in trouble with Nurse Frieda!"

Frankie stood. "All right, all right, I'm leaving. Sister Bert said that she'd let us listen to the radio after dinner anyway, and I'm missing it."

Another thing on the long, long list of things that made Sister Bert better than Sister George was the radio. Sister Bert liked *Inner Sanctum, The Shadow,* and *Fibber McGee and Molly* as much as any of the girls. Every night, she'd put the radio on and they would all gather around it, gaping at it as if the characters would come bursting out of that brown box.

Frankie ran into the senior girls' cottage, expecting the usual laughs, but instead, everyone was listening to a news broadcast.

"What's the big deal about the news—" Frankie started to say when Huckle grabbed her arm, and made her sit.

"Shut up," she said.

"What's going on?"

"Don't you know anything?" Stella hissed. "They bombed our ships!"

"What ships? Who did? Why?"

"Shut up and listen!"

"From the NBC newsroom in New York: President Roosevelt said in a statement today that the Japanese have attacked Pearl Harbor, Hawaii, by air! I'll repeat, President Roosevelt said in a statement today that the Japanese have attacked Pearl Harbor, Hawaii, by air! Now we'll go live to KTU in Hawaii."

They went to some other man who was talking on a bad telephone line, hissing with static. Even still, he sounded breathless and a little excited, and he never said his name like the announcers usually did. "The city of Honolulu has also been attacked and considerable damage done. This battle has been going on for nearly three hours. A bomb dropped within fifty feet of the KTU radio tower. This is no joke," he said. "It is a real war."

Sister Bert turned the radio off.

"It *is* a joke, though, right, Sister?" Frankie asked. "Like that program about the invaders from Mars?" It had been years before, but she still remembered it. There was a radio show about space aliens landing in New Jersey or New York or somewhere and killing everybody with heat rays. It was so real, with explosions and gunfire and a man who sounded just like the president. The sisters had them all kneeling and praying for hours before anybody figured out the world hadn't really ended, and it was all for laughs. Frankie thought Sister George was going to storm the capital, she was so mad.

Now Sister Bert said, "No. I don't think it's a joke." Her normally pale face looked even paler, and she rubbed her cheeks with both hands. "It means we're at war."

"War with Japan?" Huckle said.

"Yes. Most likely many more boys will sign up for the service."

Frankie thought of Sam sprawled out at her feet in the kitchen; she thought of Vito in Colorado. Vito was only sixteen, but what if the war lasted a long time? Would he have to go? Would he be sent all the way to Japan? Would Sam? Would they all?

I thought of my own brothers at the start of World War I, another war that had seemed as if it couldn't touch us, could never affect us. "That's Europe's problem, not ours," my father had said from behind his newspaper. "America comes first."

All of the Guardians girls started talking at once, about brothers and fathers and cousins and the boys at the Guardians, and what would happen to them, and what did it mean for the rest. Sister Bert put up her hands. "We're not going to solve all the world's problems now," she said. "We've all had a bit of a shock, but I'm sure President Roosevelt is taking the actions that need to be taken and we'll hear about them soon enough." She stood up. "How about you girls do your darning?"

"I don't have any darning," said Stella.

"Stella, a person always has darning."

"But—"

Sister held up a hand. "We must trust that God has a plan for this country, and for us. The best thing we can do is have faith and continue to do our work."

The girls made a show of getting out their torn socks and

stockings, but no one was able to concentrate on anything except for the broadcast. They talked in whispers about what it all meant, but no one knew. Soon, though, they half forgot about it, and ended up talking about the things they always did: food they wished they had to eat, the way they'd wear their hair if they could. That's the amazing thing, that you could half forget a war. But you could. Especially when that war is fought far away across the ocean, when your brother's eyesight is too terrible for him to go and your mother is so grateful that she bakes a cake herself instead of telling the cook to do it, when there's a black-haired boy with a sparkling hollow at his throat standing at your door and you can't speak for the wave of want that swamps you and threatens to drag you under.

Benno, Benno, Benno, Benno. B—

But the bad news must have stayed in the back of their minds the way bad news always does, because the girls were too jittery to sleep. Sister Bert turned out all the lights but one and told them a story that her mother used to tell her back when she was a little girl in Bavaria.

"Once upon a time," Sister said, "a man fell asleep while napping under a tree. A crow with a painfully crooked wing flapped down from the tree and pecked the man awake. The man was very angry until the crow told him that he'd been asleep for five years! The man looked down at himself and knew it was true; his thick beard reached all the way to the ground. He asked the crow how he could thank him. The crow plucked one of his own shiny black feathers and gave it to the man. 'Offer this feather to your daughters. Whoever accepts it will have her wishes come true, and mine as well.'

"The man went home and offered his daughters the feather, one by one. The eldest laughed. The middle sister scoffed. But the youngest slipped the feather into her pocket.

"Since the man had been away for five long years, his family had suffered. They had no food and nothing left to sell to buy some. The older girls were angry at their father, but the youngest said she would find work. Her sisters laughed. 'What do you know how to do?' they said.

"The youngest went to the city and got a job as a cook. But, as her sisters said, she didn't know how to cook. All her dishes were either raw or burned. The head of the kitchen beat her and told her that if she didn't do better at breakfast, she would be sent home hungry. While the girl was searching for a handkerchief to dry her tears, she found the crow's feather. Using the feather as a quill, she wrote down what she wished would happen. 'I wish that the breakfast table was filled with delicious food.'

"The next day, her wish came true. The table was heaped with one wonderful dish after another. The girl was amazed. When the head housekeeper asked her to sew some dresses for the lady of the manor, the girl wrote down the names of beautiful garments. Again, her wish came true—a half dozen beautiful gowns appeared in the lady's closet.

"Soon her reputation preceded her all around the city. She was so accomplished and so lovely that many men wanted her to be theirs. A carpenter sneaked into her room at night. She told him to leave, but he refused. She said, 'Shut the door, then.' While he was shutting the door, she quickly wrote, 'I hope he spends all night shutting the door and opening it again.' Her wish came true. At daybreak, the carpenter slunk away.

"The next night, a hunter came to the girl's room. He bent to take his boots off. With the crow's feather, she wrote, 'I hope he spends all night taking off his boots and putting them back on.' Her wish came true. At daybreak, the hunter left, exhausted.

"The third night, a crow with a crooked wing flapped into her room. Since he was just a bird, and an injured one at that, she fed it crumbs from her supper and took pity on its crooked wing. She wrote, 'I hope this crow becomes whole again.'

"With that last wish, she had broken a spell. Suddenly the crow changed into a beautiful young man clad in black velvet.

"The beautiful young man took the feather from her hand and wrote, 'I hope this girl's fondest wish comes true.' And it did."

Sister nodded, her tale finished.

"Wait, what happened?" said Huckle.

"They got married, right?" said Stella. "This girl and the crow prince?"

Sister Bert slapped both hands on her knees and stood. "Maybe. Depends on what her fondest wish was."

"What else could it be?" Stella demanded.

Sister sighed. "A piece of decent chocolate? World peace?"

"Chocolate! What kind of story is that?" Stella said.

"The kind of story that makes you think about what you'd

wish for," said Sister Bert, turning out the last light. "Now, get some sleep."

———— ✕✕✕ ————

In the dark, the girls thought about what they'd wish for if a beautiful crow man came through the window. Not all of them wished for world peace.

After a while, someone whispered, "Where's Bavaria anyway?"

Another voice said, "Somewhere in Ohio, I think."

1942

FAIRY TALES

WEAK HEARTS

THE MONTHS PASSED IN A haze of falling snow and Christmas lights and bloody battles in faraway towns with names that caught in the throat. I talked to the babies in the baby house and watched Frankie as she turned fifteen. When I wasn't at the orphanage, I wandered the streets of the city with people lumbering like bears under the weight of their coats. Or I attended the picture show where the 4-F boys went to forget their shame, too sickly or disabled for war.

One morning, as a deeper chill wrung tears from the ragged souls waiting on line at the soup kitchens, I got hungry for a different kind of story. I walked the streets, not bothering with the sidewalks. The cars drove right through me as if I were nothing, but I caught their thoughts like butterflies in a net:

What if Herbert can't find another job?

That no-good man drank his last paycheck.

Daisy, oh, Daisy, I love you but . . .

We'll have to move in with his mother.

America can't afford to be dragged into another—

But I'm starving, Mommy.
Who do you think we are, the Rockefellers?
Damn Roosevelt is useless.
The hell you say.

Finally I reached the library. I slipped through the glass doors and greeted the pretty new librarian at the desk the way I always did—Hello, Miss Books, love the sweater!—though she couldn't hear me. The old librarian, an iron-haired woman with green spectacles, hadn't been able to hear me either. Until the day she could. By then I wasn't saying Hello, Miss Books, those are some snazzy spectacles, I was saying other things, such as Better to flee from death than feel its grip, or All we see or seem is but a dream within a dream, or Most women do not creep by daylight. All to entertain myself. I was as surprised as she was when I simply whispered the word boo and the stack of catalog cards she was holding flew up in the air in a shower of oversized confetti.

She retired, which was probably for the best. Weak heart.

After I greeted the pretty new librarian, I floated into the reading room. The colder it got outside, the more crowded it got inside, but the crowd didn't bother me. More people reading, more for me to read over their shoulders. Newspapers mostly, though I didn't care for the news. The spasms of the world meant little to me—who was fighting the war, who was prepping for war, who was avoiding the war, which war, that war, or that other one—but the people here and everywhere were consumed by it, convinced that each war was different, that it wasn't one long war with the briefest of pauses between battles.

Even now, a doughy woman pored over *Reader's Digest*, lips moving as she read an old article by Charles Lindbergh, the famous aviator-turned-crank. "We, the heirs of European culture, are on the verge of a disastrous war, a war within our own family of nations, a war which will reduce the strength and destroy the treasures of the White race. . . . It is our turn to guard our heritage from Mongol and Persian and Moor. . . ." Her eyes flew from face to face, looking, I supposed, for Mongols and Persians and Moors.

I made the rounds of the reading room, searching for the man with the blond hair and crooked teeth. Well, not him exactly, but the book he'd been reading for the past few months, a couple of pages at a time. I had not been much of a reader when I was young, but I wondered if that was because I was never allowed to read anything worth reading. My favorite book of fairy tales was given away when I turned twelve, because my parents said it was time to turn from childish things. Later, my mother would confiscate the mystery magazines and love stories lent to me by my friend Harriet, saying such rubbish would melt my brain to porridge and lay my morals to waste.

Whatever brains or morals I still possessed, she'd added. She'd been horrified when she caught me and Harriet practicing our kissing instead of doing needlework as we had promised.

I found the man with the blond hair and the crooked teeth in the corner by the window. The book he'd been reading was called *The Hobbit*. Like the fairy tales I'd loved as a child, this book had monsters and goblins and riddles, but here was a grown man reading the book out in the open, as if he wasn't the least bit worried about his brains melting or his morals wasting. How nice to be a man, to be free to read a monster book in public without anyone worried that you would turn into a monster yourself. Or that you picked the book *because* you were a monster. He'd just begun chapter five, "Riddles in the Dark." I floated over his shoulder, imagining Bilbo Baggins, a tiny creature with hairy feet, stumbling upon a ring, slipping it onto his finger, becoming invisible. Magic.

Across the room, someone coughed. I looked up. Facing me, hovering over the shoulder of another man, was a girl about my age. Where I was small and fair with silvery curls—a devil in disguise, my mother said—here was a tall black girl with warm brown skin and the thickest ebony hair I'd ever seen piled high on her head. Unlike the boxy dress I wore, hers was a gold dress that nipped in at her tiny waist, skimmed her hips, and fell nearly to her ankles, making her a perfect hourglass. Despite the dress, and the hairstyle that hadn't been fashionable for nearly a decade, she was so lovely that for a moment I thought she was alive. Until she reached out and tried to turn the page of the newspaper and her hand went right through the man instead. She frowned and tried again.

I hated watching ghosts act out their last moments, hated their fruitless, frantic agitation. I wouldn't have said anything to her, but I was trying to read, and she was distracting.

That won't work, I said.

She did not reply. Of course she didn't. Her hand flicked.

You're moving too fast, I said.

Frown, flick.

Are you new? You can't be new. That dress is more than ten years out of date. I know, I've kept up. Have you seen these ads?

Frown, flick. Frown, flick.

You're trying too hard. Relax.

Flick, flick, flick.

I stamped my foot as if it could get her attention. Or anyone's. As if my own movements, my own words, weren't just as fruitless.

I said, Just read over his shoulder. It takes less energy anyway. We don't have much to begin with, you know. If you keep doing that, you'll wear yourself out.

The girl wasn't listening, wasn't looking. Frown, flick.

If you wear yourself out, you'll lose time, do you hear me? You'll lose yourself. You'll find yourself weeks from now months from now years from now, wandering in Indiana somewhere, or floating on a boat on Lake Michigan, or perched on the top of the Chicago Board of Trade or flapping around the Rookery building like all the other birds wondering how you got there. Is that what you want?

Frown, flick, frown, flick.

There was no reaching her, lost as she was in her own death. But what was lethal about a newspaper? Maybe a paper cut did her in. Maybe my mother was right and mere words could turn a brain to porridge. Or maybe this girl had a weak heart too.

She should have stayed away from newspapers, then. All that war talk could be shocking. And the heart was always the first thing to go.

Then I felt the girl's eyes on me, her glare hot, so hot. She didn't have to say anything for me to hear what she was thinking:

Who are you calling weak?

I took a step back. I didn't mean—

Her fingers flicked, and this time she jerked that newspaper right out of that man's hand. It swooped around the room like a hawk an owl an eagle spreading its wings before crashing to the table in a heap.

The patrons blinked at one another.

"Must have been the wind," said a man.

"What wind?" said a woman.

Some wind, I said.

The girl quirked a sharp brow, a hook piercing the skin.

How did you—? I began.

She put her finger to her lips. Shhh.

———⊗⊗⊗———

"Bless me, Father, for I have sinned. It's been a week since my last confession."

"Go on."

"I thought bad things about my little sister, Toni. She's telling everyone she's going to marry a duke. We don't even have dukes in America."

Father coughed. "Perhaps one day she plans to move to England."

"Like that will help."

Father coughed again but said nothing. Frankie wished she could see him better through the mesh. His face was friendly when he wasn't pounding the pulpit and going on about hell.

Frankie said, "There's something funny about Toni. But I'm not sure it's a sin to think so, because everyone says that about her."

"Everyone better confess it, then," he said. "Are you truly sorry?"

No, she thought. "Yes," she said.

"What else?"

"I almost took the Lord's name in vain. Twice."

"Almost?"

"Choppy threw a potato at me before I could get the whole name out. The second time I almost did it, she whacked me with a flipper. Choppy doesn't like it when people take the Lord's name in vain."

"A girl after my own heart," Father said, his accent making it sound like "a giurl after me own hayrt."

Frankie half wanted to be a girl after Father's own heart, but she probably wasn't. Sometimes, when the sisters weren't looking, Frankie grabbed a raw egg and sucked it out. Other times, she scooped out huge handfuls of Jell-O and slurped them down while shivering in the icebox. Was it a sin to eat when you were hungry? If Father was hungry, would he dig his hands into a vat of Jell-O? Did Father Paul actually *get* hungry, or was he too full of God's light? Frankie didn't know about his striped pajamas or how often he dreamed of his grandmother, who thought it was bad luck to put shoes on a table, to tell a mother her baby was pretty, to knit after dark unless you were certain the sheep were sleeping. His grandmother believed that since Paul had been born at night, he would be able to see both the spirits and the fairies, whom she called "the good people." Every night, she told him to leave a saucer of cream in the corner, just in case a brownie might want a sip. His mother said that this was a bunch of English nonsense, that they were *Irish*, for pity's sake, but his grandmother claimed the brownies helped everyone with their darning, especially the Irish. Once, Father woke up in the middle of the night to see a tiny wizened creature sipping at the bowl.

Father Paul loved God more than anything. But sometimes he missed the fairies.

To Frankie, Father said, "Is there something else?"

"I've been thinking about the word 'yet.'"

"What about the word 'yet'?"

"I'm thinking about doing something but I haven't done it yet."

Father said, "Ah," as if he knew exactly what Frankie was talking about. She tugged at her hair, which had finally grown a little. Not that there were many boys left to look at her hair or any other girl's. Except for the ones who weren't old enough, and some with thick glasses or a limp, the boys had been leaving the orphanage left and right for the service. Some had even snuck out in the middle of the night.

Frankie was sad to see them go. One of the jobs of the kitchen girls was to wash the dishes in the senior boys' dining rooms. At first, Frankie didn't think that was fair at all. The boys were the ones who dirtied the dishes. But after a while, she didn't mind so much. There she was, scrubbing plates and steamers and whatnot, and this or that boy would walk by, and maybe talk to her for a while, if there was no nun around. And maybe they would tell her that she was pretty and help her stack some of the dishes or carry the heavier pots. Frankie hadn't had much to do with boys, how could she? Except for Vito. And then, when she tried to picture what Vito looked like out there in Colorado, and what he could be doing, she couldn't. It was getting so much harder to see him in her mind, as if skinny Vito was getting skinnier and skinnier until he faded away to nothing, like a shadow, or the faint scribbles on the letters he sent.

But those other boys. Some smelled like the ink from the print shop, others had the bitter smell of green leaves they got from working in the orphanage flower shop, some like plain old dirt. One by one, they untied her apron, flicked bubbles at her, sang stupid songs, hid the soap, and one by one, they left for the service. Sometimes they'd tell her about it. "Fran-ces-ca," they said—they always called her Fran-ces-ca because that's what they heard Choppy called her—"it's time to ship out!"

But the one boy she really wanted to talk to was too shy to talk to her. Or maybe he didn't want to. He hovered behind the others, his hat crushed in his hands, smiling, or looking down at his shoes, but never saying a word.

"It's nothing bad," Frankie said to Father. "It's just that I've been thinking about talking to . . . a person I haven't talked to. Not yet."

"'Tis the way it should stay."

She should have expected him to say this, should have expected him to know. The Guardians worked so hard to keep boys and girls separate—even brothers and sisters. But now that she was working in the kitchens, she was allowed to go more places and do more things, talk to more people. And why shouldn't she? She had just had a birthday, the first birthday without her father. Vito sent a letter and a card he said was from everyone. As if she wanted a card from everyone. Anyway, she was a woman now.

Almost.

She said, "It's just talking."

"You have bigger, more important things to do and to think about. Your schoolwork. Your job in the kitchen, which helps the whole orphanage. And there are other things going on in the world. We are at war."

"I know," she said, though sometimes the war was easy to forget. She knew about the rationing and the recycling—they had to save the cans in the kitchen—but since the orphanage gave them their food, and since what it gave them had always been terrible, they didn't pay that much attention. Even the radio broadcasts seemed like they were talking about something that was happening too far away to be real.

Other times, though, the war wasn't so easy to forget.

Father said, "If this boy is healthy, then he'll be joining the service soon."

Frankie felt queasy and wished she hadn't run to the kitchen for an egg before confession. "Not that soon."

"Time always passes faster than we'd like it to."

Frankie thought it didn't pass fast enough. "Shouldn't I talk to him while I still can?"

"You know the answer to that."

Frankie knew Father's answer. And she knew her own. They didn't match. They rarely did.

"Ten Hail Marys," Father said. "Give thanks to the Lord, for he is good."

At Father's words, Frankie bowed her head and murmured, "His mercy endures forever," but I laughed. Father Paul thought he understood mercy, thought he understood forever, but what could he possibly know about either?

I poked at his Bible, willing wanting wishing the pages to flap, the book to lift and swoop around the confessional like a darting bird. Though the pages barely fluttered, Father Paul trapped the book against his chest.

Silly pajama man, I hissed, like the ghoul I was. Am. Was.

This is mercy, *this* is forever.

MERMAIDS OF CHICAGO

I MUST HAVE BEEN ANGRIER with Father Paul than I thought, because time stuttered, slipped, and I found myself sitting against an oak in the middle of the woods. The song of a white-throated sparrow that should have made its way south long ago bored into my ears: "Oh, sweet Canada Canada Canada."

Shut up about Canada, if you please, I said.

The sparrow was having none of my nonsense, or maybe it just wanted to hear the sound of its own voice. "Canada Canada Canada," it warbled. "CANADA."

I stood. The tree was a huge oak, bare branches raised ecstatic and saintlike to the winter sky. You learn a lot about saints when you lurk around orphanages, when you listen in on the dreams of nuns and schoolgirls. My favorite story is the one about St. Lucy, who gouged out her own eyes to discourage a too-persistent suitor who had complimented them. I'd seen a statue of her once at the lower altar of a nearby church, Our Lady of Grace. Both eye sockets were hollowed out and bleeding down her cheeks. She held a plate with her two eyes on it as if she was about to serve them as hors d'oeuvres. Something I should have tried myself.

I slipped through the woods, hoping to catch a glimpse of a wolf or a bear, but even the deer avoided me. Or maybe they were all sick of hearing about Canada too. I didn't want to go back to the orphanage just yet, so I headed for the lake. Mounds of snow still buried the sand, ice-capped water lapped thickly at the shore of Montrose Beach. I sat looking out at the great expanse of Lake Michigan. Usually it wasn't difficult to ignore the other spirits drifting around, performing their private rituals, their endless deaths. But one young black man strolling across the sand seemed fixated not on himself, but on me. Despite his neatly groomed mustache, the fine pinstriped suit he wore, and the carved cane that he twirled like Charlie Chaplin, my mother would have yanked me across the street to avoid him simply because of his dark skin.

My mother had been scared of so many things. Not much to be scared of now.

But plenty to be annoyed by. The young man passed me once, walking. He doubled back and passed me again, this time floating on a raft of mist rolling off the lake. He turned around a third time and stopped right in front of me in a spray of snow.

He pointed his cane at me. You're the whitest girl I've ever seen, he said.

I didn't answer. Once, his mother might have yanked him across the street to avoid *me*. Once, I might have been more dangerous to him.

You're whiter than the snowbank you're sitting in.

I leaned to the left, trying to look around his legs.

He peered closer. You're so white, you're almost blue.

I said, I can't see the water.

He drew back as if surprised by his own observation, said, *Definitely* blue. He took in my indigo silk dress, the length of it, the fringe of beading around my knees, my bare feet, my face. He snapped his fingers. I bet it was that flu. The one that killed all those people. Back in '18?

You have a knife sticking out of your neck, I told him.

Don't change the subject.

I'm not.

So it *was* the flu? I heard it turned some folks so dark they couldn't tell the white folks from the black ones. But it must have killed you quick, you in your fancy dress.

It had. No guns or knives required, because the sickness took me before anyone got other ideas. For a moment, my chest tightened, and even though I didn't need to, didn't have the lungs or the heart, I gasped for breath.

After I'd gathered myself, I said, If you know so much about it, why are you asking me?

Just making conversation.

Sometimes I preferred the ones like that bloody, gaping girl back at the orphanage, ones who kept leaping out of windows or jumping in front of trains in endless loops, no time to talk.

The name's Horace, he said. Horace Bordeaux. Like a fine wine, only better. You got a name, Blue Girl?

Yes.

Well, what is it?

Don't you have unfinished business you need to attend to, Mr. Horace? Haunting your brother or finding your killer or something?

He laughed. I don't have a brother, he said.

Would you please move out of the way?

Why? Can't you see through me?

He was quite solid for a dead man, but I could have seen through him if I worked at it. I didn't want to work at it. I leaned to the right.

Nothing to see, he said, but he stepped aside. His gaze followed mine. What are you looking for?

I lifted my chin. There, I said.

In the gray water chunky with ice, dark heads bobbed and dipped.

So? he said.

Mermaids, I said.

He laughed again. Those are sailors who died in a storm or something like that.

Mermaids, I repeated. Mermaids with long flowing hair and iridescent tails, peeking out of the water to laugh at the blue girl sitting in a snowbank.

He frowned. Are you crazy?

If you say so.

His features shifted ever so slightly, relaxing, smoothing out. Ah. You're playing.

I said nothing.

He twirled his cane one way, then the other. Sometimes I go to this little restaurant. Chinese place. You ever have Chinese food?

When would I have had that? I said, but I didn't take my eyes off the mermaids bobbing in the slush.

Yeah, you probably wouldn't have had the chance, gone as long as you've been. Anyway, I go to this little restaurant downtown. Been there awhile. Maybe it was the first one in Chicago, I don't know. I sit at a table with three people. I make the fourth, you understand? I don't eat alone. I never eat alone. I eat with friends. I speak their language. You can too, if you try hard enough, if you want to. It's just a different kind of music. You pick out the melody. You play along.

I cut my eyes to him, this elegant man in his fine, fine clothes and the knife sticking out of his neck, but still said nothing.

He went on: When the waiter comes over, I ask for the chef's special. None of that chop suey crap for me. That's for people who don't know any better. I want *real* Chinese food, spicy and hot. Food that lights you up from the inside. When the other folks at the table get their food, I get mine. I eat with chopsticks. I know exactly how to use them. Don't have to stab the food.

He paused, eyes closed. I eat my fill. Almost tastes good as I remember.

I said, What else do you remember?

What?

Do you remember popcorn?

He blinked, idly touching the handle of the knife. Sure do.

What about coffee cake?

I would do anything for one cup of coffee. With a little chicory.

No, not coffee. Coffee *cake*. With a heavy crumb that sticks to your lips like a kiss.

It was his turn not to answer. He looked out at the mermaids, scratching at the place where the blade had punctured his skin. I was going to ask him how he knew what had killed me, how he read me so easily. And I was going to ask him what had done him in, *who* had, who was so strong and so brutal. But such a look of sadness and surprise passed over his face that I didn't. Maybe he was remembering other things, things he didn't want to. Maybe he was thinking it would be better to be caught in an endless loop, no memories but one.

None but one. Small and precious. A jewel you can hold in the palm of your hand, a—

Pearl, I said.

Pearls? he said, voice suddenly rough and ragged. You looking for treasure now?

What would I do with treasure? I asked.

First mermaids, then treasure, he said, scratching harder at that knife, digging at it. You *are* crazy.

If I am, you are too, I said. We all are.

He didn't want to hear that. He turned and stalked away, his cane whipping at the air, his shoes rough on the snow, pushing at it so forcefully he left footprints all the way down the beach.

You can call me Blue Girl if you want, I said, the words swallowed up by the shrieks of the gulls, the crash of the water.

———⚬⚬⚬———

Vito's latest letter hadn't said much about Aunt Marion. Just that she was going to come and see Frankie and Toni—but he'd written this so many times before that Frankie was sick of reading it. Still, every time he said it, they would trudge to the waiting room the next visiting Sunday and sit there like fools. Finally one of the nuns would notice that they had no visitors and send them back to their cottages.

So Frankie spent a lot of time thinking some very bad thoughts about Aunt Marion. So bad that sometimes she said a few Hail Marys on her own, just in case.

Which was what she was doing as she sat there next to Toni, whispering the Hail Mary under her breath.

"Are you praying?" Toni said.

"No," she said.

"Yes, you are."

"I'm praying for you to move to England."

"Why would I want to move to England? Don't you know there's a war on?"

Frankie didn't answer, just finished up her Hail Mary and moved into an Our Father, mostly because she had started thinking sinful thoughts about Toni again, and figured Toni should have her own set of prayers.

"Do you really want her to come so much?" said Toni.

"No," Frankie said.

"Yes, you do."

"Funny you keep asking me what I'm doing if you know so much better."

Toni sighed and plucked at the hem of her dress. She was less jumpy today. Frankie didn't have to clamp her hand down on Toni's knee to keep her from bouncing them off the bench. She looked older than she had when their father left. Frankie did too. Maybe that's what happened when your father went away. You grew up. Not because you wanted to. Because what else were you going to do?

Toni said, "That's just it, I don't know better. When was the last time you seen Aunt Marion?"

"The same time you did. Thanksgiving a few years ago."

"I don't remember that."

"Sure you do. We went to the apartment on Irving Avenue. Daddy stuffed the turkey with spaghetti. Aunt Marion was there. She didn't say much, but she was there."

"You're not supposed to stuff a turkey with spaghetti," said Toni.

"Says you."

"When I have Thanksgiving at my house, I'm going to stuff my turkey with real stuffing."

"Good to know," Frankie said.

"You don't believe me?"

"I don't care."

Toni had the nerve to look hurt. "You don't want to come to my house for Thanksgiving?"

Frankie sighed. "Why are we even talking about this? You don't have a house. You don't have a turkey. And it's not Thanksgiving."

"Don't remind me," Toni said, gripping her belly as if it ached her. "When are you going to get me a job in the kitchen?"

"I'm not."

"Why?"

"Because you're trouble enough as it is."

"I ain't done nothing."

"Today," Frankie said.

"You should be a nun, Frankie. You sound just like one."

"Bite your tongue."

"And you're just as pretty as they are."

Frankie raised her fist. Just then, someone coughed. They looked up and there she was. Short and stout as a teapot, like the song said. Thick dark hair on top of a moon face. Holding a giant pocketbook. Scowling.

Frankie lowered her fist. "Aunt Marion?"

"I hope you weren't about to sock your sister," Aunt Marion said. She had an Italian accent like their father's, only not as strong. And she didn't skip words like he did.

Frankie's face went hot, because grown women didn't sock their sisters. "I was just fooling."

"Hmmm," said Aunt Marion. "Well, come on, then."

"Where?"

"You don't want fresh air?"

They always wanted fresh air, but no one ever asked them

what they wanted. Toni and Frankie glanced at each other and followed Aunt Marion as she walked through the visiting day crowd. One of the nuns said, "Visiting hours are over at four sharp." Aunt Marion nodded only once and kept walking, her heels clicking sharply on the polished floor. Frankie was happy to see that she was as tall as her aunt was, even with Aunt Marion's heels, and that Toni was shorter than both.

Aunt Marion reached the door that led outside, pushed it open, and marched through. She was marching so fast that they had to skip some to keep up. They didn't even have time to put on their coats.

Over her shoulder, Aunt Marion said, "Your father says hello."

It seemed to Frankie that the only people saying hello to each other were Vito and Aunt Marion. Who really knew what her father said? But thinking about him gave Frankie a pain in her head, so she stopped thinking.

The sky was blue as a robin's egg. There was a ferocious bite in the air, but it was all right by Frankie. It felt good to walk in the chill. It made her feel clean.

"I'm cold," Toni whined.

"We should walk faster, then," said Aunt Marion. "It will warm you up."

Toni didn't like it, but she didn't complain again. Maybe she was still hoping that Aunt Marion had some treats banging around in that big pocketbook. Or maybe she thought Aunt Marion was going to walk them right off the grounds to a fancy restaurant where they served turkeys stuffed just the right way. But Aunt Marion kept walking. It was only when they got to the courtyard angel that she stopped.

"Bella," said Aunt Marion, and Frankie felt another pain. But Aunt Marion was looking up at the stone angel, not Frankie. And that stone angel was beautiful, anyone would think so.

"Who is she?" Aunt Marion asked.

"We just call her the angel," Toni said. "The nuns say she looks out for us."

Aunt Marion held her pocketbook high and found a bench near the statue. "Let's sit."

"Aren't we going somewhere to eat?" Toni said.

Aunt Marion frowned. "Didn't you have supper already? It's half past two."

"We had supper, all right. If you can call gray meat and rainbow potatoes supper," Toni grumbled.

"What are rainbow potatoes?"

"Potatoes so bruised that they're about a million colors. Like a rainbow," Frankie said.

"Hmmm," said Aunt Marion. She nodded, still staring at the courtyard angel like she expected the angel to start singing or playing the harp. She set her giant pocketbook on the ground, then thought better of it, and put it back on her lap. It really did look like a suitcase. Like she'd been traveling. Then Frankie remembered that she had traveled at least once.

"When did you get here?" Frankie said.

Aunt Marion looked surprised. "Right before two. I took the streetcar."

"No, I mean, when did you first come to America?"

"Oh," Aunt Marion said. "That. In 1920. Two years after my brother—your father—did. A long time ago."

"Were you scared?"

"You mean was I scared to ride on a boat for three weeks with a bunch of stinking men? Was I scared to go to a country where no one spoke my language?"

"Yeah. Were you?"

Her lips twitched. "Not at all."

Toni said, "Why do you speak English better than Daddy if he was here longer than you?"

"Sometimes it works that way," she says. "Some people learn a new language very fast, some people can't let go of the old one."

"I spoke Italian once," Frankie said. "At least, that's what Vito tells me. I don't remember."

"Yes," said Aunt Marion. Her lips opened as if she was going to say more, but then she snapped them together before they let loose.

"Did our father say anything else?" Frankie asked.

"About what?"

Frankie shrugged. Toni said, "About us."

"He misses you," Aunt Marion said.

Frankie could only see one side of Aunt Marion's face because she was sitting next to her on the bench. "That's what he told you?"

Aunt Marion gazed up at the angel. "Yes."

Toni got up from the bench and rolled a rock with her shoe. Frankie scooted away from Aunt Marion. She didn't say that

Marion was going to have to confess her lies at her next confession. Frankie assumed Aunt Marion knew that already. Or maybe she didn't care.

Aunt Marion stood the pocketbook on her lap and opened it. "I can't stay long today, but I have something for you both. From your father."

From inside the enormous pocketbook, she pulled something wrapped in tissue paper. "Here," she said, offering it to Toni.

Toni stopped kicking the rock and took it. She shoved Frankie aside to sit back down on the bench and dug through the tissue paper. "A hat!" she said, fingering the soft blue felt, the glossy black feathers. She put it on and turned to me. "How does it look?"

"Real swell," Frankie said. And it did, too, nestled in her dark hair. Frankie thought about Vito's letters, about how Ada's girls couldn't get enough of hats. Frankie wondered if they had hats like Toni's. She wondered if they had *lots* of hats like Toni's. She wondered if it was one of theirs. A castoff.

"And this is for you, Frankie." Frankie expected Aunt Marion to pull out another hat, but she didn't. She handed Frankie a thin metal tin with no label.

"What's this?" Frankie said. "Cigarettes? I don't smoke."

"Open it."

Frankie opened the container to find a bunch of crayons. No, not exactly crayons. She picked up the red one.

"Careful," said Aunt Toni. "You don't want to get stained."

It was a cross between a crayon and paint so thick they made sticks out of it.

"It's a pastel," Aunt Toni told Frankie. "Artists use them to draw."

An artist *had* used these, at least a little. There was only half a black stick, and some of the other colors were worn down here and there. A cast-off set. But that was all right with Frankie. I wondered about the artist who had been forced to sell them. I wonder how how hungry and desperate that artist must have been.

Frankie said, "My father wanted you to buy me this?"

"And this," said Aunt Marion. She pulled out a small sketch pad with the thickest, nicest paper Frankie had ever seen and gave it to her. "He sent me the money. He said you liked to draw. They're used. We couldn't afford new. But they're still good."

"That's okay," she said. "This is, this is . . ." She trailed off, trying to decide exactly what it was. How she felt about it.

Just then, a tall man in a brown coat passed by, walking with a boy. *The* boy. Her boy.

Frankie froze right in the middle of her sentence. He—the boy, Sam—glanced at her. He tipped his cap and said, "Hi, Frankie," with a smile just deep enough to show his dimples. His voice, lower than she'd expected, slipped under her skin, vibrating there, as if someone had just moved a bow across the strings of a cello and left her yearning for a whole symphony. The man and Aunt Marion exchanged good afternoons. Then the man put his hand on Sam's neck and steered him around the other side of the angel, and out of sight.

Toni watched them go, stroking the feathers on her new hat, the sly smirk on her face aging her a thousand years. Aunt Marion nodded at the angel, as if they were talking to each other, but only in their heads, no time for dimpled boys. Frankie sat there, oblivious to them all, the pastel warm between her fingers, thinking about the fact that Sam knew her name, thinking about the way his lower lip curled under his teeth to pronounce it, thinking about his lips and teeth and hair and bones and all the other truths of a body that seem so mundane when that body is yours, and so fascinating when that body belongs to someone else.

Frankie smoothed a page in her book and sketched an apple, round and red and good enough to eat.

WHAT DIDN'T BURN IN THE FIRE

I WENT TO THE BLUE house in the sea of brick and watched Berry Girl and her boxer boy eat a quiet lunch at their kitchen table. They did not speak, but held hands through the entire meal—cheese sandwiches, cups of canned tomato soup. While I was watching the two of them, cozy in their quiet, shabby kitchen, I thought about the new chapters of *The Hobbit* I'd read over the shoulder of the blond man with the crooked teeth. With the help of the magic ring, Bilbo Baggins escaped the goblins and the creature Gollum, made his way out of the Misty Mountains, and ran straight into Gandalf the wizard and the dwarves. But Bilbo didn't tell anyone about the magic ring that could render him invisible. Hobbits had secrets too. When the wolves found them, and then the goblins, the eagles came and swept up the hobbit and the wizard and the dwarves and flew them away. But no eagles came to my rescue when the red fox found me again.

Shoo! I said.

It snuffled at my feet like a dog. It was beneath the dignity of a fox to snuffle at the feet of a person with no actual feet. Which is what I told him.

He stopped snuffling and looked up, reproaching me with eyes like the amber in my mother's bracelets.

Fine, I said, it's beneath my dignity to peep into people's windows.

Of course it wasn't. But watching Berry Girl and Boxer Boy hold hands over lunch hurt like a splinter a pin a shard of glass, so I drifted to the next yard, the fox trotting after me, the stupid, beautiful thing. The people in the next house were also getting ready for lunch, each in their own way—a pale woman heating something on the stove, and a paler man behind her, a hand on her hip and the other furiously kneading one of her breasts as if it were a lump of dough. Maybe this happened every day. He came home for lunch, kneaded one of her breasts like a lump of dough while she stirred the pot and tried not to roll her eyes. Except now she was rolling her eyes.

She's rolling her eyes, I told the fox.

The fox smiled a foxy smile, because nothing in the whole wide world was new.

I moved to the next window, where a tired woman fed four children under the age of six; the next, where a lone man ate a lone sandwich at a lone table with a lone chair; the next, where a young boy cuddled a striped cat that strained to get away; the next, where a young woman curled up on a homemade rug, crying and crying and crying; the next, where a man pulled on a dress and carefully painted his lips red; and the next, where two other men kissed so passionately it was hard to tell one man from the other. Faster I moved from window to window—a woman a man a girl a boy a cat eating and feeding and kneading and holding and clawing and crying and painting and kissing—looking in on all that life, the happy-unhappy thrill of it, and I wanted a cheese-and-lettuce sandwich, a cup of hot soup. I wanted someone to hold my hand as I ate. I wanted a breast to knead, a cat with a desperate heart clawing blood from my skin. I wanted my own wings so that I could swoop in and save myself.

I might have cried a little, or I might have punched the window with my not-fist, I might have clutched at my chest trying to take a breath, but I couldn't be sure. One minute I was standing in the yard of a stranger and the next I was slumped at the foot of the angel, telling her about the fox, that stupid beautiful thing.

It won't leave me alone, I said. One day someone will see it, and then what will happen?

You know the answer to that, the angel said.

What?

What happens to you all. Blood to stone, stone to ash.

I'm not *ash*, I said.

Her laugh was kind. Aren't you, though? You're what didn't burn in the fire.

I said, I don't remember a fire.

Again, the kind laugh. There's always a fire.

Frankie confessed everything. Not to Father, but to Loretta and Huckle. The first time she saw Sam skidding across the kitchen floor. The way he hovered behind the other senior boys twist-ing his hat but never saying a word. And then out of the blue, "Hi, Frankie," as if they'd known each other forever.

The whole cottage was lined up, waiting for Sister Bert to check their hair for lice. Loretta, Huckle, and Frankie were all the way in the back, whispering.

"Why didn't you tell us you had a fella?" Huckle demanded.

"Shhh!" Frankie said.

"Well, why didn't you?"

"Because I didn't. I don't."

"Sure sounds like you do."

"I don't," Frankie said. And then she added, "yet."

"Oo-la-la!" Huckle said.

"Shh!" Frankie shook her fist at Huckle as she giggled.

"Please don't shake your fist like that, Francesca, it makes me nervous," Sister Bert called as she inspected Joanie McNal-ly's hair for nits. They had two new girls in the cottage, and whenever there were new girls, there were nits.

"Aw, come on, Sister Bert. Nothing makes you nervous," Joanie McNally said, talking while bent at the waist, almost upside down. "You could probably take on Hitler hisself!"

Sister Bert pursed her lips and held up something pinched between her fingertips. "Just as I thought. A nit. I believe I shall call him Hitler," and she squished him between her fingernails. "All right, Joanie, you can stand up straight. Unless you prefer spending your time looking at your own knees."

They all knew what was up now, and started moaning even before Sister Bert left the cottage to scare up some kerosene. If one of them had it, it usually meant all of them had it. Frankie's scalp suddenly felt itchy, and she scratched at it. Soon all of them had their hair soaked in kerosene and wrapped up in towels.

"Gosh, we *stink*!" said Huckle.

"You always stink," Stella said, and then she said, "Ow!" when Huckle socked her on the arm.

Immediately Stella started moaning. "Sister Bert! Huckle hit me!"

"Oh, that's terrible," said Sister Bert as she unscrewed the cap off another can of kerosene. "Huckle, please don't hit Stella. It makes her yell and that gives me a pain between my eyes."

Stella stopped whining and watched Sister Bert with a sad look on her face; Frankie could see that it wasn't just another one of her acting jobs. As much as she couldn't stand Miss My-Name-Means-Star-in-Italian-and-Isn't-My-Blond-Hair-Swell? and as much she liked it when Sister Bert said things like that to her, she couldn't help but feel just a little sorry for Stella; you could tell that Sister Bert didn't like her any more than any of them did. She wondered if there was a person who truly liked Stella.

There had been, once. Stella was an only child born to a silvery sylph of a woman even more beautiful than her own daughter and a man so handsome that both men and women would stop on the street to stare. They knew they were beautiful, and they knew their child was too, so they'd spent all of their savings to commission a painting of the three of them. They'd sat for the artist for weeks, little Stella still and quiet as a porcelain doll on her mother's lap. Once the painting was done, they'd hung it over their fireplace and spent their evenings admiring it, and one another. But when the silvery sylph caught a strange sort of cough, grew thinner and thinner till she was more spirit than flesh, they'd had no money left to treat what consumed her. During her last months, she'd taken to sleeping outside in the yard to take the edge off her fever, snowflakes gathering on her eyelashes. And then one morning, she was gone to the angels. Stella's father sat by the fire, drinking and staring at the portrait of his family, too beautiful for this life. And though his own beautiful daughter was hungry for food and for solace, though she brushed her own hair till it shone and dressed herself as nicely as she could, he gave all his attention to his bottle until he too was in the ground.

Now, at fifteen, Stella liked herself, *loved* herself, because there was no one else to do it. And one day she would convince someone else to take the job, through sheer force of her considerable will.

It would, in fact, take a lot of someone elses to make up what she had lost.

When the kerosene had set long enough, Loretta unwrapped her own hair and plopped herself on the floor in front of me. Frankie combed through Loretta's hair with the lice comb, looking for the little white eggs and the bugs. When she found a nit or a bug, she squeezed it between her fingernails.

"Look at us. We're just a bunch of nitpickers!" Joanie McNally said.

"Funny," Loretta said. Frankie knew that she hated the lice and the smell of the kerosene. "We don't look like people. We look like monkeys," she said, which made Frankie think of the boys and all their monkeying around, which *then* made her think about washing dishes in the senior boys' dining room, which led her to the boy, her boy. Sam. She sighed.

"Hey! Are you looking for nits or what?" Loretta said.

"No, she's just mooning over what's-his-face," said Huckle. She would have said more, but Frankie kicked her.

"Who?" Stella said. "Who is Frankie mooning over?"

"Oh, I'm sure Huckle is talking about Jesus," said Sister Bert. "Francesca is obviously praying to Our Lord and Savior so that we never get nits again." She opened a drawer and took out a pair of scissors. "I suppose now is as good a time as any to give everyone a trim. When you're all finished combing through each other's hair, I'll trim you up. Then we'll go down to the shower room and rinse the kerosene out."

Frankie didn't cry much, but that was what she wanted to do right then and there. Nobody but orphans wore their hair up around their ears. And she still had so little hair that she couldn't stand to lose even a tiny bit of it.

"Ow!" Loretta said. "Don't tug so hard!"

"Sorry," Frankie told her. "I don't see why we have to get our hair cut so short."

"To keep away the nits," Loretta said matter-of-factly.

"It doesn't work too well." Frankie pulled a tiny gray bug from a strand of Loretta's hair and killed it with a pinch. "What boys are going to look at us with orphan's hair?"

Huckle snorted. "Maybe that's the whole point."

When Sister got done trimming everyone's hair, they gathered up the kerosene-soaked towels and dropped them at the laundry. Frankie didn't complain, though; none of them did. What would be the use? When she got out of the orphanage, Frankie thought, she would grow her hair as long as Lana Turner's, and curl it every night so that it fell into her eyes the way Lana's did. That kind of hair would make any boy sit up and pay attention. Then she thought about how she'd have to confess having impure thoughts on Sunday.

It took about five minutes to walk out of the cottage and down to the shower room. They changed into their tights—the sack dresses they wore into the showers—in the dressing rooms, and then all forty of them crowded into the shower room. Sister Bert passed out the soap, and they each picked a showerhead. Most girls tried to get the ones in the corners because they thought they got more privacy that way, but the truth was that there wasn't any privacy when you were soaping up with forty other girls. It was the tights—those dresses—that kept them decent and modest, the nuns said. To wash, they turned their back to the other girls and reached underneath the dress and did the best they could. If you asked me, sticking your hands underneath a wet dress seemed far more lewd and far less effective an act than simply washing a naked body, but no one was asking me, a scandalous and shameless girl, not nearly dead enough.

After they washed, they took that strong brown soap and

scrubbed their hair with it, too, making sure that they rinsed out all the stinky kerosene. Basically, they were trading one kind of stink for another kind of stink, kerosene for the brown soap. In the wintertime, Frankie's skin was always itching from one or the other.

As they got ready for bed, Huckle said, "So what are you going to do?"

"About what?"

"About him," she said, as if Frankie was too silly for words.

"What can I do?"

"You're going to have to talk to him."

"When?"

Loretta said, "In the yard."

"In the yard?" Frankie squeaked. Some of the other girls glared at them because the radio was on. Frankie lowered her voice. "I can't talk to him in the yard. If the nuns see me crossing the yellow line, they'll beat me for sure."

"He ain't worth a beating?" said Huckle. "I don't know if I'd want a fella that ain't worth a beating."

Loretta shrugged. "And you can get beat for a lot less around here."

"I don't know," Frankie said. But they were right. She had to do something. What if his eighteenth birthday was next month? What if it was next week? What if he was shipping out tomorrow and Frankie would never see him again? How can you miss someone you never really met?

But as soon as she could, Frankie climbed to the top of the slide, where she used to sit to see her brother, Vito. Since so many older boys had gone, it was easy to spot Sam. There he was, kicking a ball across the yard to another, shorter boy. Sam looked up, and waved. Frankie glanced around, making sure he was waving at her, before she waved back. And she realized that Sam was the boy who was with Vito the last day he was here, the boy who'd gotten hit upside the head for waving at her. Maybe Sam thought *she* was worth a beating. The thought made her feel warm inside, as if she were sipping hot chocolate after coming in from the snow.

She climbed down from the slide. Her skin was sweaty and she wasn't sure if she could do it, wasn't sure if she could stand there by the yellow line. But she did. The slip of paper was in her pocket. Just a short note in pencil—no hearts, no flowers. Loretta and Huckle thought she should put *Frankie + Sam* on it, but she couldn't—it seemed both too bold and too childish. And, as wobbly as her knees were, as much as her hands were shaking, she didn't want to sound that cheap.

She waited by the fence for a long time, so long she thought he wouldn't come. For some crazy reason she started thinking about Vito again. She wondered if there was ever a girl who had caught his eye, and if he ever stood by the fence, risking a beating for that girl. Maybe he did what Frankie was doing right now lots of times. But Frankie had never asked.

A rock skidded over the top of her shoe. She didn't turn around. She didn't look. She crouched and fooled with the buckle of her shoe with one hand. With the other, she dropped the note on the yellow line. She saw a hand snatch it up, heard footsteps walking away.

"What are you doing?"

She tipped over onto the pavement as if someone had pushed her. Sister George blocked the sun like one of those eclipses.

"I'm fixing my shoe. I think the buckle's broken."

Sister George grabbed her by the collar and hauled her up. "There's nothing wrong with your shoe."

"There was," Frankie said.

Sister gave Frankie a good pinch on the meaty part of her arm. "Don't get smart with me."

Frankie hated when Sister said that. She hated when any of the nuns said that. What did they want the girls to be, dumb?

"I'm not trying to be . . ." Frankie trailed off, because she wasn't quite sure what she was trying to be.

"Do you think I don't know what you're doing?"

Frankie's brain started to chatter. Had she seen her drop the note? Had she just gotten Sam in trouble? Was Sister going to cut off all Frankie's hair again? "I wasn't doing anything."

"Those boys have enough to worry about without you girls running around acting like trash."

That made Frankie mad. She wasn't acting like anything, especially not trash. "What boys?" she said.

Sister leaned in. Frankie could smell the onions on her breath. Frankie knew she'd had onions, because she'd helped Choppy make the nuns' supper. Liver and onions and a side of potato, plus real coffee with a little sugar.

Sister George said, "Do you want to go to hell?"

The warm feeling in Frankie's guts was replaced by the kind of cold she got when she stood in the icebox, a scoopful of

Jell-O that hadn't had enough time to set sliding through her fingers. "No."

"Are you sure?"

"Yes."

"Good," Sister said, and shoved her back toward the girls' side of the play yard. "Then stay away from the yellow line. I catch you over here again, you'll wish for the devil to take you."

Sister stomped away, but not before tearing a jump rope right out of another girl's hands for no good reason. The girl looked at her empty hands, then shrugged. Who knows how many things had been ripped from her.

FAIRY TALES

ONCE UPON A TIME, I was a small girl in a big house on a big lake in the middle of a big country. I was fourteen when a German submarine sank the *Lusitania*, killing over a hundred twenty Americans; sixteen when the United States entered World War I; seventeen when the first cases of the flu were reported in Chicago. Death was everywhere, but it seemed to have so little to do with me; nothing but a bunch of scary stories that my parents spoke about in hushed tones when they thought their children were asleep. Besides, I had my own battles, caught as I was between my stuffy older brother, William, he of the thick glasses and the thicker head, and my younger brother, Frederick, of the quick smile and quicker fists.

Frederick said to my mother, "I don't know why I go to the trouble to get into a fistfight with the Jensen twins when all you do is fret over Pearl. *She* didn't get into a fistfight."

"I haven't forgotten your fight," my mother said. "But others will forget it soon enough. People will never forget a young woman behaving like a wild animal. I don't understand what's gotten into you, Pearl. That you keep—" She scissored off the end of her own sentence, tugged her lips tight.

I was sipping hot tea in front of the window, admiring the view of our large front lawns. So I liked to take walks in the woods behind the house. I liked to *run* through the woods. I liked to wade in the lake after running through the woods. I'd come home disheveled and damp, but no more disheveled and damp than I always had.

But I was seventeen now, not seven. Mother said it was unseemly. Mother said it was scandalous.

"Nobody saw me," I said.

"Everyone saw you," my mother said.

"You're worried about my prospects."

"*You* should be worried about your prospects."

"It doesn't matter," Frederick said. "The war and the flu will kill all the young men, and she'll end up a spinster anyway."

"Nonsense," said Father. "The flu will pass and the war will end and Pearl will be married like any other girl."

"What a pearl, our Pearl," Frederick sang. He held his wineglass to the light, turned it, appraising. "She is a treasure, something you lock up in a box and only take out on holidays."

William peered over his thick glasses. "That's what all women are. Treasures."

Frederick laughed, said, "I pity the woman you marry, William." He knocked back the wine in far too practiced a manner for someone only sixteen. My mother frowned.

I wondered what Mother would have done if she'd been the one to find the box stowed in the back of William's closet. All those French postcards, all those slyly grinning young women bent this way and that, the sight of them setting my bones to thrumming. No one worried if *they* went running in the forest, leaves churning up around their plump, bare thighs.

William snapped the paper he wasn't really reading. "Charles Kent won't allow Pearl to gallop through the woods."

"Charles Kent," I spat.

William continued as if I'd never spoken. "So she better get used to staying indoors and behaving like a lady."

My turn to laugh. "And you'd know all about ladies, William."

"He's a respectable young man," said Mother.

"William?" I said.

"Charles Kent!" barked Mother.

"You mean he's richer than Midas," said Frederick, already slurring a little.

"Charles Kent," I repeated, conjuring up his slicked-back dishwater hair, the down-turned mouth, overly pink lips in a pallid face, the petulance that emanated from him like musk. "He stares too much."

My mother jerked a red thread through the hide of her needlework. "It's a compliment to you, Pearl."

But that's not what it was.

That's not what it was.

The thought of Charles, the revulsion, caught in my throat, and I coughed. Once I started, I couldn't stop. I coughed until a smear of red marked my knuckles, as if I had been in a fistfight after all.

"Pearl?" my father said. "Are you all right? Pearl?"

"Pearl?"

"Pearl?"

"Pearl?"

———⊷⊶———

Frankie pushed the gig down the hallway toward the boys' slop house, her heart pounding up a storm. But the room was empty. Dinner was over, the porridge bowls and spoons thrown every which way. Swallowing the disappointment, she started stacking the bowls onto the gig.

"We're slobs, aren't we?"

She whipped around. There he was, standing in the doorway, hat crushed in his hands as usual.

"You can say that again," Frankie said.

"Doesn't seem fair that we should make the mess and you should clean it up."

"Nuns always say life ain't fair."

"Need some help?" he said, his voice hoarse, as if he didn't use it much. She had never seen a body who looked so nervous. But then, her heart was about to pop out of her mouth.

"Sure," she said. "I'm just putting all the dishes onto the gig."

"Gig?"

"This cart here. So I can bring them back to the kitchen."

He shoved the hat in his back pocket and walked toward Frankie. He helped her stack some of the dishes. "I bet these get heavy."

She nodded. That was what she'd written on the note. *Those dishes sure get heavy.* Frankie figured that if anyone else picked up the note, even a nun, that one sentence wouldn't give her away.

It was hard to look at him. She had to tilt her head back, she was so short. She tried to find something to say, something to talk about, but she was distracted by the scant whiskers that darkened his chin, one small cut on his jaw.

He said, "Sister George didn't seem so happy with you out in the yard. Are you all right?"

"She just gave me a pinch and a shove. I've had worse."

He gave Frankie another few bowls, and she set them on the gig. "She the one who cut your hair?"

Her hands flew up before she could stop them. "Yeah."

He turned red, the flush traveling from his neck into his cheeks. "I didn't mean to say that it looked bad! It didn't look bad at all. And it looks real nice now that it's grown in some."

She forced her hands back to the table. She picked up some more bowls and spoons. "Thanks."

"Sister George ain't the worst nun I ever saw."

She almost dropped the bowls. "She's not? Who is, then?"

"One time, this kid sicked up his food? An old nun, I forget her name, scraped the sick back into a bowl and made him eat it."

Now her hands flew up to her mouth. "No."

"Yeah," he said. "Made us all sick to watch. But I guess that was a long time ago, when I was just little. I haven't seen anything like that in a while."

"Well, that's something," Frankie said. "Vito never told me about that."

115

"Vito. I remember him. He's your brother, right?"

"Yeah."

"But he's not around anymore. He go into the service?"

"No," Frankie said. "He's in Colorado."

Sam handed her another couple of bowls. "What's he doing in Colorado?"

"My father moved there."

"Your father moved to Colorado and took your brother?"

"Yeah."

"But not you."

She didn't answer. She didn't need to.

"That doesn't sound right," he said.

She shrugged like the girl in the yard who'd gotten her jump rope ripped from her hands. "What can you do?"

He tilted his head and looked down at her. She could see a tiny reflection of herself in his big brown eyes.

"I'm Sam," he said.

"I know. I mean, I'm Frankie."

"I know," he said, smiling a little. "If it makes any difference, Frankie, I'm glad your father didn't take you away."

He held out a fistful of spoons like a bouquet. The blush was back, pinking up his cheeks, but he held her gaze.

"Me too," she said. She held out her hand to take the spoons. When her fingertips brushed his knuckles, he dropped the spoons, which clattered on the table and floor. They snatched back their hands as if they'd both been burned.

There's always a fire, I said.

WHAT FRANKIE DIDN'T CONFESS

THAT SHE'D TAKEN THE LORD'S name in vain before Choppy could whack her with a towel or hit her with a tomato. That she'd stolen spoonfuls of soupy cake batter before she popped the cake into the oven. That she'd left Sam that note in the yard. That he'd come to the boys' slop house after dinner. That her hand had brushed his. That she wanted more brushing everywhere. That he'd been coming to see her every day after. That she thought about him all the time. That thinking about him pushed everything else out of her head, like the rest of the world didn't matter anymore. That Hitler could have bombed Chicago and she wouldn't have noticed.

What she did confess: that Toni's cottage had gotten too crowded, so the nuns moved her up to a girls' senior cottage. That the cottage they moved her to was Frankie's. That Toni was doing her best to drive Frankie and everyone else batty. That it was working. That Toni should be sent to Germany to spy for America because ten minutes in a room with her would be enough to crack Adolf like an egg.

"Who was that fella I saw you talking to?"

Frankie and Toni were at the back of the line, following Sister Bert as she walked across the street. On Saturday afternoons, Sister Bert liked to march the girls around town for about an hour or so, letting them look in the shop windows and letting whoever had a penny get some candy in the candy store. Usually Frankie talked to Loretta on these outings. Instead, Toni was killing Frankie with questions.

"Huh?" Frankie said. "Who?"

"That tall fella you were talking to. Who was he?"

"I wasn't talking to any fella," Frankie said.

"Yes, you were. I saw you. In the yard, by the yellow line."

"Are you crazy? I wouldn't cross the yellow line," Frankie said.

"I didn't say you crossed it, I said you was standing by it."

"That's a crime, now?"

"Who was the fella?"

"What fella?"

"The one who was across the yellow line," Toni said, getting louder.

"In case you hadn't noticed, all the boys are across the yellow line. That's where they keep them at the Guardians."

"Course I noticed that," Toni said. "I was just wondering when *you* noticed. It's not like you ever noticed before."

"What would you know about what I notice?" said Frankie.

"You're my sister," Toni said.

"So?"

"That means I know you better than you know yourself."

"You don't know nothing."

"I know you were talking to a tall fella with brown hair and a gray cap. So what's his name?"

"St. Anthony. I was asking him where you lost your mind."

Sister Bert stopped abruptly, and all the girls slammed into one another. She turned and glared down the line. "Francesca! Antonina! All your bickering is enough to bring down the Allies!"

"What?" said Toni. "I don't—"

"Sorry, Sister," Frankie said.

"But—" Toni began, but Frankie elbowed her so hard that she fell against the butcher's window. Sausage links swung behind her.

Toni got the message. "Sorry, Sister," she said.

"And?" said Sister.

"We'll try to keep it zipped," Frankie said.

"Do more than try," said Sister Bert. "This heat is giving me headache enough." She whipped around and waved us on toward the candy shop.

"She don't have to be so cranky about it," Toni muttered, rubbing her ribs. "We were just talking."

Loretta, who'd been quiet up till now, said, "That wasn't cranky. If she was cranky, she would have threatened to call President Roosebelt."

"It's President Roose*velt*," said Toni, in her snottiest voice.

"No," said Loretta. "It's President Roose*belt*. What she'd smack you with if she was really mad."

Toni's mouth dropped open. "But all the other girls said Sister Bert wasn't the type to beat on people."

"Maybe you'll be the first," Frankie said.

Toni scowled and marched ahead, falling in next to Stella, her new best friend. Now there was a match made in heaven. Which got Frankie thinking about matches made in heaven, which got her thinking about Sam, which made her knees feel like rubber, bending every which way.

"Hey, Loretta?"

"What?"

"Do you confess everything?"

"What do you mean?"

"When you go to confession, do you confess everything?"

Loretta bit her lip. "We're supposed to."

"That doesn't answer my question."

"Most times I do," she said. "But sometimes I don't." She turned a little bit pink. "Some things are too embarrassing. But then I confess them in private to God at night. And I say my Hail Marys and my Our Fathers right then. Right to God. That should count, don't you think?"

"I guess." Frankie wanted to ask her what was too embarrassing to talk about, but she figured that if Loretta wasn't going to tell Father, she wouldn't tell Frankie either. "How do you know how many Hail Marys to say?"

"Father never gives me more than ten, so I always say fifty, just in case."

"Fifty!" Now Frankie really wanted to know what Loretta

was thinking. If there was someone she had her eye on, someone who made her all shivery just to look. Which there was. It was nothing Loretta could confess, either.

"Girls!" yelled Sister Bert, who was waiting with everyone else up at the corner. "Stop lollygagging and keep up, please!"

They ran to catch the rest of the group but had to wait for a streetcar to pass before they could start walking again. Because everyone else was around, Frankie didn't want to ask Loretta more questions about confessing, but she didn't have anything else to talk about, so she just stayed quiet. That was the nice thing about walking with Loretta, because she didn't have a problem with quiet. Some girls just had to chatter their heads off, whether because they couldn't stand the silence or maybe they didn't like to keep themselves company. Frankie liked talking, but she also liked silence, especially with it being a little warmer now, the air so heavy with rain, and Loretta was the same way. As she looked into the shop windows, admiring shoes and dresses as they walked, Frankie read the posters pasted on some of the door and walls.

"Buy war bonds!" Which was fine, except Frankie didn't have any money to buy anything. And she wasn't sure what bonds were.

"Books are weapons in the war of ideas!" She knew they were in a war, but she didn't think it was about ideas. Unless it was about the idea that bombing people was a really bad one.

"Defend your country. Enlist now."

This last billboard had a picture of Uncle Sam rolling up

his sleeve to show a big arm muscle. Frankie looked around and saw a gaggle of sailors walking around in their crazy, wide-legged uniforms, but they all looked too young, younger than Vito even, to have such big muscles as the Uncle Sam in the picture. When they spotted the girls, they started pushing and shoving each other. Stella started to giggle and waved at one of them. The sailors waved back.

Sister Bert herded them into the candy store because a couple of the girls had pennies that their relatives gave them. Frankie didn't have any pennies, but she loved the smell of the candy store and the pretty colors of the candy. Even with the war on, there were jars of licorice whips, suckers, rock candy, gooey-looking fudge and caramels, though not as many as there used to be. How the candy store could keep making candy with sugar being rationed she didn't know, but she figured that a candy-store owner probably was allowed to buy more sugar than everyone else.

Loretta was mooning over the candy case with Huckle, so Frankie wandered over to the window display. They had pretty white boxes tied up with bows, but if you looked close, you could see that the boxes and the bows had dust on them, and that there was no candy in them, because it was too hot in the window. Frankie pulled at her collar. She wondered if it was warm in Colorado. In his last letter, Vito hadn't said.

> *Dear Frankie,*
>
> *Thanks for the drawing—I never seen anything so swell. I could almost taste that bowl of fruit! I'm glad that Aunt Marion*

made good on her promise and went to see you. I didn't know Dad was sending her money to buy you and Toni a present, but I'm glad to hear that, too. I told you that Dad misses you and Toni a lot. He talks about you all the time. "Belle!" he says. My beautiful girls.

Things are pretty much the same around here. Half the time Ada acts like she can't understand a word I say, the other half she acts like what I say is the worst thing she ever heard. She's an awful cook, did I tell you that? (She put ketchup on the spaghetti once. I thought Dad was going to keel over.) The girls are still spoiled rotten, but they complain less because Dad got mad at the younger one and whacked her for mouthing off. I don't want anyone to get beat, but I can't say that she didn't deserve it. The boys are terrible as always. Mostly I stay out of everyone's way and they stay out of mine. Not a lot of presents here, except for what I buy myself. Not that I'm complaining. It's good to have a job, good to have a little change in my pocket so that I can do what I like. (Most of the time.) And it sure is nice not to have a nun always following me around, waiting to smack me upside the head just for blinking.

But I miss Chicago. I miss the smell of it. I even miss that stupid orphanage, if you can believe that. The yard with the yellow line down the middle. The sound of the rain on the windows. Denver is nice enough, but it's like living on some other planet, with all these crazy mountains all around. I'm antsy all the time. I keep up with the papers, so I know this war is going to last awhile. I figured that I'll be eighteen soon enough, so why not just join up now? Get on with it. I asked Dad, and he said no.

Can you believe it? I couldn't. I said, "Why not?" and he couldn't come up with a good reason. Finally he just said that it was dangerous. Did you hear that, Frankie? War is dangerous. Call the papers!

Anyway, Ada is calling me for who knows what, so I gotta cut this short. Keep your chin up and your nose clean.

Love,

Vito

Frankie turned away from the window. The other girls were crowded around this display or that, even though they'd been to this candy shop a million times before. There wasn't anything new, but there was something nice about coming here and see-ing the same things you saw the last time. Something safe. You weren't ever going to follow Sister Bert into the candy shop and find out that the candy man was selling dresses instead. Or furniture. Or cars. And after, they knew that they'd go back to the Guardians and watch a picture. Sometimes it would be a good one, *The Philadelphia Story* maybe, or *Fantasia*, with the scary devil rising from the mountain, or something glamorous or scandalous with Greta Garbo or Hedy Lamarr (if Sister Bert was the one picking the film). Sometimes it would be an old or boring one. But it didn't much matter. You knew what was going on. You knew what would happen next. You weren't con-fused or antsy, like Vito.

Frankie turned back around to look out to the street and saw that Stella and one of the other girls had slipped outside the candy store when no one was looking. They were across the street talking to the sailors. As she watched, Stella grabbed the arm of one fellow, a tall boy with red hair, and squeezed with both hands. He didn't seem to mind. He pulled off his little sailor's hat and dropped it on her head. Where did Stella learn to be so bold? But then, she was always so full of herself, always telling everyone how pretty she was and how much better she was, why wouldn't she be bold in front of sailors?

"What are you doing?" Loretta and Huckle crowded around at the window. Frankie pointed to Stella and the sailors.

"Look at her!" Loretta said as Stella rubbed the sailor's biceps. "Cheap as they come."

"I don't know," said Huckle. "That sailor's all right. Maybe if he wanted to talk to you, you'd act cheap."

Loretta blushed again, for reasons that Huckle wouldn't understand. "No, I wouldn't."

Huckle saw the blush and smiled, slow and lazy. "Say, you sure would."

Outside, Stella threw a glance at the candy store and opened her handbag. Frankie didn't know if she saw the other girls staring through the window, but Stella took out a scrap of paper and a pencil, and the red-headed sailor wrote something down on it. When he was finished writing, she took the paper back and shoved it into her handbag before running back across the street to the candy store.

She and the other girl slipped back inside and made a big

show of looking at all the candy, maybe to make Sister Bert think they'd been there the whole time. But Sister Bert wasn't paying attention to them anyway, she was standing in the corner reading a book. She was always reading a book—sometimes the Bible, sometimes a prayer book, sometimes other books, like today. Sometimes when she was reading the books, she would laugh, or frown, or nod, or smile in a way that made Frankie think that whatever was going on in those books was more real to Sister Bert than the people around her. That if she could choose, Sister Bert would dive into one of those books and never come back out again.

Today, Sister was buried in a copy of *All Quiet on the Western Front*, a book banned and burned by Joseph Goebbels when the Nazis came to power in 1933. Goebbels thought that the book made German soldiers seem weak.

Sister Bert turned the page in the book. Then she threw her head back and laughed.

"What's so funny, Sister?" Huckle asked.

"One of the nuns is described as a beautiful tea cozy," said Sister Bert. "Don't I look like a beautiful tea cozy?"

Frankie thought Sister did, a little.

Loretta frowned. "But isn't *All Quiet on the Western Front* about war? What's funny about war?"

"Nothing is funny about war," Sister said. "But one must find reasons to laugh anyway, especially when nothing is funny. Sometimes joy is the only defense you have, and your only weapon. Remember that."

Frankie looked again at the sailors, who were still on the sidewalk. She remembered how Stella laughed with them. Stella's joy, it seemed to Frankie, was a different sort of weapon.

"What are you all staring at?" Toni said.

"Nobody," Frankie said, but Toni had already shoved her out of the way. "Ooh, boy! Look at them!"

"What do you care?" Frankie said. "None of those boys are dukes."

Frankie figured Toni would just get steamed again, but all she did was smile. "Neither is that fella you were talking to in the yard."

"How many times do I have to tell you that I wasn't talking to any fella?"

Toni shrugged. "At least those fellas are something to look at."

Frankie almost socked her one right there, but Sister Bert had closed her book. "All right, girls, I think we've all had enough of the candy store," she said. "This infernal rain is making us all edgy."

They lined up outside to shuffle back to the orphanage, all of them limp and damp as a pile of washrags. Toni stood next to Stella again. She was whispering something to Stella, maybe something about the sailors. Stella opened up her pocketbook and showed Toni some slips of paper. They both laughed like it was the funniest thing ever. And then Toni pulled two lollipops from her pocket and gave Stella one of them.

Frankie gripped Loretta's arm.

"What?" she said.

"She didn't have any money for those. She went and took them."

"What? Who?"

As Frankie glared, she thought of the P.S. at the bottom of Vito's letter. It had looked like he'd erased it once, changed his mind, and then written it out again:

P.S. I ask Dad all the time when we'll be able to come and get you and Toni out. He says that he doesn't know. But I have to tell you, Frankie, there are some days that I think you're a lot better off where you are, and that's the God's honest truth.

And it was. Frankie knew that it was. She didn't want to be trapped by any mountains. She didn't want to talk only to have Ada shake her head at everything that came out of her mouth. She didn't want to live with spoiled girls and terrible boys. They had those at the Guardians, but at least they weren't strangers. And she really didn't want to leave Sam before . . . before . . . what? Before she could draw him. Before he was hers. She needed to have something of her own for once.

And then there was the thought that wormed its way up out of the dark recesses of her brain like something out of a fresh grave: *Your father doesn't want you. Why do you think he'd take you in even if you had nowhere else to go?*

As she watched Toni and Stella lick those stolen pops, so bold, bolder than anyone, she could see that Toni didn't much care about being safe, about knowing what came next. That Toni didn't much care about anything. That Toni could do something to get herself thrown out of the orphanage, just as easy as breathing.

And if they threw her out, they'd throw Frankie out too. Like a shower of dirty handkerchiefs over a fence. Like so much trash.

GOLDEN ARM

MY FATHER KEPT A SMALL collection of books in his study, books I was not allowed to touch. Only British writers would do for my father's shelves—Charles Dickens. Thackeray. Hardy. A smattering of women, too: Brontë, Austen. My father didn't read any of the books; he displayed the rows of embossed spines to impress the men who came to discuss business over cognac and cigars. He thought the shelves of books made him appear cultured, a man of many interests, even a man of secret passions.

He wasn't.

When I was twelve years old, I crept into the study and stole a book. I thought that if the books were so special, then reading at least one of them might make me special too. I took Mary Shelley's *Frankenstein* to the lake and struggled through the prologue. . . .

I passed the summer of 1816 in the environs of Geneva. The season was cold and rainy, and in the evenings we crowded around a blazing wood fire, and occasionally amused ourselves with some German stories of ghosts, which happened to fall into our hands. These tales excited in us a playful desire of imitation.

. . . only to learn, years later, that Mary Shelley hadn't even written that prologue, that her husband had. But back then, I grew frustrated with the book. The lake beckoned the way it always did, and I left the book in the sand. By the time I was done swimming, the water had found poor *Frankenstein*, tried to drown him. After the book was dry, the pages stuck together as if with glue. When I tried to peel the sheets apart, they tore, leaving fragments of themselves adhered to the other pages. At first my father was angry, but what did he care? The spine still looked handsome enough in the row of unread books.

Sometimes I remembered that waterlogged book when I moved through Chicago, with all the bits and fragments of other eras, other lives, stitched here, there, everywhere—a patched-up monster shambling along. I saw all these people in their uniforms and their smart modern suits, living and breathing, and then I saw all the dead beside them, in and around them, in their raccoon caps and breeches and hoopskirts and bustles, from 1750 and 1800, 1850 and 1880. The two black women dressed in homespun cotton, fleeing Missouri or Kentucky, looking over their shoulders, clutching each other's hands. The exhausted Civil War soldier riding through the streets on his starving horse. For a while, I even looked for Jean Baptiste Point du Sable, a black man who arrived around 1780, the first non-Native to settle here, but I never saw him.

I never saw the Natives who had passed, either, though I saw the living. The Indian Boundary Lines were meant to keep the Potowatomi, the Fox, the Shawnee and Winnebago, out of the city of Chicago, but there were still some trying to survive here on the land of their ancestors. Yet their dead were invisible, at least to me. Maybe those spirits had moved on, like many of their people.

Or maybe the ancestors of the Natives had better things to do than show themselves to ruined girls who liked to read about monsters.

The library was hushed except for the rasp of turning pages. In *The Hobbit*, Bilbo and the dwarves were about to enter the forest of Mirkwood, where there seemed to be eyes everywhere. And giant lurking spiders. I could almost hear their stealthy approach, the kaleidoscope click of their feet.

Thunk!

Everyone in the library looked up. The young librarian in her crisp blouse and skirt leaned over the desk to peer into the stacks. A lone book lay on the floor. The librarian sighed, walked around the desk and into the shelves. She picked up the book and slipped it back into place, returned to the front desk. All was quiet until another book slammed to the floor.

That was when I saw her, the girl in the golden dress. She was lying on her stomach on the very top of the bookshelves, cheek resting on her forearm, her other arm dangling loosely over the rows of books like someone trailing her fingers in a stream. The girl watched the librarian retrieve the fallen book, tuck it back on the shelves, and sit once again at the front desk.

Then the girl in the golden dress reached down and pulled yet another book off the shelf and tossed it to the floor. The librarian jumped, the patrons started, everyone started mumbling about faulty shelves and incompetent employees and drafty old buildings.

That's just cruel, I said.

For a moment I thought the girl wasn't going to answer, but then she said, As if you haven't done the very same sort of thing.

Not to her.

To someone, she said.

What's that book? I asked.

Only a book, she replied.

According to my mother, no book is only a book. A book can improve your mind or it can break it, I said.

Your mother must have been an . . . interesting woman.

Still is, I assume.

You don't know?

I said, I don't want to know.

Her eyes walked my form head to toe and back, then again to the book on the floor. She said, None of these books are the books I want.

What kind of books do you want?

Good ones.

I like the one he's reading, I said, pointing to the blond man with *The Hobbit*.

The girl picked up her head, glanced at the cover of *The Hobbit*, wrinkled her nose. She said, I'm not interested in little men with hairy feet.

So you know it?

She smiled. I don't want to know.

I want to know how you pulled all those books off the shelves, I said. I usually can't move anything that heavy.

You've never slammed a door?

I said usually.

So you've never slammed a door, she replied. Like a cat, she vaulted off the shelf, righted herself in the air, and landed on her feet. Said, I haven't met many of us who can converse.

I was irritated about the books and the doors. I said, Converse?

Talk. Speak. Opine, she said, drawing out the I.

Opine, I said. How is it that you can opine?

Her voice took on a faraway twang as she said, I don't know. I reckon I'm special.

Converse? Reckon? Not from around here, then?

Where's here? she asked.

The public library on a beautiful Chicago day, I said.

Or maybe we just believe we're at the library. Maybe we're somewhere else entirely.

Like where? I said. Heaven?

My father always said that there would be plenty of books in heaven, but I don't think that's where we are. She drifted closer. She was even more beautiful than I'd first realized. Smooth brown skin, large liquid eyes. Full lips. Flawless.

You don't have a mark on you, I said.

Excuse me?

A mark. A wound.

Not all wounds are visible.

How did you die?

Don't be rude, she said.

We're dead, I told her. We don't need to stand on ceremony.

Besides a good story, I haven't figured out what I need.

I have a good story, I said.

She drifted even closer to me, the yellow fabric of her dress seeming rich and thick enough to touch. Let me guess, she said. Poor little rich girl wasted away for want of love. What was his name? Percival? Reginald? Was he a banker, or a banker?

I thought we weren't being rude.

I thought we weren't standing on ceremony.

A tasteful gold cross winked from the hollow of her throat; jeweled combs sparkled in her dark hair. If anyone knew any bankers, it was this girl.

I wasn't talking about *my* story, I said. I have *a* story.

Please don't tell me about the hobbits. I don't want to know about the hobbits.

No, this one is about a crow prince.

What would *you* know about the crows? she said.

Once upon a time, I began.

She rolled her big dark eyes, but she listened to Sister Bertina's whole tale. When it was done, she said, That wasn't particularly terrible. It makes you think about what you might wish for.

I already know what I would wish for, I said.

Percival or Reginald?

Percival, definitely, I said. He wore much tighter trousers than Reginald.

She snorted, surprised, and covered her mouth. Then she dropped her hand, said, I have a story too.

What's his name?

Not that kind of story, she said. A ghost story.

You're joking, I said.

Once upon a time, there was a cruel miserly man who lived in a castle at the very top of a hill.

Was he a banker? I asked.

Shhhh! This is a library and you have to be quiet. As I was saying, the cruel miserly man lived in his castle with nobody but a bear and a bobcat.

A bear and a bobcat?

He'd trapped them as cubs, kept them chained up in the house just because he could. He liked the idea of taming wild things. He also liked counting his money.

One dark and snowy winter's night, while he was checking that there was the same number of silver pieces in his safe that there had been the night before, there was a knock on the door. The cruel man was far too miserly to keep a butler, so he answered the door himself, along with the bear he called Crunch and the bobcat he called Tear. On the doorstep stood a young woman in a threadbare cloak, shivering in the chill. She was on her way to her auntie's house, but she had lost her way in the storm. She begged for the chance to warm herself by the fire. She didn't seem to be afraid of Crunch or Tear.

Now, this cruel and miserly man never would have allowed just any wandering urchin in his castle. But through the holes in that threadbare cloak, he could see glimpses of the purest gold going all the way from her hand to her shoulder. And this miserly man knew real gold when he saw it. He realized that she must be a clever girl, to hide so much jewelry beneath a tattered cloak and disguise her riches.

So he let her in the castle. Sure enough, when she removed her cloak and sat by the fire, her gold gleamed bright. But it wasn't jewelry that gleamed in the light, it was her arm. Her whole arm, in fact, was made of gold. And not just any kind of gold, a malleable sort of gold that let her move the arm, wiggle the fingers—the sort of gold that gleamed brighter than any sun. She explained that she had lost the limb as a child. Her mother had had this one made especially for her, with gold and with magic. She wept just a little when she told the cruel man how her mother had died, penniless because she had spent every single one of her coins and every ounce of her magic on her girl child's beautiful golden arm. Some mothers do things like that, you know. They sacrifice for their children, because they know how much their children will have to sacrifice.

Some mothers do perhaps, I said. But I've never met any.

She put a finger to her lips, continued. The cruel and miserly man couldn't take his eyes off that arm. He knew it was worth a fortune, perhaps more money than he'd ever had in his life. This seemed outrageous to the miserly man. What use was such a thing to a girl? Girls were ridiculous creatures, good for nothing, easily led, easily finished. She would simply give the arm to the first liar who told her he loved her. Look how she trusted *him* so quickly!

The miserly man convinced the girl that it was far too dangerous to go out again and offered her a bed for the night. She eagerly accepted, but after she had fallen asleep, he smothered her with the bedclothes. Crunch and Tear growled and howled, refused to help him, refused to even go near him, so he dragged the body alone out into the woods behind the castle. He stole the golden arm right off the body, and then buried the girl underneath an old pine tree.

When he arrived back home, he decided to chop off his own arm and replace it with the golden one. It was messy work, but soon he was done and the golden arm and hand gleamed in the early dawn light. He wiggled the fingers, admiring. Now, instead of merely possessing riches, he was a rich man in the flesh. The richest man alive.

The next evening, the man was sitting by the fire, the bear and bobcat eyeing him warily from across the room. The castle was still and quiet, with only the crackling of the wood in the fireplace. But then the man heard a strange sound, like the hoot of an owl.

Whooo

He got up and peered out the window, but saw nothing. When he sat again, he heard:

Whooo whooo whooo

Stupid creatures, owls, he thought. *Go catch a mouse!*

But Crunch growled. And Tear shivered. They pulled against their chains.

Who has, the owl said.

But it didn't sound like an owl anymore. The sound was as dry as the tearing of paper, the crunching of leaves beneath heavy, lurching feet.

Who . . . has . . . my

Crunch growled louder. Tear pawed at the floor and howled.

Who . . . has . . . my . . . golden

The man's hair stood on end. Something scratched on the other side of the door, like the scrape of broken fingernails.

Who . . . has . . . my . . . golden . . . arm.

Get back! the man shouted.

Who . . . has . . . my . . . golden . . . arm.

Go away! the man bellowed.

The voice wailed: *WHO . . . HAS . . . MY . . . GOLDEN . . . ARM!*

The miserly man leaped from his chair and ran upstairs to his bedchamber, where he huddled under the covers. He heard a terrible booming sound, a crack and a splinter as the front door gave way.

Crunch, whispered the voice.

Tear, whispered the voice.

RUN!

The man heard the snap of the chains and the scrabble of claws on the floor as the animals fled into the night. The man pulled the blankets all the way over his head. He couldn't see anything in the dark but he knew it was there, he knew *she* was there, climbing the stairs, stealing down the hallway, stepping into the room. She moved, getting closer and closer to the bed, her footsteps creaking on the floorboards. And then she was *on* the bed, creeping up the bedclothes until her face hovered over his, her breath the smell of a new grave.

Who . . .

has . . .

my . . .

golden . . .

ARM?

The man screamed, You don't need it! You're dead!

She said, That's true. And so are you.

Some say she took back her arm and then tore him limb from limb, leaving nothing but scraps behind for the animals. Others say she swallowed him whole and spat out the golden arm like a bone. Either way, no one ever saw the man again. But to this day, if you travel down a certain lonely road, stumble upon a certain hill, and make the trek up to the castle at the top, and you knock on the door, you'll hear howling and growling, and a woman's voice will whisper, *Crunch*, will whisper, *Tear*, before opening the door. You will be blasted by a beam of golden light, and you'll wonder if you are in heaven or hell.

I was so lost in her story that it took me several moments to register that she was done telling it. Let me guess, I said. She was some sort of witch, or avenging angel?

The girl in the golden dress shrugged. Mark Twain told this story a long time ago, she said, but he got it wrong, turned it into a cheap scare, so I fixed it. The girl with the golden arm was a woman like every woman. Sooner or later, someone always tries to take what's yours. She just got mad enough to do something about it.

I said, Well, that's silly.

Pardon me?

There's nothing you can do to stop it. Getting mad doesn't help.

Anger can be righteous.

I said, Are you angry?

She lifted her chin. Sometimes.

I thought about visiting the babies, I thought about the girls, about poking their feet.

I'm not angry, I told her. There's no one left to be mad at.

She laughed, a trickle of honey. Look at how you lie to yourself.

Now I was mad. I said, I do not lie.

Yes, you do.

I'm the only person I've never lied to, I said, but even as I said it, the world pitched and buzzed. A strange static filled my head, a voice barely audible, *You lie to yourself, don't lie to yourself, don't lie to ME.*

Above us, a light bulb blazed hot and bright. Then it burst, showering patrons with glass.

The girl in the golden dress glanced up, then at me with her huge brown eyes. Did you do that?

No, I said.

I think you did that, she said. What else can you do?

Nothing, I said, watching the library patrons brush glass

from their shoulders, blink frightened eyes. I can't do anything.
I'm dead.

So?

So? What do you mean, *so*?

She stared at me long and hard. Then she sighed, said,
Never mind then. She turned and walked away, waving one
hand over her shoulder. Enjoy all the little men with the hairy
feet, she said. She drifted into the stacks, leaving me with the
startled patrons and the hobbits and the blanket of shattered
glass.

NO AND YES

I TRIED KNOCKING A BOOK off a shelf for hours for days for weeks, but I couldn't do it. And I couldn't burst a light bulb either, of course I couldn't do that, no matter how irritable I got. The world wanted nothing to do with me. I wasn't the story, my story had already been told. The people I watched, *they* were the story. Frankie was the story. She moved in one direction, she had a beginning and a middle and a possible painless end. Here she was, in the nuns' section of the kitchen, lifting the cover from a steamer to steal a few carrots, sweet and garish as candy. Here she was, handing the steamer to Sister Cornelius, who was waiting just inside the dining-room door. Here she was, turning the gig around and heading back down the long hallway toward the kitchen with Choppy.

"How old are you, Choppy?"

"Me? Sixteen. Why?"

"Were you always big?"

"Sure," she said. "My brothers are big too. Bigger than me."

"Bigger? How big are they?"

"I don't know," said Choppy. "Eight or nine feet tall." She

smacked the back of Frankie's head the way she always did. "You have any brothers, Fran-ces-ca?"

"One brother. Vito."

"He's here too?"

"He was."

"What happened to him?"

"Nothing. My father took him to Colorado."

Choppy gave Frankie a look and asked the same question that Sam had asked. "Your father took your brother and not you?"

"Yeah."

"That's lousy," she said.

"Yeah, well." Frankie didn't really want to talk about it. "So what do you think you'll do when you get out of this place?"

Choppy knotted her shaggy brows. "I dunno. Maybe get a job in one of them factories, if the war's still on. Maybe I could build airplanes." She stopped the gig to roll up her sleeve and flex a biceps.

Frankie whistled. Choppy did have some spectacular muscles. Must have been that good nun food she "tasted" all the time. "You could *lift* airplanes," Frankie said. "Maybe you could fly them."

"Girls can't fly airplanes, least not war planes. How about you? What are you gonna do when you get out?"

"I don't know," Frankie said. "I don't even know what 'out' looks like, you know?" She trailed off. She wouldn't know where to go. She wouldn't know where to shop or where to live or work. She wouldn't know how to talk to people who hadn't been raised in the orphanage. What do those people talk about? She thought then of what Vito had said in one of his letters, that maybe she was better off where she was, and she wondered if he was right. If she was so dumb that she wouldn't even know where to get groceries, wouldn't know how to talk to anyone, maybe she was better off.

"Well, you're only a half orphan. Maybe your dad could help you."

Frankie shrugged. Vito was writing all the letters. She wasn't sure if her dad would help her do anything. She wasn't sure if she'd ever see him again. All of a sudden, she felt a sting in her eyes. They were gearing up to cry, and it hurt the same every single time.

"Here," said Choppy, motioning with her chin. "Get on."

"Get on what?"

"The gig, stupid. What do you think? You're going for a ride."

Frankie looked around. The halls were dark and quiet, even though it was the middle of the day. "We'll get in trouble if we're caught."

"So then, we better not get caught," she said.

Frankie climbed up on top of the gig and held on as Choppy took off. Choppy really was as strong as she looked, and faster than Frankie thought she'd be. They went flying down the hallway fast enough to blow back Frankie's hair, and Frankie had to keep herself from shrieking or giggling out loud. Giggling was sure to bring the nuns out of their hiding places. If they were having too much fun, then something was wrong.

They flew past the doors to cottage after cottage, girls' cottages, boys' cottages, senior cottages. As they whipped past the senior boys' cottage, the door opened, and Frankie thought she caught a glimpse of Sam, and she hoped he saw her too, with her hair ruffled and laughing so hard that she was close to bursting. But there was sadness twisting through her laughter, woven into it, a grief she couldn't name, a fear that the future would never come and a fear that it would, a strange sense that she wouldn't be strong enough to meet it.

Choppy stopped short right in front of the kitchen, and had to grab Frankie's shoulder so that she wouldn't go flying off the gig. They stood next to the gig, trying to catch their breath. Frankie swiped the tears from her face, pretended they were happy ones.

"So," Frankie said, "are you going to get married?"

"Huh? I may be big, but I'm only sixteen," Choppy said.

"No, I mean when you get out of here. When you're older."

"Absolutely," Choppy said. "I'm going carry my man down the aisle."

Frankie laughed. "I bet you will."

"What about you? You gonna get married?"

Frankie thought about Sam, his eyes big and surprised as they raced by on the gig. "Yeah. Doesn't everyone?"

"Not everyone. There's the nuns. And my aunt Ethel."

"What's wrong with your aunt Ethel?"

"She's got a mustache. Plus she's mean as a snake."

"Your aunt Ethel couldn't take you and your brothers in?"

Choppy snorted. "Are you kidding? She hates kids. It's a good thing she ain't married. I'd feel too sorry for the babies. She'd send that stork packing as soon as it showed up."

Frankie laughed. "Babies don't come from storks."

Choppy smacked her. Again. "I know that, chooch. They pop out of your belly button."

Frankie didn't correct her. Lots of the girls believed such things. When they turned twelve, each Guardians girl got a book called *It's Your Day, Marjory May*. But the book didn't explain much beyond how to wash out your rags. And it didn't help the eleven-year-old who came into her monthlies in the showers and started screaming that she was dying before the other girls could calm her down.

Frankie knew better because Loretta had set her straight about everything—at least, about what went where. But, according to Loretta, people were endlessly creative about their whats and wheres and even whos. She described acts that made Frankie blush—but not Loretta, not anymore.

And maybe not Frankie, either.

Choppy delivered a note, and Frankie met Sam in the greenhouse after hours. Outside the greenhouse, the world was just waking up, green buds just forming on the trees. Inside the greenhouse, however, was riotous with tulips and daffodils. Even the rosebushes were showing signs of life. The sun setting over the glass ceiling gave whole place a soft, warm glow that made Sam's eyes glitter in the fading light. All her twisted feelings whipped through Frankie at once, and she almost fell to her knees at the sight of him standing there. How beautiful the flowers, how beautiful this boy. How terrible this place that worked so hard to keep them apart, to keep them all from one another. How horrible a war howling across the ocean that could whisk him away as easily as the wind tears a leaf from a tree.

Her vision blurred again. If he'd asked, she wouldn't be able to say what she was crying about. *I'm scared I'll be stuck here forever, I'm scared I won't be, I'm scared you'll die, I'm scared all the time, and being scared makes me so mad, when I think about the future there's only smoke and fog and I can't see my way through it.*

His voice brought her back. "Hey," he said, the faint growl in his tone dancing along her nerves.

"Hey," she said.

"You looked like you were having fun."

"Huh?" she said.

"Before, when you were running around on that cart with Choppy. Haven't seen anyone look so happy since the nuns took us to the carnival a few years ago."

"Oh, that," Frankie said. "Yeah."

"You okay?"

"Sure," she said. "Why?"

"You have a funny look on your face, is all." Quickly, he added, "A funny *expression*. Your face is pretty as always."

She laughed. "Yours too."

"What?"

She shrugged, touched the pink cup of a tulip. "It even *smells* green in here."

He didn't speak, just stared. Then he bent and lifted a watering can. "I need to finish watering."

"I'll help you," she said.

"You don't have to."

"I don't mind."

"Okay." He set the can under a spigot in the corner and filled it. Then he brought it to her. "Hope that's not too heavy."

Her muscles weren't as big as Choppy's, but she was almost as strong. She laughed, hefting the can over her shoulder. "What's too heavy?"

He smiled. "Not much, I guess."

He filled another can for himself and then pointed to the end of the row by the windows. "You only want to dampen the soil. If you water too much, the roots will rot." He poured a bit of water into the nearest pot. "Like that."

She nodded, the scent of the flowers and the earth and the wool of his coat making her just a bit dizzy.

"You start over there, I'll start here," he said. "We'll meet in the middle."

Frankie moved to the end of the row and watered some daffodils. "So you water the plants in here. What else do you do?"

"Well, we grow the seedlings that we'll plant out in the garden later." He hooked a thumb at rows and rows of pots in the middle of the greenhouse, many spiky with green shoots.

"And we have to clean up all the garden beds outside. Clear them of leaves and sticks and rocks. We already planted the first crops of the season."

"What did you plant?"

"Cabbage and beets mostly. Some broccoli too."

She wrinkled her nose. "Father likes cabbage, but he's the only one."

"I like cabbage."

"You do?"

"Red cabbage. With apples."

"Cabbage and *fruit*? That sounds kinda strange."

"My mother used to make it."

"Oh," Frankie said. "When was that?"

"A long time ago."

Frankie nodded. She wanted to hear more about Sam's family, but didn't know how to ask. Whatever had happened to his mother was bound to be sad. She was poor, she was lost, she was dead, she left and never came back. Frankie had heard these stories from other orphans over and over, and they were never happy ones.

If Frankie had asked, though, Sam might have confessed that his mother hadn't gone anywhere and *was* perfectly happy, that she'd been happy ever since she'd handed him over to the nuns when he was seven. Having children was his father's idea, she said, and once that son of a bitch had taken off, why would she keep the boy, especially since Sam would probably turn out just like his daddy?

And maybe, if Frankie had asked some more questions, different questions, Sam might have confessed that he'd noticed Frankie because of all the ways she was unlike his tall and pale and angry mother, no matter how delicious her cabbage and apples. Frankie was tiny, with dark hair and darker eyes slanted up at the outer corners like a cat. And no matter how she was feeling inside, she always looked as if she was about to laugh.

But Frankie didn't laugh, and she didn't ask any other questions about Sam's mother. She said, "What kind of food do you like besides cabbage?"

"Oh, I'll eat almost anything. But my favorite food is cake."

"What kind?"

"Any kind! Chocolate, strawberry, lemon. Not much cake anymore."

"Not enough sugar. We have to use honey," said Frankie.

"We should probably get some beehives for the orphanage so we can have more cake."

"Would you take care of the bees?"

"Sure. Why not?"

"They sting."

"So do the nuns," said Sam. "And the nuns hurt worse."

Frankie laughed. She watered a pot full of perfect tulips, the blooms a bright pink-red.

"You know, tulip bulbs used to be worth more than gold," Sam said, nodding at the blooms. "A long time ago. In Europe. People traded them like money."

"They traded flowers like money?"

"People believed they symbolized love and immortality. Kind of funny, because the blooms only last a few days."

Frankie didn't say anything, because the word "love" was shuttling around her brain, knocking on the sides of her skull.

"And these," Sam said, pointing to a row of green bushes with buds that had not yet bloomed, "are roses. Roses are related to fruit like raspberries, cherries, peaches."

They got quieter and quieter as they got closer. Sam was in a swirl of emotions too. He wanted to tell Frankie what he was going to do when he got out of the orphanage. He wanted to say that he would buy his own plot of land and grow things like fruit and flowers, that he would have beehives and a little house all his own. He wanted to say that he would play his trumpet in a band on the weekends, and walk home when the sun was rising. He wanted to tell her that the war encroached on his visions like a nightmare, and sometimes he woke up panting in a tangle of blankets. He wanted to say that sometimes he dreamed of tulips and wondered if that was a bad omen, or a good one.

Frankie wanted to say something, anything, but "love" sounded too small and "immortality" sounded too long and she didn't know what word could capture all the moments in between.

They watered the flowers in silence until they finally met in the middle of the row, standing side by side. Sam went still, his eyes darting to her and darting away, like bees that refused to be kept by anyone, even well-meaning young men. Frankie put her can on the ground. Then she took the watering can from Sam's hands and set that down too. When they had met before, wherever they had met, Frankie usually stopped a few feet away from him, waiting for him to approach her, but it was spring inside and outside and in all her wheres, so she didn't stop. She laid a hand on his elbow, turned him toward her, stepped so close the buttons on their coats touched. He was so surprised his arms spread like the angels in the stained windows of the church. Her nose filled with the scents of good earth and wool and a salty, woodsy note underneath, sweat and strong soap.

When they kissed it was like riding the gig, and even in the moment Frankie understood what Sister Bert had meant about joy, a way of saying no and yes at the very same time.

So lost were they, so intent on each other, they didn't see the white and twisted face pressed to the glass behind them.

1943
WOLVES

THE SONG OF SOLOMON

DAYS, WEEKS, MONTHS, BLURRED. The girls in the senior cottage bloomed liked so many flowers, closer to the women they would become than the children they used to be. Frankie stole food and stole kisses in the back of the green-house, in stairwells, behind buildings. Loretta did too, but was far better at hiding it. Toni burst like a kernel of corn, and hid as little as possible.

I wandered the Chicago streets, I sat through film after film at the picture show. I went to the library and read fairy tales and novels and *The Hobbit*. Bilbo, still invisible because of his ring, travels the tunnels through the Misty Mountains and makes it to the other side of the range. He stumbles upon Gandalf and the dwarves, takes off the ring, and surprises them. The group journeys on, but as night falls, they hear the howling of wolves. They barely have time to climb some trees before the wolves, called Wargs, find them, along with the goblins, who light fires under the trees. Before Gandalf can attack, the eagles come swooping down, carrying the company to safety.

I did not hear the howling of wolves, but I could hear the voice of the girl in gold: *You lie to yourself.* Or maybe it was just the voice in my head. Or the voice of the angel, who had taken to telling me things about the spasms of the world, things I didn't want to hear, things I couldn't bear to know. She told me about the Japanese Americans rounded up and sent to camps for the duration of the war, though they had done nothing wrong. She told me that the United States surrendered the Bataan Peninsula in the Philippines and thousands of troops were forced to march sixty-five miles to prison camps, and that many died in the process.

She told me that the Jews in the Netherlands were ordered to wear the Star of David, that they couldn't ride bicycles or trains, that a girl named Anne Frank went into hiding with her family. Anne wrote in her diary that she'd packed curlers, schoolbooks, a comb, and some old letters instead of clothes, because memories meant more to her than dresses.

The angel told me that scientists were working on a secret scheme to build a powerful bomb, and that soon some of those same scientists would have nightmares every night, and wake up in a sweat, eyes cranked wide.

The world keeps many secrets from itself, the angel said. But it can't keep secrets from you without your permission.

I liked knowing everyone's secrets, but it seemed as if the angel wanted me to do something with them, something *about* them, that they were supposed to mean more to me. I'd been resting my head on her feet, but I sat up and stared at her. What's the point of my knowing anyone's secrets? I'm *dead*.

That's not an excuse, the angel said. Go back to the library.

Find the girl in yellow. Or better yet, go back to the blue house in the sea of brick, remind yourself why you're there.

I didn't go back to the library, not then. I didn't go to the lake, I refused to visit the blue house.

The bar I found was the type of place that opened in the morning for those who planned to be drunk by noon. I drifted through the door into the dark, dank space inside. The wood paneling was stained a dark brown from cigarette smoke, red leather jacketed the barstools and booths, a dusty piano sat in the corner. You couldn't have called it crowded, but you wouldn't have called it empty, either. I found a seat between two men perched at the long, scuffed counter, shot glasses already piling up in front of them. The bartender, a tall, stooped man with an unfashionably bushy beard, poured them two more. He snatched up the coins they threw on the bar, then turned and walked right through the woman behind him. She was also tall, white arms thin and wiry, with brown hair and blue eyes so bright they burned with a strange energy. As the bartender passed through her, she stiffened, yelled, Kiss me where I sat on Saturday, you loping ape! Of course, the man paid her no mind.

At first I thought she wore some sort of printed blouse and stockings underneath her short black dress, but as she moved toward me, I realized they were tattoos, and that they danced and shifted across her skin—a flower into a dragon, a dragon into a fish, a fish back into a flower, words and symbols twining and unwinding and twining again.

What will you have? she said to me.

What do you mean?

What are you drinking, dear?

Drinking?

This *is* a bar, love.

Are you playing with me?

She leaned her elbows on the bar top, said, You want a drink or not?

I shrugged. Wine?

The wine we serve at this place isn't worth scrubbing the pots with. You'll have some bourbon if you know what's good for you, she said. She set a glass in front of me, poured it full of a rich amber liquid.

I can't pick up a glass.

You can pick up that one, she said. Try it.

She was right. Tentatively, I took a sip of the bourbon. I could swear I tasted the fire of the liquor hitting the back of my throat, scorching me all the way down.

There's a good girl, she said.

I set the glass back on the bar. Said, My brother Frederick would be proud of me.

Yeah? Where's ole Freddy now?

Not here, I said.

And why are you here?

I don't know.

It's all right if you want to tell me, love, the woman said. And it's all right if you don't. It's just that we don't see many of your kind around here.

My kind?

Rich girls in fancy gowns usually drink at home.

This is not a gown. And I'm not a rich girl.

Whatever you say, she told me. The fish on her chest snapped its tail at me before diving into what Mother would have referred to as her "décolletage."

I said, He delivered a package to my door.

The tattooed woman did not ask who "he" was. She said, Package. Delivered. Never heard it put that way.

No, I meant he was a delivery boy.

She winked, and the fish peeked its head up from the neckline of her dress and winked too.

Stop that, I said. He brought a delivery for my father. A parcel wrapped in brown paper, tied with string. Normally our maid answered the door, but—

I thought you said you weren't rich, she said.

What?

You think poor people have maids?

We had to let the maid go a few months before that. Mother said it was because we were perfectly capable of opening our own doors. But it was because Father's business was failing. But I didn't find that out until later.

Business, schmisiness. Why don't you get back to the boyo at the door?

I'm trying, I said. I felt a little lightheaded, a little woozy, though there was no reason I should have felt that. The alcohol wasn't real. The bartender wasn't real. I wasn't.

I tried to center myself. I asked her, What's your name? Do you know it?

She took a step back and bowed. Mad Maureen Kelly at your service.

Mad Maureen?

I have a bit of a temper, she said. Snakes shivered up and down her legs. The words "Credo quia absurdum" wound themselves around her biceps. The tattoo of an eye that had been sitting on her shoulder migrated to her forehead and peered at me. I couldn't decide which of her eyes to focus on, which just made me even more dizzy.

She said, It's normal to introduce yourself, you know, and rude to stare.

I wasn't . . . , I began, but of course I had been staring. Pearl, I told her. Miss Pearl Brownlow.

Pleased to make your acquaintance, Miss Pearl Brownlow of the Not-Rich-Enough-to-Keep-a-Maid Brownlows, she said. Now, are you going to tell me about this boyo or not? If not, I'm going to start drinking myself.

I was home alone, I began. Well, not alone exactly. Cook was in the kitchen, baking a pie. I was bored and tried to help, but I wasn't really helping as much as stealing little bits of pie dough to eat, spoonfuls of blueberries and sugar. Cook grew tired of me and sent me outside where she said I could do less damage. But I could always find a way to do damage, especially to myself.

Mmmm, murmured Mad Maureen, making a twirling motion with her hand to hurry me along.

So I tucked a copy of *Detective Story* given to me by my friend Harriet into the bodice of my day dress and took myself to the woods. I found a sunny place in a clearing and read "The Yellow Claw" for a while. My mother would have burned that magazine for trash had she caught me with it, but I found it only mildly diverting. Soon I got bored. I went exploring in the woods instead, looking for a glimpse of a deer or a bear or a fox or a wolf, gathering flowers and leaves I might press in between the pages of my Bible, the only book my mother wanted me to read. Which is funny, considering all the killing and the blood in the Bible. Considering the Song of Solomon. Especially the Song of Solomon: *I am sick of love.* Which confuses me: Who is sick of love?

You'd be surprised, said Mad Maureen.

I don't know how long I spent gathering flowers and looking for wolves—I had myself convinced that if I found a wolf pup I could raise it to be my pet; I would name it Tarzan and it would adore me, protect me. But I didn't find any wolf pups. I never did. And I got as scratched up and dirty as always happened when I went where I wasn't supposed to. So I decided to clean up a bit before going home. I walked from the woods to the edge of the lake. There weren't so many houses back then. Most of the place was a vast stretch of woods and grass and rocky shore. It all belonged to Father and, I thought, to my brothers and me. I left my magazine and my shoes and dress on the beach and waded into the water. It was shockingly cold, but the cold numbed my cuts and the scrapes, and the gentle lapping of the water lulled and cradled me. I stopped feeling the cold. I started to swim, remembering how much I'd loved it as a child. I swam as far as I could go, until the shore was just a memory and I was alone and adrift in a deep, dark sea.

I forgot myself, lost in every stroke of my arms, every kick. And then when I had swum so far out that I might be too tired to get back, I panicked. I flailed and screamed at the birds overhead. They screamed right back, but I couldn't understand them, and they couldn't help me. No one could help me. I imagined sinking, choking, drowning, my own mother at my funeral saying that I never thought about anyone but myself, I never thought before I acted, I was a wild thing that came to a wild end and that was God's own will, God's own judgment, and that made me so angry that I got back to swimming, following the paths of the gulls back to shore. When I pulled myself up on the rocky beach, I was so exhausted that my arms and legs were as liquid as the pie filling I'd sucked through my teeth. I barely managed to pull my dress over my head, put the shoes on my feet. I left the magazine where it was—Harriet wouldn't miss it and neither would I—and walked home. Though the trees would have concealed me, though I should have, I didn't walk through the woods. I walked straight up our drive to our door, bold as anyone. I was still mad at my mother, you see, the mother in my head. I didn't care who saw me.

And that's when I saw *him* standing on our porch, his hand on the lion's-head knocker. I had a few seconds to watch him before he heard my shoes slapping against the stones. Do you know how long a few seconds can be? So long. So long. He

THE SONG OF SOLOMON

wasn't that tall, though everyone was tall compared to me. Hair so black it looked blue in the bright sunlight. He had broad shoulders and a narrow waist emphasized by a crisp white shirt tucked neatly in his linen trousers. A small parcel was tucked under one arm. He knocked again—once, twice, three times. No answer. He must have heard my footsteps, because he turned to look at me. And I . . .

You? said Mad Maureen.

I had forgotten I was in a bar. I had forgotten Mad Maureen was there too. Her fish had turned into a mermaid, and they both waited for an answer.

I said, I got dizzy and had to stop walking.

Dizzy, like you had a few shots of bourbon?

Yes. And hot too, like settling into a fresh bath. Bible verses tingled on my tongue: *His eyes are as the eyes of doves by the rivers of waters, washed with milk, and fitly set. His cheeks are as a bed of spices, as sweet flowers: his lips like lilies.* Except his eyes weren't like doves at all, not pale like that, not soft. They were as black as his hair, black as the wings of crows wet with rain. And didn't smile the way that other boys, other men had smiled at me, the way they would have smiled at a girl so damp and disheveled, wrecked and wretched. He didn't smile at all. He was almost . . . frowning. As if I had disturbed him somehow. As if I were threatening. When I reached him, when I said hello, all he did was nod to acknowledge it. I asked him if the package was for Mr. Brownlow, he nodded again, holding the parcel out to me with one hand, but the way you'd hold out a scrap of meat to an animal, perhaps wanting to feed it but still afraid it will bite. I thought, *Please don't be scared of me, why are you scared of me, you've never met me before, you don't even know me*, and, at the same time, *That's right, be scared of me, be terrified.*

So, said Mad Maureen Kelly. Who was the wolf?

Stella might have looked more like a starlet than ever, but she was a pup who dreamed she was a wolf. She liked to write her servicemen just after church in the early afternoon. She'd take out all the little slips of paper she'd collected and transfer the names and addresses to index cards she'd gotten from Sister Cornelius (she lied and said she was using them to study). In an old cigar box, she kept the cards in alphabetical order, along with all the letters the servicemen wrote her. Some days, she read parts of the letters out loud to the other girls, mostly the parts that said something about her being beautiful (if she'd sent a picture) or talented (if she'd sent a hand-knitted scarf) or smart (who knows why?).

"'I showed the fellas your picture,'" she read, "'and they all say you look just like a movie star.'" Stella put the letter down in her lap. "Isn't that just the sweetest thing you ever heard?"

Loretta looked up from her book, Steinbeck's *The Moon is Down*. "Which serviceman was that one?"

"That was Robert C.," she said. "There are three Roberts. Robert C., Robert M., and Robert R." Stella folded up the letter and dropped it into the box.

Loretta flipped a page in her book. The intervening year

had sharpened her cheekbones, gilded her strawberry-blond hair with bright veins of gold, and given her gaze a knowing calm that made some of the girls believe she could read their minds. "If you were as careful with your schoolwork as you are with those letters," she told Stella, "you wouldn't have to spend so much time staying after class with Sister Cornelius."

Stella took a fresh piece of paper and licked the tip of her pencil. "You're just jealous that nobody's telling you that you look like a movie star."

"True," said Loretta. "Frankie, remind me to start lying to a bunch of servicemen, okay?"

Stella's smile got even wider. "The other day I got a marriage proposal."

Toni nearly flipped right out of her chair. "No! A marriage proposal! What are you going to do?"

"Do? Nothing! What do I need to do? Sam W. is on a boat in the middle of the ocean."

"But what if he comes back?" said Toni.

"Oh, he's got eighteen more months, at least," said Stella. "And who knows, maybe I'll want to get married by then."

"You won't even be eighteen in eighteen months," Loretta said.

"But I *look* eighteen now," said Stella, raising her eyebrow. "And what do you care anyway? You don't even like boys, do you?"

A muscle in Loretta's cheek jumped. Stella's practiced giggle sounded like the clink of a knife on a wineglass. Toni laughed hard enough that one of the buttons straining to contain her bosom gave up and popped from her blouse. Toni made a great show of being upset about it. (She wasn't upset about it.) Frankie scooped up the button and tossed it to Toni, who missed it. She and Stella crawled after the button, snickering at Toni's open blouse and visible cleavage, while Frankie rolled her eyes.

Frankie turned her chair away from her sister and opened Vito's latest letter, expecting more news about the shoe shop, more complaints about Ada's spoiled kids, more lies about their father saying hello and sending his best. But that wasn't what the letter said, because this letter was the one Frankie had been pretending would never come.

> *Dear Frankie,*
>
> *Thanks for the birthday card. But you know what that means. It's the army for me. I'm shipping out in a few weeks. Not sure where I'm going and I probably won't be able to tell you when I get there. I wish I had the time to visit before I go, but it's not in the cards.*
>
> *Still, I don't want you to worry about me. Hitler is the only one with something to worry about.*
>
> *I'll write again soon.*
>
> > *Your brother,*
> > *Vito*

She stood and paced back and forth, folding and refolding the letter. Maybe the war wouldn't last, maybe Vito wouldn't even have to go. Vito would be okay, everyone would be okay.

She wasn't okay.

"What is it, Frankie?" Loretta said. "You look like you've seen a ghost."

"Vito," Frankie said. "He's . . . he's . . ." She could barely choke out the words. "He's going overseas."

"Vito?" said Stella. "That handsome brother of yours? You just tell him to write me and I'll be—"

Frankie dropped Vito's letter and shoved Stella hard enough to launch her out of her seat.

Look at that, I said. A shooting star.

THE THREE SPINDLES

EVERY TIME I VISITED THE blue house in the sea of brick, I promised myself that I wouldn't go back. And then I proved myself a liar. I hovered at the back window, hoping to catch a glimpse of Berry Girl and Boxer Boy. Was there a word for that, a word for wishing for exactly the thing that caused you the most pain? Perhaps the Germans had one. They probably did.

There was no one in the bedroom. No one in the kitchen, either; no one in the living room. Before I had the chance to think better of it, before I could remind myself of my own rules, I pressed inside. Doesn't take much, to move through a wall when you're dead. You take a step and let go of yourself, release the thought or the dream or the belief that binds you together. Then, once you are through, you gather yourself back, the way a woman gathers up a sheet that has fallen from the bed.

It doesn't take much, but it does take a while to learn.

Not pleasant, being trapped in a wall, mice running over your feet.

Once I was through, once I had gathered myself, I stole through the darkened, empty rooms on my ghostly tiptoes. I swept my not-fingers over the dishes drying in the rack—simple white bowls, scratched juice glasses. I pressed my not-palms on the spotless counters, the threadbare furniture. I breathed my not-breath on the photographs on the coffee table, where the two of them smiled at their wedding, smiled in their swimsuits at the beach, smiled at a party, smiled and smiled and smiled. There were pictures of her family, and his, and everyone was so happy. Their happiness hurt. There was probably a German word for that, too.

I stood, still and mesmerized by those wide white smiles until a key turned in the lock and the front door swung open. I'd expected to see him, home from a job where he added up numbers in endless, numbing columns, but it wasn't him. *She* walked in, the same girl she always was, and a completely different girl. Instead of spilling down her shoulders and back, her long glossy hair was tied up in a red kerchief. No dress today, no posing like a starlet; she wore blue trousers and a denim shirt with the sleeves rolled up. Oil-stained work boots on her feet. She stomped past me into the kitchen, where she dropped her lunch pail on the counter. She rummaged in the icebox, brought a beer back into the living room, and slumped in the nearest chair. She put her booted feet up on that table and sipped the beer.

Your mother wouldn't approve of the beer, I said, a ridiculous thing to say, both because she couldn't hear me and because what did I know of her mother? Maybe her mother loved beer. I was too astonished by the trousers and the posture and the boots to make sense. Where did she go in that outfit? What did she do all day? *Rivet* things? How did one rivet a thing? What kind of thing needed to be riveted? A boat? A plane? But she was so delicate, so fine boned and ladylike.

I tried to imagine myself coming home in trousers, putting my boots up on my mother's coffee table, but the vision wouldn't keep in my head, kept dissolving into cloudy wisps for its sheer lunacy, its impossibility. My mother would never have allowed it—well, also ridiculous because everyone insisted I act like a lady, and look what I'd done instead. I'd been a riveter too, in my own way. I giggled at my own joke, more lunacy because there was no Mad Maureen here to appreciate it, and also because I'd died because of it. Divine intervention, my mother called it, divine retribution. The pretty girl coming to an ugly but satisfying end, delirious and feverish and hacking blood up on herself. Tragic, but was anyone really surprised, considering? I wasn't ill long, just a few hours, not even long enough to soil my dress. Maybe not so much retribution as intervention, then, because it had been so quick. Or maybe the reverse, as I was still here, still trying to sort my own boundaries, the lines of myself.

When I first crossed over, I didn't understand anything I was seeing. Everything had a queer sort of vagueness, a haziness, a fuzziness, a flatness and a brightness at the same time. As if I had stared at the sun too long and then tried to make out the outlines and the colors of a thing—a flower, a dog, a bird, a person. Nothing came together, people and animals and plants and things spat and sparked, flesh or spirit coming off them like bits of ash floating up a chimney. I might have screamed a lot. Difficult to be sure. It took me a while to understand that I couldn't just rely on my senses the way I had when I was alive, I had to use my imagination. I had to focus, I had to concentrate, apply my own will to gather the people and the things into coherence, fill them all with substance and color. They almost looked real now, as if I could touch them.

I could touch her.

She finished her beer and set the bottle by the array of pictures on the coffee table, laid her head back, and closed her eyes. I would not enter her mind, I would not sift through her thoughts like the thief I was, the criminal, but I wanted . . . what did I want? For her to see me, the spirit coming off me like sparks from a fire? For her to scream and scream and scream? No. And yet.

I wanted her to know.

I took a step toward her. She didn't move. I took another step. A few strands of glossy hair had escaped the kerchief. If I could just smooth them from her cheek, I—

Her eyes opened and she gasped, clutching her chest. My not-heart hitched and ran. Don't be afraid, I told her, I won't hurt you, I could never, I will tell you a story if you want to listen. Listen. Listen. Li—

She leaned forward, staring. "Where did you come from?"

Shock that she saw me, shock that she heard me, made the words tumble out in a torrent. I've been here before, I said, I've been here longer than you remember, I can't stay away, I wish I could.

"What do you want?"

Once, there was a noble's young daughter who got herself in trouble and her parents threw her out of the house. She wandered around aimlessly because she had nowhere to go. The world is cold, you see, cold and gray and deader than dead, and so this girl ended up in the woods all alone. She found a tree stump with three crosses carved into it and sat down to rest there, because what else was she to do? All of a sudden, a fairy no bigger than a cat burst from a clump of trees. Hot on her heels was a band of hunters, all dressed in red, all on fiery red horses whose sharpened fangs champed at silver bits. Demon hunters on demon horses, come to kill everything that was good, everything that was magic, including the fairy. The girl pulled the fairy behind her so that the demons wouldn't see her. They raced by without a backward glance. The fairy thanked the girl and asked how she might help, considering the girl had just saved her life. Through her tears, the girl explained her trouble, and the fairy said that all would be well. The fairy led the girl to a little house in the middle of the wood. Inside the house was a tidy bed, a warm hearth, and a spindle. The fairy told the girl to spin moss into yarn every day, and every day, when her work was done, she would be paid in food and wood for that hearth. She had never worked before, this nobleman's daughter, so the yarn wasn't very fine at first, but she grew to love her work, grew to love herself for working. Every day, she spun, and every night, the fire in her hearth burned cheerily, a full pot bubbling over it. Then one evening, the fairy came by and found a beautiful baby wrapped in swaddling on the rug by the hearth. The child was so calm and lovely that the fairy asked if she could keep the baby in exchange for bringing the young woman home. The young woman agreed. The fairy brought the girl back to the tree stump carved with three crosses and left her there with three spindles of her own beautiful yarn. The fairy said, The child will never want for anything. And neither will you. If you ever find yourself in real need, just unspool a bit of the yarn from the spindle. You'll find that there's always the same amount of yarn left on the spindle, you'll find that you'll never run out.

Do you see? I said. Do you hate me?

I reached for her then, for that lock of hair that had come loose from the kerchief. I thought she was seeing me, I thought she was hearing me. When she got up from the chair and moved toward me I thought she might ask my name, and I thought I would tell her, I thought I would tell her everything, anything she wanted. She stepped through me, and it was as if I'd jumped from the top of a skyscraper as if I'd jumped from an airplane as if I were drowning in a lake and the lake was her. Not-tears streamed down my cheeks, but she kept going, through me, then past me, moving instead to the window, where a little furred face was perfectly framed, as if in a painting, or in one of Frankie's drawings.

"What are you doing out there?" she said to the little furred face, laying a palm on the window. "Are you spying on me?"

The fox smiled, its tongue lolling like a party favor.

No, no, no! I shouted. Go away!

"Look at you, you sweet thing."

You're ruining it, you stupid animal!

"Aren't you cute?"

My vision went hazy, fuzzy, white. On the coffee table behind us, the photographs shook, then fell to the floor with a crash.

The girl was picking up the pictures, setting them back on the table, when the door opened, and he limped in. His pale skin, the exaggerated limp, told the story of the trials of the day, but his cinnamon eyes blazed for her, they always blazed for her, a fire that would never run out.

"What happened?" he said, seeing her crouched there by the chair, a chipped frame in her hand.

"I saw—" She gestured to the window where the fox had been, frowned. "Never mind," she said. "Whatever it was, it's gone."

———— ∞ ————

An accident, just an accident, I muttered to myself as I walked back to the orphanage. But it hadn't been an accident. I had just wanted her to see me. I had knocked those pictures to the floor, and I hadn't even been near them. But why couldn't I figure out how I'd done it?

Instead of finding the orphanage comfortably, soothingly,

punishingly gray and somber, stark and sad, churchy and still, I stumbled into a parade, the Parade of Corpus Christi. The June sunlight shining over everything was the same bright, buttery color as the new dresses the orphan girls had made for themselves.

"It's your color," said Loretta.

"What is?" Frankie asked.

Loretta lifted the hem of dress she wore, revealing one knee red and pitted from kneeling to scrub this or polish that. "Yellow," she said. "I'd look better in blue or pink, but you look like a princess or something."

A flush crept up Frankie's neck, but she was pleased. It couldn't hurt to look like a princess if she caught a glimpse of Sam, if he caught a glimpse of her. She scanned the boys, who were lined up in their best suits just a few feet away. Normally they didn't let boys and girls get this close, but the Parade of Corpus Christi was different. They were celebrating "the real presence of Jesus Christ in the bread and wine of the Eucharist, the real presence of Jesus Christ in the world," Father Paul said every year, had said after mass that morning. They were marching for Jesus, and they were going to do it all together. Frankie wasn't complaining.

Loretta was plucking at her collar.

"What's the matter?" Frankie asked.

"You know I can't sew," Loretta said. "Of course I made my collar too tight."

"Unbutton one button in the back."

"I already did," she said.

"It's nice, ain't it?" A boy's voice. Scratchy and low.

Frankie whirled around. Saw him. Sam. Smiling.

"What?" she said dumbly, her mouth hanging open. She couldn't help it, she kept thinking of the day before, when they'd sneaked into the greenhouse and kissed behind a lemon tree until her lips were numb. She could still taste the lemons.

"The sky," Sam said. "It's nice today."

"Uh . . . yeah," she said. "It's real nice."

Sam pointed to a cloud. "Now, my friend Clarence says that that cloud looks like Sister George, but I say it looks like the witch from *The Wizard of Oz*. What do you say?"

"I say that there isn't much difference, is there?"

He laughed, and for a minute she could see his teeth, big and white, straight on top, a little jumbled on the bottom. She had run her tongue over those teeth. The thought made her shiver.

"I think I've seen you washing up in my cottage after dinner. Do you work in the kitchen?" he said, as if they didn't know each other at all, as if their hands hadn't worked frantically at buttons and zippers and skin.

"Yeah," she said. "I work in the kitchen."

"So how come they make you wash our dishes?"

"Maybe they think you don't know how to take care of yourselves."

"They're probably right," he said, still grinning. "We can be hopeless on our own. Without . . . you know . . . women."

Frankie was just warming up to the conversation, just getting used to the idea of being called a woman, when Sister Cornelius marched up to them and shooed Sam back to his place on line. After she marched away, he smiled at Frankie and waved. She made sure no one was looking before she waved back.

"Be careful, Frankie."

Loretta. She'd forgotten Loretta was there. There was something wrong about that, but Frankie wasn't sure what it was. "What do you mean?"

Loretta sighed. "You know what I mean."

The trumpets swelled and the rest of the band started to play, and the parade began. Frankie couldn't describe why she liked it so much, parading around the orphanage like that— it could take hours—but she did. Something about the fancy gowns, the warm summer air, the smell of the flowers that they carried in baskets and tucked in their hair, the sight of the colored banners made her, made all of them, feel special. Maybe it was Jesus. Maybe it was the angels. Maybe it was all of it. It seemed impossible that there was a war going on anywhere, with the sun so bright. It seemed impossible that she'd ever felt sad about the future. She wondered how she would describe it to Vito in her next letter.

Just as they were passing the girls' cottages, the boys' line passed them. Before she knew what was happening, Sam plucked a flower from the basket Frankie held. His fingers brushed her hand a little before he took that flower and put the stem between his teeth so that the bloom hung out of his mouth.

Frankie had to clench her own teeth to keep from laughing out loud.

Loretta poked her arm. "Where's your sister?"

"I'm sure she's around here somewhere," Frankie said, staring at her hand where Sam's fingers had touched it.

"Frankie, I mean it. I don't see her anywhere in the line. Do you think she's sick?"

"She could be," Frankie said, but even as she said it, Frankie knew that Toni would have to be *very* sick to miss the parade. And if she was that sick, someone would have told Frankie so that she could go visit Toni in the infirmary. "We probably can't tell who she is because we've all got the same dress on, you know?"

"Yeah," said Loretta. "You're probably right."

As much as Frankie wanted to be right, she kept her eyes peeled as they circled back toward the main building. There were so many of them, so many yellow dresses, how could she tell anyone from anyone? That was when she saw Toni sneaking away from the line of kids, a boy right behind her.

"Aw, hell," she said.

"What?" Loretta said.

"Toni just ducked behind that building with some boy."

Frankie slowed down her pace to a crawl and Loretta did too. A couple of kids behind them thumped them in the back to get them moving again, but when they didn't, streamed around them. They edged closer and closer to where Toni had disappeared, then slipped out of the line and around the brick wall.

Nothing. An empty patch of grass running between buildings.

"She's not here," said Loretta.

"Well, she wouldn't just stand here, waiting to be caught. She's not that dumb. No, she'd be hiding somewhere with that boy." Frankie pointed ahead. "Let's try over there. Around the next corner."

"We're going to get caught," said Loretta, but she followed her anyway.

They rounded the corner and there they were. Toni and a boy Frankie hardly recognized, snuggled up against the wall, nuzzling like newlyweds.

Toni looked up, smirked. "Why, it's my sister, Frankie!"

Frankie grabbed the boy by the collar and peeled him away.

"Hey!" he said, pinwheeling his arms, probably surprised that a girl as small as her could be so strong.

"Just what in the name of Pete do you two geniuses think you're doing?" Frankie said.

Toni put her hands on her hips. "What does it look like, Frankie? God, you are such a pain!"

Frankie still had the boy's collar in her fist, and she shook him a little. "I'm a pain? *I'm* a pain?"

The boy reached around for Frankie's hand and yanked it off. "Would you mind not doing that?"

"Who the heck are you?" Frankie demanded. She thought she'd seen him around. Blond hair, pale skin, blue eyes.

He straightened his collar. "I'm Guy."

"A guy named Guy," Frankie said. "That's like something out of a children's book."

"You're a barrel of laughs," Toni said. "Why don't you two just get out of here?"

"Sure," Frankie said. "But you're coming with me."

"I don't have to," Toni said, crossing her arms over her big bosoms.

"You do too," Frankie said. "I am not going to get stuck scrubbing out all the toilets on account of you!" She took a step forward and stuck her big nose in Toni's face. Part of her wondered why she was so mad, part of her knew she had no right, but the larger part of her was just too mad to care. "I am not going to be thrown out of the orphanage on account of you!"

"Come on, Frankie," Toni said. "You hate the orphanage."

She hated the orphanage, she didn't hate the orphanage, it didn't matter either way. "We don't have anywhere else to go!" she spat.

Loretta tugged at Frankie's arm. "Simmer down, okay? We don't want anyone to hear you yelling like that."

Frankie took a breath and said more quietly, "We have nowhere else to go."

Toni shrank back against the wall. "We could go to Colorado and be with Dad—"

Frankie cut her off. "He doesn't want us. We have to stay here, we have to get diplomas, we have to get jobs. We have to learn to do things for ourselves, you got that?" She turned and jabbed a finger at the blue-eyed boy. "You listen up, *Guy*. You stay away from my sister, you hear me? Or I'll tell. I swear on my mother's grave I will."

He kicked at the grass. "I hear you."

"Good." Frankie looked at Toni. "I hope you hear me too."

Toni tossed her head. "Go to hell, Frankie."

Sam's kisses burned on Frankie's lips, her skin. "I guess I'll see you there." Frankie could not feel guilty, she wouldn't. What she had with Sam was different, special. She wasn't trying to get attention, like Stella, or showing off, like Toni. Sam was her future. Who had brought Sam to her if not God?

But the devil had his tricks; he played them on us all. I followed as Frankie hauled her sister around the brick wall and back into the sunlight.

"Let go, you dumb ape!" Toni said, yanking her arm away. "You want something to boss around, why don't you go yell at that dog over there?"

"Dog?" said Loretta. "What dog?"

In the middle of the sea of yellow dresses, a flash of red fur. *Red* fur.

Loretta said, "Is that a fox?"

The fox, that stupid beautiful thing, wove through the crowd, heading right for us. For *me*.

What are you doing? I yelled at it. Go home!

"Why would a fox come out during the day?" said Frankie.

"Do you think it's sick?" said Toni.

I waved my arms, I stamped and shrieked, but the fox kept coming, ignoring the gasps and shouts of the orphans, who had by now noticed the wild animal in their midst and were backing away.

Behind the fox, the nuns bellowed orders. The girls in yellow dresses scattered like chicks. The fox dodged and darted, evading outstretched hands, as if they were nothing but branches and brambles, insignificant and harmless.

NO! I screamed at it. Get out of here! GO! Don't you understand? Don't you understand anything?

It kept coming, the silly, beautiful thing, determined to break itself, ruin itself. Whatever power had knocked the pictures from the table, whatever power had burst the light in the library, was nowhere to be found. I could do nothing when Sister George ran up behind the fox, a shovel poised over her head.

LIGHT, MORE LIGHT

I SAT IN THE MIDDLE of the table at the library, every ounce of my energy focused on the light bulb.

Burst, I thought. Burst. BURST.

Who's your friend? said a voice.

The golden girl stood on a desk just a few feet away. Unlike the bright yellow dresses worn by the girls at the orphanage, this girl's dress burned like the sun right before the sunset, fiery and furious and sad at the same time. Or maybe that was just the girl herself.

Hello? she said.

I wanted to ask her where she'd been for so long. I wanted to know what she'd been doing. I wanted to hear more of her stories. I wanted to know if she'd been lonely as I'd been. But all I said was, What?

Your friend, she said, pointing to the fox curled at my side. Where did you find him?

As soon as the shovel had come down, the spirit of the fox rose up, trotted right to me as if nothing had happened. I didn't know if he recognized the difference. He probably did. Or if he didn't, he would by now. The only smells here were remembered ones.

I didn't find him, he found me, I told the girl.

What's his name?

I thought about the wolf pup I'd been so determined to find in the woods of my home. But Tarzan didn't seem like the right name for such a wretched thing, a stupid beautiful thing, a truly wild thing and not a pretender.

What's *your* name? I asked her.

I can't tell you, she said.

Why not?

It will give you power over me.

Nonsense, I said.

She said, Well, what's *your* name?

If you won't tell me your name, I'm not going to tell you mine.

See? she said.

I rolled my eyes and focused on the light fixture.

Are you trying to burst it again?

Don't worry about what I'm trying to do, I said.

You *are* trying to burst it. She leaped up onto the table with me. The fox raised his nose and sniffed at her hem out of habit. She said, What did you do the last time?

What do you mean?

Right before it burst, what happened? What were you thinking?

You were making me angry.

So we just have to make you angry again. That shouldn't be

too difficult. You are very angry, generally.

I already told you, I said. Getting angry doesn't help anything. I was angry when . . . I trailed off and pointed to the fox. I was angry when he got hurt. He still got hurt.

Hurt?

You know what I mean, I said.

Whoever promised you that you would never get hurt was lying, she said.

No one promised me anything.

Oh? she said. That's a shame.

Why? Did someone promise you something?

She pursed her lips, didn't answer. She jumped from the table and drifted out the door. I scrambled to catch up. The fox loped beside me.

Outside, it was as bright and sunny as it had been the day of the Corpus Christi parade, but much warmer now. Men had their collars open. Women wore dresses in shades of candy. Looking at the bustling streets, the lines of coupon-bearing women at the bakery and the butcher, you would never know that some people were still poor and desperate enough to sell their own children for a few dollars. That black men signed up for the service in droves but were assigned the dirtiest and most dangerous jobs and weren't allowed to be officers. That America had turned away so many Jews trying to escape the Nazis before the borders were closed. And if not for the posters advertising war bonds, you would have never guessed that across the ocean, bombs crashed into buildings, bullets tore into bodies, men with shadows for souls shot their arms out in mindless salutes and ordered the deaths of thousands.

I caught up to the girl in gold at the end of the block. I said, Where are you going?

I walk sometimes, she told me.

Where?

Nowhere and everywhere, nowhere and everywhere.

Fine, don't tell me, I said, desperate for her to tell me.

I used to walk with my father every evening, she said. We lived downtown, in Bronzeville. Twenty-Second Street. The house where I was born.

In that moment, I remembered our first meeting, when she'd said the words "I reckon" with the slightest drawl woven into them.

As if she could read my mind, she explained, My parents came up from Georgia.

Why did they leave?

There was no work. And it was awful. You had to step off the sidewalk to make room for a white person, you couldn't vote, you couldn't testify in court because no one believed a black man, she said. Her eyes cut to me, a slice of a knife. A man or even a boy could be lynched just for looking at a girl like you.

No one ever believed me about anything, I said.

A girl like you could murder one of those men, one of those boys, she said, as if I hadn't interrupted. All you'd have to do is cry.

I wasn't the type to cry, but I didn't tell her that. I reached down to pet the fox. I imagined I could feel the rough fur beneath my fingers, the scrape of his teeth against my skin.

My father was a learned man, she went on. He and my mother started a pharmacy. He had a head for numbers, but she was the one who compounded the medicines, she was the one who knew how to heal. She was . . .

What?

Everything. She was everything.

You miss her, I said, not a question.

By the time I came along, she said, they owned two pharmacies. Some people considered us rich folks. Not rich like you, of course, but richer than some.

You can call me Pearl.

Her eyes cut to me again, but this time, they lingered. Pearl? It suits you.

I was named after my mother's favorite jewel.

A treasure, then, she said.

Oyster spit, I said.

Her fine brows flew up, opening and softening her whole face. Then she said, I'm Marguerite.

Lovely to meet you.

She gave me a rueful smile. I haven't introduced myself in a very long time, she said. I wondered if I would ever do it again. The people here . . . She trailed off. Well, you know.

I know. Not a lot of people to converse with, Miss Marguerite.

For a moment, she stopped drifting, stared at me, the not-fabric of her not-gown floating around her like a golden cloud.

What? I said.

She shook her head and then began to move again. Said,

You can call me Marguerite. Just Marguerite. Though I have— had—many names. My father always called me Marguerite Irene, always had the time to say the whole thing. My mother called me Margie. My brothers and sisters called me Mags or Magsy, especially when they were teasing me.

Did they do that a lot? Tease you?

Yes. I am—was—the baby. The last of five.

Where . . . ? Are they . . . ?

She glanced away, running a hand through the passersby, none of whom noticed. My family is fine, she said. They're all fine without me.

I wanted to ask her what that meant, how she would know if they were fine, if she visited them sometimes and watched through the windows, if she chose what to witness, but then, I was sure my family was fine without me, happy, even, that the devil had taken me.

I died from the flu in 1918, I told Marguerite. I wouldn't be surprised if my family had a party to celebrate my passing every year.

She laughed, a bright chirp of surprise. Do you always give everything away so soon?

Never, I said. Then: Always.

Me too, she said. Me too.

We walked through the streets of Chicago with the crowds of candy people. Every once in a while, a ghost performed his or her ritual, tripping into traffic, breaking a neck in the gutter, choking on a sweet. We didn't try to talk to them, we didn't mention them. We admired the dresses and the hats on the living ladies, marveled at the men's suits, so plain and narrow now that wool was restricted. Because all the young men were away, few couples strolled about the streets, but we did notice a handsome older gentleman helping his pretty blond wife from a cab.

I wonder if she knows, Marguerite said.

Knows what?

That man is passing.

Excuse me?

He's black, she said.

He is? You can tell by looking at him?

Yes, of course.

Marguerite watched the two walk arm in arm down the street, watched as he opened the door of a nearby restaurant, put a hand on the small of her back to guide her inside. I watched Marguerite.

I said, Did you have . . . someone?

My parents had a young man in mind for me, she said. A fine, upstanding man. He went to our church. He was a lawyer so skilled that he had both black and white clients. He was bound for great things. My parents thought he could be a senator one day.

Marguerite had her hand out again, wafting through the passing people. But hearts sometimes want what they shouldn't, she said. Such is the way of hearts.

She told me that though the lawyer was tall and brown and safe and right, though everything about him made sense and wasn't she a sensible girl? Marguerite opened the door one day and on her front porch stood a white boy so stunning it was as if he'd been carved from marble. He had a petition for her to sign, he said. He was from a long line of abolitionists and ministers, he said. He didn't see the color of her skin, it didn't matter to him at all. Not at all.

Until it did.

Until it did.

———— ✸ ————

Another door, I said.

What?

Doors can be dangerous. You never know what's on the other side, what you're letting in.

True, she said.

In stories, girls are always opening doors, always the wrong ones. Always crossing thresholds thinking they're getting away free. Nothing is free.

Marguerite ran a finger down the side of her face, as if remembering someone else's touch. It doesn't matter which door you open, she said. Three or ten or thirteen doorways, there are wolves behind them all.

———— ✸ ————

We had walked all day and into the night. We sat on the beach, my favorite haunt, or one of them, and watched the ships come

in, their winking lights making the skin of the lake shimmer
and sparkle. The dying words of Goethe, Marguerite said after
a while, and then she sang:

"Light! more light! the shadows deepen,
And my life is ebbing low,
Throw the windows widely open:
Light! more light! before I go.

"Softly let the balmy sunshine
Play around my dying bed,
E'er the dimly lighted valley
I with lonely feet must tread.

"Light! more light! for Death is weaving
Shadows 'round my waning sight,
And I fain would gaze upon him
Through a stream of earthly light."

Not for greater gifts of genius;
Not for thoughts more grandly bright,
All the dying poet whispers
Is a prayer for light, more light.

Heeds he not the gathered laurels,
Fading slowly from his sight;
All the poet's aspirations
Centre in that prayer for light.

Gracious Saviour, when life's day-dreams
Melt and vanish from the sight,
May our dim and longing vision
Then be blessed with light, more light.

I didn't tell her about the fairy lights that led the hobbits astray, how they had become lost from one another. I didn't tell her that maybe the lights were just one more door that we should hesitate to open.

Instead, I asked, Did you write that song?

No! That's a poem by Frances Ellen Watkins Harper. *She* was an abolitionist and suffragist. My mother read that poem to me. My mother always saw me for exactly who I was. She always knew. I couldn't hide a thing from her.

The fox sat between us, panting the way he liked to do, even though there was no need for breathing anymore.

I decided to call him Wolf.

It was as right a name as any.

LITTLE RED RIDING HOOD

THE GIRLS OF FRANKIE'S COTTAGE were subdued. Not because of Wolf, though the horror of his death occupied them through the summer and fall—*Did you see Sister with that shovel did you see the blood did you see did you see did you see?*—and some would bring it up for years afterward. But because Huckle insisted that someone kept mumbling and poking her throughout the night, that the cottage was haunted. "There are no ghosts but the Holy Ghost," Sister Bert said wearily, without much conviction. Sister was tired these days—less tart, less pert. She read *All Quiet on the Western Front* over and over again. When someone suggested another book, she'd say, "Yes, yes, as soon as I'm done with this one."

But Sister Bert seemed energetic enough when she and the other sisters marched every girl and boy who was old enough to the Granville Avenue "L" station and herded them onto the train headed to Jackson Park. The sisters kept shouting for everyone to stay together, and took a head count every few minutes. They didn't count the girl with the shattered face and the hair ropy with blood who rocked and moaned in the seat by the door. It wasn't me poking and mumbling, I said to her. Was

it you? Did you like it too much when they heard you? Did it
thrill you? And then, Where did you come from? What's your
story? But the girl just kept rocking and moaning, unhinging
her jaw in that disconcerting manner of hers. Next to me, Wolf
yawned—in imitation or in boredom, I couldn't be sure.

A cipher, that Wolf.

"Think you could get a little closer? My face is in your arm-
pit," Frankie said to Loretta, who was hanging on to one of the
bars over their heads for dear life. Even so, Frankie practically
broke her neck jumping and looking around the car for Sam.
So far, she hadn't seen him in the crush of orphans on the train.
Maybe he hadn't come.

Loretta crashed into Frankie as the train lurched. "How
long are we going to be on this thing?"

"At least it's warm in here," said Joanie McNally, scratching
at her freckled nose. "I don't know why they always make these
trips for days when it's too hot or too cold. How come they can't
pick a nice day?"

"'Cause that would make sense," Loretta said.

Joanie McNally scrunched up her nose. "Huh?"

Loretta sighed. "Never mind."

Huckle, who had been hunched in one of the seats, sulking
because no one believed her story, said, "I'm telling you, it was
nibbling on me, like some kind of animal."

I nudged Wolf. Nibbling? I said. He licked his not-lips and
yawned again, showing me his not-teeth. I told him the story
of Little Red Riding Hood, but I had to stop halfway because it

was so silly. Who wouldn't recognize their own grandmother? Who didn't know a wolf when they saw one?

They rode to the end of the line, Sixty-Third Street and Stoney Island Avenue, filed out of the trains and onto the street. Frankie supposed it could have been colder, but it was cold enough to make her nose go numb as they walked toward Jackson Park.

"I hope we're having lunch in the park," said Joanie.

"It's only about ten o'clock now," Loretta said, stuffing her hands in her pockets. "We probably won't be having lunch until we get to the museum. And who knows how long that's going to take, with all these people. We won't have hardly any time to see the exhibits."

"How much time do you need?" Joanie said. "This isn't even the good museum."

"You mean the one with all the paintings?" Frankie said, thinking about the one time they had taken a bunch of the girls to a place filled with beautiful, colorful pictures painted by all sorts of famous artists.

"What? Oh, no, not *that* boring old place," said Joanie. "I'm talking about the place with all the dinosour bones."

"It's dino*saur*, not dino*sour*," Loretta said.

Joanie frowned. "But that's what I said."

They walked the rest of the way to the park as Joanie chattered on about dinosours and their very big bones and foot-long teeth. I couldn't remember ever being in a dinosaur museum, so I wondered if she was just making it all up.

Ahead of us, Sister Bert turned and shouted, "Chop, chop, people! We want to make it to the museum in time for lunch." Sister George just shot them all a glare that said they would regret their whole lives if anyone made her late for lunch.

Joanie muttered, "She's worse than the Nazis."

A strange but interesting little building loomed up ahead. "What's that?" Frankie asked Loretta.

"Is it a bathroom?" Joanie asked. "I hope it is, 'cause I really gotta go."

"I don't think it's a bathroom," Loretta said. "Look at how it's landscaped. With all the little trees and everything. Oh, wait! There's a plaque."

"I don't want to read about anything but a bathroom," said Joanie, but they slowed down as Loretta read, "'The Ho-o-den Pavilion. A replica of the famous Phoenix Hall in Uji, Japan.'" She shook her head. "It was put here a long time before the war."

"What about Japan?" said a boy behind them. He wore a gray cap pulled low over his eyes and a blue scarf that looked as if moths had nested in it.

"Nothing, really," said Loretta as we started walking again. "That building's a replica of some building in Japan. This whole place is supposed to look like a Japanese garden."

The boy in the gray cap said, "Oh yeah?" He reached out and grabbed a pretty little bush and yanked it clean out of the ground. "I don't think we need no Japanese *anything* in Chicago, now do we, fellas?"

The boys around him nodded, and all at once started pulling out plants, uprooting bushes, and throwing rocks into the little ponds. Wolf whined and pawed at the ground, but no one heard him.

One of the plants landed at Sister George's feet, and she whipped around. Frankie was sure she'd start shrieking at them, maybe march back to where they were, grab someone by the ear. But Sister George just looked at the boys, then looked at the plant crumpled at her feet the way a bird looks at a worm it's just bitten in two. All she said was, "You heard Sister Bert. We have to make it to the museum in time for lunch." She scooped up the plant, ripped it in half, and stomped on it with such ferocity everyone stopped to watch.

Frankie waited until Sister George was far away before she said, "Forget the boys. They should send *her* overseas."

Too cold outside, too hot inside.

"I'm baking in this sweater," Joanie said, already upset because Sister Bert had made her wait until after lunch to go to the bathroom, and she already had to go again. Plus, she was mad that there were no dinosaurs, no bones. Sister Bert had herded a group of them right beneath an old airplane hanging from the ceiling and made them crowd around a piece of an old lighthouse instead. They couldn't have been more bored if they worked at it.

"Now," she said, "this lens was recovered from a very old lighthouse on Barnegat Inlet—that's on the shore of New Jersey."

She droned on and on and on while the orphans shifted their coats from one arm to the other. "It was brought to the museum in 1934. And," she said, "it cost fifteen thousand dollars."

That, we heard. "Fifteen thousand dollars!" said Joanie. "For this old piece of junk?"

"It's hardly junk, Miss McNally, and if you'd been paying attention . . . Oh!" All of a sudden Sister Bert gasped and clapped her hand over her mouth.

At first I thought she was staring back at the airplane itself, but that wasn't it. She was staring at the boy in the gray cap who'd somehow climbed up into the plane and was waving at them from the cockpit.

"Daniel Konecky! Get down here!" Sister George yelled. "Now!"

I didn't know if Gray Cap didn't hear her or didn't care, because he just kept waving as Sister George turned red, and then purple. I was mildly curious if she would have an embolism and have to haunt the museum, forever flapping and shouting at a wayward orphan in an airplane. Sister shoved the orphans aside and ran underneath the plane, back and forth, like Gray Cap might jump out and she would be the one to catch him. The rest of orphans giggled, but then tried to stifle themselves when Sister Bert came over.

"Goodness," Sister Bert said in that mild way she had. "We can't take you hooligans anywhere, can we?" A uniformed museum guard dragged a ladder under the plane. As he was pulled from the plane, Gray Cap gave them the thumbs-up and all the orphans clapped until Sister Bert told them to knock it off.

"You think it's funny? It won't be so funny when that boy has to go up in a plane for real, will it?"

Frankie remembered some of the letters Stella had read to them. Boys talking about bombs bursting around them, hitting the wings, shrapnel cutting through the metal skin of the plane like it was nothing but tissue paper. Suddenly she was very happy Vito wasn't flying in any airplanes and had both feet on the ground, as if that were the thing that could keep him safe, as if any one thing could.

Frankie had a stream of letters that Vito had written, but it didn't occur to her how little he wrote of the actual war. She knew he was in Italy somewhere, but she didn't know he was a part of Operation Avalanche, the main invasion of Salerno. She knew they were fighting, but she didn't hear the crash of the bombs, she couldn't know what it was like to try to sleep to the sound of men screaming. Vito had talked of listening to a radio that one of the boys had found in town, but she didn't know that they listened to Axis Sally, who signed on to her show by saying, "Hello, Suckers!" and told them that their wives and fiancées back home were sleeping with any man they could find—you know girls, girls will trick you every time—but that it wouldn't matter, because they'd all be wiped out anyway when the Germans rolled in. Frankie didn't know that the boys opened every letter, any letter, as if it were a dispatch from another world, a kinder one, a pleasant dream they'd once had when they were young.

She didn't know they weren't young anymore.

The next exhibit they were dragged to was better than the lens, and got their minds off the plane, off the vague and nagging fear of war. It was the Santa Fe Railroad exhibit, the biggest model train set any of them had ever seen.

"Danny's gonna be sore that he missed this," said one of Gray Cap's friends, watching the locomotive pull a line of cars along the track. There was a cement factory and an oil field. Even some of the houses and buildings had working electricity, just like real houses.

"You ever been to the Grand Canyon?" said someone next to Frankie. Sam.

She was so surprised to see him that she forgot what he had asked. "What?"

"The Grand Canyon. Have you ever been?"

Was he making fun of her? "Um, no, what do you think?"

"Here," he said, and grabbed hold of her hand. He led her over to where the museum people had set up a miniature Grand Canyon next to one of the train tracks. "Now you've been there. One day, we'll go for real. All around the country, all the around the world."

He meant it, she could see that. He squeezed her hand, she squeezed back.

Loretta squeezed between them. "Give it a rest."

"What?" said Frankie.

"Sister George is *right over there*," said Loretta. "She's going to see you, and then what will happen?"

She could be beaten. She could be thrown out of the orphanage for good. But would that be the worst thing? Choppy had left the orphanage last fall, had taken a job at a factory in Forest Park, where she was helping to make torpedoes, living it up in a boardinghouse with a dozen other girls. On Saturday nights, they took the train to the Christian Servicemen's Center downtown to dance the night away with petty officers and marines. "Anyone can find a man, cut a rug," Choppy told Frankie on her only visit, her last. "I'm telling ya, Fran-ces-ca, it's the life. I'm going to join up, Frankie. They have a women's auxiliary."

Frankie had no father, Frankie had no mother. She would have to make a life in any way she could. With Sam, she could manage. She wouldn't be alone. And Toni would be okay. Toni always was. They wouldn't punish her for anything Frankie did; Toni was too young. Maybe Toni would even be glad to see Frankie go.

Luckily for Frankie, Sister George wasn't watching them. Not then. Her eyes were still on the plane that hung so high above them, swaying slightly with a phantom weight. The ghost girl with the broken face sat in the cockpit, trying desperately to fly away.

WHAT ARE YOU DOING, WHAT HAVE YOU DONE?

MY OLDER BROTHER WILLIAM'S HERO was Theodore Roosevelt—bear-hunting, horse-loving, gun-slinging Teddy Roosevelt. My father said it was Teddy's fault William was so desperate to go to war. William hated horses—or rather, the horses hated him—he was a terrible shot, and any bear worth its salt would have eaten him and used his bones for toothpicks, but he read Roosevelt's books the way religious men pored over scripture: *The Rough Riders, The Winning of the West, The Conservation of Womanhood and Childhood, America and the World War.* After the Germans sank the *Lusitania*, William couldn't believe Woodrow Wilson wasn't leading the whole of America's military straight to the German border. He believed a man wasn't much of a man if he didn't have a gun in his hand, if he wasn't willing to protect home and country with his very flesh and blood, with the blood of others, no matter how far he had to travel to do it. When the service rejected William for poor eyesight, he took it as a judgment not on his vision, but on his manhood. So many boys did. As if a person's worth could only be measured in the number of people he was willing to kill. William was willing.

Not everyone was so eager.

"Hey," said Sam, pulling at Frankie's arms, which were around his neck. "Not so tight. You're choking me."

"Sorry," she said. Lately, when she was with him, she got a cold, cold feeling in the pit of her stomach. His eighteenth birthday was coming up, and the war wasn't over yet. But maybe it would be, soon. Maybe the Allies would beat back the Germans and the Japanese. Maybe she'd be listening to the radio tomorrow or next week and hear the announcers interrupt the regular programs to say that Hitler had surrendered and that not one more boy would have to leave.

"Come on, Frankie. Let go." Sam stood up and ran his fingers through his hair. His face was wan and drawn, and there were lines around his eyes, like he'd gotten old overnight.

"What's the matter?"

"I don't know," he said. Then he shook his head. "I do know. I have to sign up."

She knew what he was talking about, but she asked anyway. "Sign up for what?"

"The service, goof."

"Don't call me a goof," she said, though she was acting like one, and on purpose. "You don't have to sign up yet."

"I will in a few months."

He walked over to the window and looked out. He had a handprint on the back of his dark shirt, hers. She'd been making dough for pie crusts and still had flour all over herself and she

went ahead and left it on him. She decided not to tell him, decided to leave him marked.

"Everyone has to enlist," she said after a while.

"*You* don't," he said, over his shoulder.

She didn't know what he wanted her to say to that. "My
brother Vito did. And he's okay."

"Not everyone stays okay, Frankie."

"I know. But Vito will, and you will."

"Just because you want it doesn't mean it will happen," he
said.

Anger flared up in her like a struck match, melting the cold
spot. "Why are you saying things like that? Why do you want
me to worry about my brother? Why do you want me to worry
about you?"

He shoved his hands into his pockets and said something to
the window that she couldn't hear.

"What?" she said.

He turned his head a little, so she could only see half his
face. "I said, *I'm scared.*"

Frankie opened her mouth, but nothing came out. Vito had
never said he was scared, but maybe he was.

And then Sam scared *her*: he started to cry.

She didn't know what to do except take his face in her hands
and kiss him until the salt dried on her own skin.

———— ∞ ————

At the bar, Mad Maureen poured me a bourbon. She set a bowl
of water for Wolf, showed him the tattoo of a fox she had on her

thigh. When she flexed her muscles, her fox seemed to tense, ready to pounce. Wolf jumped up on the stool next to me and lapped at the bourbon. I let him have it.

I said, Every time there was a knock at the door, I ran to answer it myself, just in case it was him, standing there with a message or a package for my father. He told me that his name was Benno. But that wasn't his real name. He didn't want to tell me his real name.

Mad Maureen wiped down the bar in big sweeping circles, told me exactly what Marguerite had told me: Names have power. He didn't want to give away what little he had.

I wanted more, I said. I wanted everything. When I looked at him, I felt . . . strange inside, blurred and watery and indistinct, as strange as I felt when I first found my brother William's French postcards buried in the back of his closet. As if I'd discovered some secret that everyone else was keeping from me. As if *he* was the secret. There was an itch under my skin I couldn't reach, no matter how much I scratched. My mother saw the red marks on my neck at the dinner table. What are you doing to yourself? she asked me. What have you done?

THREE LETTERS

IN THE KITCHEN, IN THE hallway, in the yard by the angel, in a classroom used by the music students for practice—every time and every place they could get away, Frankie met Sam. They would find a place to sit, they would talk a little about what they had done that day and what they wanted to do the next one, and the next. They would kiss, and time fell away as if it had no meaning at all. Sometimes, if there was no one around, he'd play her a song, low and sweet, on his trumpet. Frankie liked the trumpet, it was sad, but strong too. Like she thought she was.

But who is ever as strong as they believe?

"No," Frankie said. "No, no, no!"

"Frankie, we knew the letter was gonna come someday," Sam said.

"When?"

"Tomorrow."

The word tore through her like shrapnel. "Tomorrow! You can't be going tomorrow!" She gripped the front of his shirt as if she could make him stay if she held on tight enough.

"I would have told you sooner," he said, "but I didn't know

either. They just told me to report downtown."

"It's not fair," she said, and it wasn't, but that didn't change anything. Because this was war, and because Sam himself had changed. He had steeled himself. He didn't dream of tulips anymore. He had told himself that the war might leave scars, but scars weren't the worst things to mark a man. He had told himself that even if the war took a bigger bite, an arm, a leg, he had other arms and legs—Frankie's. Frankie would hold him up. He had told himself that if he were destined to die, God would see to it that his death was quick. And if God wouldn't, the bombs would.

If he had to, he would pray to the bombs.

"Come on, Frankie," he said. "You'll write me, won't you?"

She tried to get ahold of herself, swiping at her eyes. "Yeah, sure I will. You know I will."

"And I'll write you. Every week, how's that?"

"You promise? Every week?"

He kissed the top of her head. "You bet." He looked up at the clock. "We don't have long. I told Sister Cornelius that I forgot my coat. She's going to start wondering where I am soon."

"Play me a song first," she said.

"I don't—"

"Please," she said. "Just play me a song before you go."

"What do you want me to play?"

"I don't know. Anything. A goodbye song."

He thought for a minute, then put the trumpet to his mouth, closed his eyes, and started to play. Frankie didn't know the song, but it was a happy song, filled with notes that skipped and danced like butterflies. Somehow hearing that happy song at such a sad time made her that much sadder, as if happy songs were nothing but wishes, fleeting as the first blooms of spring.

When he was done playing, he gave her the trumpet. For safekeeping, he said. They found his coat in the closet, they used it for a bed. In the dark of that tiny room, they broke against each other—detonated, shattered.

Frankie tried to play that trumpet, but she didn't know how. She settled for holding the mouthpiece against her lips, where Sam's had been.

———∞———

Frankie was supposed to be doing her chores, she was supposed to be practicing her shorthand. She was supposed to be doing her part for her family and friends and country, keeping her chin up and a smile on her face. Before, she had been riding the gig through the hallways, she was at the top of the class in her secretarial course, she was stealing kisses in the greenhouse, but now that Sam had been called, now that Sam had gone away, she couldn't think, she didn't know who she was. If she kept her chin up, something else would punch her in the jaw. Lights out.

So Frankie put her head down and tried to write Sam a letter. Not about the war. She hated the war. No, she wanted to write about where she and Sam would be in a year, after she got out of the orphanage. By then, the war would be over, of course it would be over, and everyone would get jobs. She could work for an important businessman, Sam could open his own flower shop. Maybe he could play the trumpet in a band in a club where people danced all night. They'd get an apartment, and then a house, and then—

"Earth to Francesca!"

Frankie looked up from the letter she'd been writing for days. Sister Bert dropped two letters in front of her, both, Frankie figured, from Vito. She tore into the first envelope.

Dear Frankie,

We're here in ████████████████████ *and the weather's finally been good to us. You'd think it would be cold in January, but it's not, not here, anyway.*

But better than the not-so-cold weather is the quiet. I love the quiet! We haven't seen any action in a few days, so finally we have some time to write letters to all our friends and families that we all miss so much.

Last night, some of the boys in my unit went on a mission to ████████████ *and brought back a few carrots, onions, potatoes, and a chicken! (They must have traded all their cigarettes for the chicken!) We made a big pot of chicken soup. I couldn't believe how good it tasted. It had been so long since I had homemade chicken soup, it seemed like the best soup I've ever had, even though it was fixed up by a bunch of guys who could rebuild an engine and fire a gun but probably couldn't make a slice of toast without burning it.*

Anyway, how are you? All the guys liked the drawings of the museum that you went to, especially the one with all the trains in it. And they just loved that story about the crazy boy who got himself up in that airplane. And like you said, it is kind of funny that that same boy ended up shipping out just a month later. I wonder if he went into the air force. (Probably not.)

Speaking of funny boys, who's this Sam who you mentioned twice in your last letter? I hope you're keeping your head. Wait a minute, I'm not hoping, I'm telling you to keep your head, you get me? I've already got one out-of-control sister. I don't want to worry about the sensible sister too.

Well, it's just about time for me to hit the hay, so I'm going to have one last cigarette and say good night.

Write again soon!

Love,
Vito

Sensible. Responsible. In control. What if she wanted to get a little out of control? What if she already had? What if she was tired of being so responsible all the time? Didn't she deserve more?

She stuffed the first letter back into the envelope and ripped open the second one. Right away she was scared—*did something happen to Vito?*—because she didn't recognize the handwriting, and nothing was blacked out by the censors. But then she saw who it was from.

Dear Francesca,

Your father wanted me to write and tell you that we decided to move back to Chicago soon after the New Year. Your father's health is much better, he misses Chicago, and we think that it's a good time to open up another shoe shop. People won't want new shoes, but we should do enough business in repairs to keep us going. We plan on getting a place with a little apartment upstairs or in the back.

The space will be small. Even with your brother and step-brothers gone to war, there isn't going to be enough room for you or for Toni, so I don't want you begging your father, he feels bad enough already. Besides, you're almost old enough to be out on your own, aren't you? I'm sure you understand.

As soon as we get settled, your father will visit you.

Regards,

Ada

When I got to the library, Marguerite was already there, reading a newspaper over another woman's shoulder.

I said, The Germans captured Erich Maria Remarque's sister, Elfriede.

What? Who?

Remarque. He wrote *All Quiet on the Western Front*. He escaped Germany, but his youngest sister, Elfriede, stayed behind with her husband and children. She was arrested and found guilty of undermining morale. The Germans couldn't catch her brother, but they caught her. They had her beheaded.

Marguerite stared, silent. Then she said, How do you know this?

I shrugged. There are things I just know, I said. And there

were. But not this. The angel had told me, the way she told me many things. I didn't want to share the angel with Marguerite just yet.

In 1932, we thought Hitler was a ridiculous little man, Marguerite said. No one took him seriously. We were too busy with our own worries.

I guess the devil wears a clown nose, I said.

Or a funny mustache and a silly haircut, said Marguerite. Speaking of haircuts, how's Wolf?

Wolf is fine, as you can see. Where's the man with *The Hobbit*? Is he here today?

I told you, I don't care about *The Hobbit*.

I wanted to read a bit more. There are wolves in it, called Wargs. They are friends to the goblins.

Lovely, said Marguerite.

They're not lovely at all. Goblins are horrible. Wargs are horrible.

Then why did you name your fox after them?

His name isn't Warg.

Thank goodness for that, she said.

There is a character in the book called Beorn the Skin-changer. He is called Skin-changer because he can change himself into a bear.

A handy talent, I'm sure, said Marguerite. Why do you like this story so much?

Perhaps I wish I could turn myself into a bear. Or a Warg. Or anything else.

Have you ever tried? Marguerite asked.

To turn myself into a Warg?

To assume another shape.

No, I said, astonished at the question. Well, maybe. Have you?

She bit her lip. She didn't want to share either.

It's all right, I said. You don't have to tell me.

She hesitated, then said, I would tell you another story. A true story, but I can't imagine you'll believe it.

I'll believe it! I said.

Hmmm, she said.

It's your story, though, I told her. I won't pester you. As much as I'd like to hear it.

A slight smile played across her mouth. She said, This is you not pestering me?

This is the least amount of pestering I've ever done in my life. Or death.

She thought for a moment. Then she said, I will tell Wolf the story, but I won't mind if you listen as well. If you promise to be quiet as I tell it.

I promise I'll be as silent as—

—a ghost? she said.

See how well you know me?

Shhh. You promised. So, listen:

Long ago, fifty years before the Civil War, a group of men and women were stolen from their homes in West Africa. Slavers packed the people into a boat for the long journey to

America, a nightmare journey full of starvation and abuse and all sorts of horrors too terrible to name. At a slave market in Savannah, the people were auctioned off, sold to a plantation. They were once again forced into a boat, this one a smaller vessel, and confined belowdecks for the trip down the coast to a place called St. Simons Island, off the Georgia coast. But something happened during the journey. The people rose up against their captors and threw them overboard. Then they landed that boat on the shores of St. Simons Island.

According to white men who witnessed it, as soon as the boat landed, the men and women walked into Dunbar Creek and drowned. But that's not the whole story. Because back in Africa, some of the people were conjure men and women—they knew magic. They could make a buzzard row a boat, they could boil a pot without a fire. And some were skin-changers. They could change into lions, they could change into crocodiles. And when that boat ran up on that shore, some of them remembered who they were. They whispered the magic words one to the other, rose up into the sky, and flew right back home to Africa.

The ones who did not know the magic words, the ones who could not fly, cast their eyes to the sky, their eyes saying *Don't leave us, help us, take us.* But though the magic ones were heartbroken for those they were leaving, they didn't have the time to teach the magic words, didn't have the time to teach the others to fly. The others would have to find a chance to fight, to run.

And one day they would.

By the time Marguerite reached the end of her story, we had

left the library and made it all the way downtown to 209 South LaSalle Street, Chicago's first skyscraper, called the Rookery. We sat in the light court, the muted sunshine through the glass ceiling burnishing everything in gold.

I love your stories, I said.

They're not just mine. My mother told me the stories like her mother told her, and her mother before.

Still.

If this is the Rookery, Marguerite asked, where are the birds?

After the Great Fire, I said, there was a temporary city hall on this site. Some said it was so shoddily built, crows built their nests everywhere. My father told me that since city hall was full of crooks, any citizen who entered was bound to be rooked. The architects never cared for the name, but it stuck.

Was your father rooked?

I shrugged. He was the rook.

Marguerite nodded, and we turned our attention to the people passing by. Smart-suited men, gloved and hatted women, some with lines drawn on the backs of bare calves so it looked as if they were wearing nylons, though their legs must have been freezing. One of the men caught my eye, one of the finest-looking men I had ever seen, alive or dead. Sandy hair rippling like a wheat field, pale skin rich, blue eyes deep, not too tall or too short. It was as if he'd been carved from—

Marguerite gasped, clutched at her chest, her throat. Wolf, who had been lounging on the floor, snapped to his feet, paced.

What is it? I said. Do you know that man?

Marguerite paced along with the fox. I shouldn't have come here, she said, why did you bring me? She pressed the back of her hand to her mouth, mashing her lips against her knuckles.

You were talking about birds, so it reminded me of—

I wasn't talking about birds, I was talking about *magic.*

Yes, but—

I need to go, she said. She stepped into a shaft of light, rendering her in a shimmering wash of gold that blazed so bright it almost hurt to look. The man suddenly stopped walking as if he'd hit a wall of glass. He turned around, slowly, so slowly, and his creamy skin went as gray as lake water. He gaped at the place where Marguerite was standing, though he couldn't have seen her. Couldn't have, because she was—

"Rita?" he whispered. His eyes rolled up, knees buckling. The smart-suited men and the hatted women swarmed, catching him before he hit the floor.

1944
JEZEBELS

THE BOYS OF WAR

MARGUERITE VANISHED. I POKED AND prodded the children of the Guardians, but none of them would listen. The yellows and reds and browns of late fall turned into the icy blues and whites of another war-torn winter. As the days marched forward, Frankie made bargains with God: please spare Sam and Vito. I'll pray every day, I'll confess every sin, I'll repent, I'll be nice to Toni, I'll be nice to *Stella*. Please, please, please.

But it was from Stella that Frankie heard about the dead boys. Stella had been writing to an orphanage fellow named Clay every week for a year, and all of a sudden the letters stopped coming. She could feel it in her bones, she told the other girls, the day she got the mail and there wasn't a letter from dear ol' Clay. Loretta had scowled and said, "How could she miss one with fifty others in the stack?" But Stella insisted that Clay must have been killed in action, and for once in her life, Stella was right.

Soon after Stella had pulled Clay's address from her card file, Sister Bert announced that a special service would be held for Clay and for three other Guardians boys who'd died overseas.

On a clear, cold Sunday in early March, Frankie and the rest of the orphans found themselves in church for the third time, listening to Father Paul eulogize each of the four boys. When he got to Clay, Stella threw herself on the floor. "Poor, poor Clay," she wailed, sobbing into her crumpled hankie as Toni patted her back. A couple of people turned around in their pews just to watch, she was making such a spectacle of herself.

Frankie felt sorry for the boys, and their brothers and sisters still at the Guardians, but she wouldn't feel sorry for Stella, considering that she had whole battalions of boys convinced that they were her only love, and that she was milking it for all she was worth. Considering that Frankie's one and only love had been shipped out and Frankie was doing her best to stay strong.

What if something happened to Sam? What if—

No. *No.*

Tired of watching Stella hamming it up, Frankie unfolded her program and read:

A Patriotic Tribute to Our Servicemen

"Greater love than this no man hath,
that a man lay down his life for his friends."
John 15:13

KILLED IN ACTION
Roderick Butz
Clayton Jackson

Robert Keys

Henry Zimmer

Eternal rest grant unto them, O Lord. May they rest in peace.

Listening to Father Paul, you'd think that Clay was brave and generous and helpful and loving, willing to give his life for his country, and so were all the rest of the boys who died. But Clay didn't sound like that in the letters he wrote Stella, the ones she read out loud. In those letters, he sounded sweet and nervous and a little silly. He talked about his feet a lot, how they hurt all the time because of the blisters, and how the thing he missed most about America was sleep. He talked about wishing Stella was with him so that he could kiss her "peachy little nose," whatever that meant. And he talked about the nightmares he had when he did sleep, filled with monsters and witches and flying monkeys just like in *The Wizard of Oz*. How, thought Frankie, could a boy who believed Stella had a peachy *anything*, a boy who was terrified of flying monkeys, be the same courageous soul Father Paul was going on about? How could this boy be Captain America with his knockout punch?

Frankie had to wonder if anyone really knew anyone. Poor Clay didn't know Stella, Father Paul didn't know Clay. Frankie's own father was a mystery, gone for years and then he was back and wanting to visit after the memorial service, like some kind of twisted magic trick. It was too confusing to think about, so Frankie tried not to.

After Father Paul was done with his eulogies, after the sisters and cousins had gone up to the altar to light candles for their brothers, one of the boys got up from his seat and went to stand at the communion railing. He lifted his trumpet to his lips and started to play "Taps," low and slow, pausing at the end of each phrase so that another bugler in the bell tower could play the exact same part. Except the bugler in the bell tower wasn't so much a bugler as a bungler, and kept getting the notes all wrong, or sour. Some of the kids in the church smiled and some of them even laughed. Sam, who was a kind boy, the kind who willed flowers to grow, who wanted to coax vegetables from the ground, would have been offended that these brave boys' funeral was turned into a joke.

But maybe Clay and the rest weren't brave at all. Maybe they'd made mistakes and that's why they were killed. Sam didn't make mistakes. Frankie knew that about him. She already had a stack of his letters. The air force had sent him to Mississippi for training, and he liked to talk about the food and the weather and the mess-ups of guys who would man the transport planes with him. *Yesterday*, he wrote,

> *during mail call everybody was quiet reading their letters when suddenly somebody cursed in a loud voice and shouted, "Alice got married!" So that's how Eugene learned he's out in the cold. I'd feel bad for him if he hadn't gotten us all latrine duty because he's a slob who can't make a bed right. . . .*
>
> *We got a night off and went out for gumbo. Do you know what that is? A spicy kind of stew with shrimp in it. I thought I*

wouldn't like it, but I did. Reggie didn't like it, but that's because he drank enough for ten guys and spent the rest of the night sick as a dog.

I got your letter, the one with the self-portrait. The fellows all agreed that you were as pretty as I said you were, and a crackerjack artist too! Hank said you looked as good as Hedy Lamarr. (He's wrong. You look better.) Can you believe he tried to swipe your picture? As if I wouldn't notice. I nearly broke his fingers. (But I didn't.)

He signed all his letters "Love, Sam."

Frankie would write to Sam about this service, make him see that everyone messes up and that it was okay, that you had to find something to laugh about, especially during a war. *Sam,* she'd write,

it's a funeral and all, but maybe after all the sadness and flowers and speeches, the boys would hear it up in heaven and they would laugh like we were laughing, and they would understand that there is joy in everything, like Sister Bert said. Remember Sister? She looks like a beautiful tea cozy. Have you seen any nuns over there? I bet you don't miss them, even the ones who look like beautiful tea cozies. Do you miss me? I miss you. I think about the greenhouse. I think about our garden, the one we'll have together. We'll plant those tulips that you said were worth more than gold. The bees will visit us, or maybe we'll have a hive. The bees will never sting, and if they do it will feel more like a kiss. I'll make you any kind of cake you want with the honey. Or with sugar, when we can get it. Or that dish your mother made, the funny one with the apples and the cabbage. Gumbo? Gumbo! Ham and beans so green they'll make your eyes hurt. Fluffy mashed pota-toes. Real butter over everything. You can play for me while I cook, you can play for me always. A song as happy as we are, as we will be.

—∞—

Toni wasn't happy. She had never quite forgiven Frankie for screaming at her and her boyfriend back on the day of the Corpus Christi parade. Sitting in their best dresses, waiting for their father's first visit in two years, they were quiet as clouds. Frankie kept tying and retying the scarf around her neck, thinking about the love bites her scarves always used to hide, feeling like a heel.

"Not a heel," Loretta had told her. "A hypocrite."

"I'm not," Frankie muttered, though she felt as terrible as a hypocrite and a heel probably should.

"What did you say?" Toni said.

"Nothing."

Toni looked at her with her big dark eyes. "You're going to strangle yourself with that scarf."

Frankie let go of the scarf. "I'm just nervous, is all."

"Do you think he forgot?"

"He never forgot visiting Sunday before," she said. "But I almost did." She didn't say that she had gotten used to spending Sundays hanging out with Loretta and the other girls. That now that their father was coming, and probably would be every other Sunday, she couldn't help but feel disappointed, as if they would be missing everything good. And then she felt guilty. And then mad. Everything was all mixed up.

"I almost forgot too," Toni said. "It just feels funny after all this time."

"Yeah," said Frankie.

Toni smoothed the skirt of her blue dress. "You think he'll be surprised when he sees us?"

"Probably," Frankie said. "You've grown about a foot."

"A foot wider maybe," she said. "Still, I'm taller than you."

"There are girls in the eight-year-olds' cottage who are taller than me."

Toni smiled just a little bit, and Frankie could see that maybe her sister still hated her, but not as much as she did before. That was all right.

They had waited just a few minutes more in their quiet, all right way, when their father swept into the waiting room, hat at an angle, like the movie star he always was, like the Italian Clark Gable. "Belle!" he said. "Belle!" and dropped the bags of food onto the floor. Hugging them, he rubbed their faces with his rough, scratchy cheeks, even teared up a little, as if he'd never learned that men don't cry about anything, that real men were never sad.

He stepped away from them and held Frankie by the shoulders. "Let me look, eh? So big! So grown up!" He let go and turned to Toni and whistled. "And you! No Toni for you! Mia

Antonina, a woman!" He picked up one of the paper bags he had brought, dug around inside, and brought out two carefully wrapped sandwiches. They could smell the meatballs even through the layers of newspaper he'd wrapped them in, and Frankie's stomach gurgled, though she wasn't hungry at all.

"Yes!" said their father. "This will fix you."

They took their sandwiches and he shooed them over to a table so that they could eat them. As they unwrapped the packages, he talked about the new apartment and the customers he had at the new shoe shop. He told them about Ada and her kids, how the two older boys got sent off to war, how Dewey would sometimes tap dance on the sidewalk for a few coins, how the girls got jobs in a typing pool somewhere, that they were special because they worked in an office and not a factory.

"That's what you do, eh? You type important letters."

Though it was probably what Frankie would do, what they both might do, what the orphanage had trained them to do, Frankie shrugged and did her best to eat that sandwich. He was acting like nothing had ever happened at all, that he had never left, that he hadn't picked Ada and her army of brats over them, that he wasn't going home to them afterward. There he was, sitting in front of them, talking and talking and talking, and Frankie felt so far away from him, as if she were Sister Bert with her face in a book so much more interesting than the real world.

And that's how it went. For weeks after, the missing-him part of Frankie fought with the mad-at-him part, and every time she thought she had it figured out, it turned out that she hadn't. She loved him, she hated him, she wanted him to visit, she wanted him to stay away. And either way, she thought more about Sam than she did about when her father was coming to visit. Huckle said that all that meant was that Frankie was a red-blooded American gal, but Frankie figured that was just one more reason she was going to burn.

Join the club, I said.

I couldn't find Marguerite anywhere. As soon as the pretty white man had fallen in the atrium, she had fled from the Rookery, taking her golden blazing light with her. The other men and women lifted the man to his feet and he'd shaken them off. He was fine, he told them. He just slipped, that's all. Nothing life-threatening, he was sure of that. Nothing wrong with his heart.

Wolf and I had followed him from the Rookery to an antiques shop on the north side of town. Porcelain table lamps. Ornate carved furniture with animal feet. Rare books bound in leather. Sparkling jewelry tucked away in glass cases. If I could have smelled the place, I was sure it would smell of must and lemon oil and money. I could imagine my own father shopping in just such a place, not because he valued old things but because he thought other people did, that a rich man who wanted to be richer should always look the part, even if he had to go into debt to do it. When Charles Kent started coming to call on me, too rich and too important for war—even a Great one—my father had my mother order a dozen new dresses for me, and three pairs of handmade leather shoes. I needed to play my part, too—the beautiful, dutiful daughter, soon to be a richer man's wife. It didn't matter that I wasn't yet eighteen. *I* didn't matter.

Once upon a time, a banker and a banker arranged a merger, traded a girl for a stake in a corporation, agreed over a handshake and a scotch. And on a chilly afternoon, while my parents were out, Charles Kent tore one of those lovely new gowns off my back because I didn't want to play. He laughed as I shivered in the sudden cold, he laughed as I gathered myself by the fire.

He stopped laughing when I hit him with the poker. He cried when I hit him again.

War is hell.

But in that musty, dusty shop, there was no fire to warm me, no fire that could. A sleek black cat dashed out of the stacks to greet the beautiful fair man, and still shaken from his encounter, he bent down to scratch her between the ears. The cat's large jewel eyes, an acid green, regarded Wolf and me placidly, fearlessly. We were no danger to her, and she let us know this with a twitch of her tail, an unhurried saunter as she followed the man to the very back wall of the shop. She jumped up onto the large mahogany desk there, and the man sat down behind it, breathing, breathing, as if the mere fact of breath was a feat in and of itself. On the desk were photographs of him and his family. As he did in the flesh, he looked in the photos like something hewn by Michelangelo, freed from the stone with chisel and hammer. No wonder Marguerite couldn't refuse him. The

redhead posing with him in the pictures couldn't either, I supposed. A wide-eyed and bow-mouthed little thing, unassuming
as milk.

He was beautiful, but I could see the truth. I knew what
he'd done.

The black cat settled herself on the desktop, closed her
acid eyes, shutting us out. After the man had proven to himself that he could breathe just fine, he fished inside his jacket
pocket, removed a snowy handkerchief. He took off his glasses
and rubbed each lens slowly, methodically, the way you might
if you'd seen the ghost of the girl you murdered more than a
decade ago and you were trying to convince yourself you hadn't.

BAMBI

MOVIE NIGHT AT THE GUARDIANS.

"*Bambi* again?" said Frankie.

"They think we're all a bunch of babies," Loretta said in Frankie's ear.

"Some of us are," Frankie told her, looking in Joanie McNally's direction. She was crying up a storm because Bambi's mother had died.

"Did Joanie's mother die?" Loretta asked.

"I don't know. Maybe? But my mother is dead and you don't see me acting like that."

"Hmmm," Loretta said. The last time Loretta's mom had come to visit, she forgot to put her dress on under her coat again, and sat talking to Loretta in her stained old slip before one of the sisters made her put her coat back on. Later, the girls found out that she'd been sent to Dunning to "rest." Loretta said that the asylum was the last place anyone should be sent to rest. The last place anyone should be sent, ever.

Frankie searched for something else to talk about, something safe, but everything seemed loaded these days. Loretta's mom, Sam, Toni, the war, the sisters all so on edge. Stella sat a few rows down, dabbing at the corners of her eyes with a white hankie. Her lipstick was perfect. "Some of us are babies, and some of us are regular old Sarah Bernhardts," Frankie said, nodding at Stella.

Loretta scowled and pushed her strawberry-blond hair from her eyes. "She got so much attention by crying at that funeral, now she just cries all the time, as if it's the same. What was she saying yesterday? 'I've only got two Roberts left?' I could have slugged her."

"I wish you would."

Someone must have opened the back door of the theater, because a beam of light cut across the screen, slicing poor Bambi in half. A bunch of the little kids started shouting, and a bunch of the older girls twisted around to see who it was.

A young man was limping slowly across the auditorium. He wore a uniform and a green coat, and he looked rumpled as a bed, as if he'd been traveling a long time. As he got closer, Frankie saw that he was scanning the audience in the dark, looking for someone. Brown hair fell across his brows, and an ugly scar ran from his ear to his chin. He held a piece of paper or an envelope or something in his hand like it was precious, a will, a treasure map.

The sisters, napping as usual in their chairs against the back wall, started to poke and nudge one another. Sister Cornelius pushed her glasses up her nose, stood and flapped her wings at the boy running the projector. The movie stopped, and the kids booed. "Be quiet!" boomed Sister Cornelius, and the girls shut up.

But the soldier with the scar didn't seem to notice that the movie had stopped and the lights went on. And he didn't notice Sister Cornelius zooming up behind him like a wasp getting ready to sting. He kept scanning the audience, looking for the one face he wanted. He stopped at Stella's row and his split face broke out in a smile, though it must have hurt to grin like that.

"Young man!" barked Sister Cornelius. "Young man! You cannot just come in here! This is private property! There are designated visiting hours!" She yammered on and on, but he didn't hear it. Stella's eyebrows flew up almost into her hair as he stood there with that envelope—it was an envelope, I could see it now—smiling like that, his big scar fresh and raw and red.

"Stella," he said, sighing her name. Then he looked at the girl on the end of the row and said, very politely, "Excuse me. I need to speak with Stella."

"Young man!" shrieked Sister Cornelius.

The girl stood up, and so did all the girls next to her. The soldier stepped past them, nodding at them as he went thank you, excuse me, thank you, until he reached Stella and Toni. Toni jumped out of her seat, letting the man take it. "Thank you," he said to her, and turned to Stella.

"Young man! I *will* call the police!"

"Stella," the soldier said, sliding the envelope into his pocket and taking her hands in his. Frankie could only see her profile, but she wondered what Stella was thinking, looking at that poor handsome boy's messed-up face. "You're more beautiful than in your pictures, more beautiful than ever," he said to her, and he brought her hand up to his lips. Though he hardly had the room, though it seemed to pain him to do it, he got down on one knee. All the girls held their breath. Even me.

"Stella," he said. "I promised myself that if I made it home, that the first thing I would do was come and look for you. And here you are, so pretty. Just like I knew you would be. You are my angel."

Even Sister Cornelius seemed to realize that something big was going on and stopped yelling for a minute, listening along with the rest. They watched, fascinated, as he let go of Stella's hands and pulled something else out of his pocket, a box.

"It's not much, but after I get a job we'll get you something as beautiful as you." He opened the box, as if everyone didn't already know what was in it. They expected him to say something like, "Will you be my wife?" the way they always say it in movies, but all he said was, "Please."

The room was quiet as a church as they waited for Stella's answer. "Well," she said. "This is certainly a surprise. A lovely surprise, of course." She probably realized that she should be paying attention to the ring, and she reached out to touch it, but stopped, her hand hanging there in the air.

Something in his face fell, his smile drooping a little. "I'm sorry it's so small," he said. "I just got home and this was all I could find."

"Oh, no!" she said. "It's just beautiful. Really, it is."

"You kept me alive, Stella. You did."

"I didn't," she said.

"You kept me alive. I wouldn't be here if it wasn't for you. You got me through."

"Stop saying that," she said, her voice tightening as she finally figured out what she'd done. "It's just that it's such a big surprise. A shock, even. And so fast, I don't know what to say."

He grabbed her hand again. "Say that you'll marry me. We love each other, right? That's all there is to it. What else do we need?"

"Of course we care for one another, but—"

"What do you mean, *care* for one another?" His scar got redder, along with the rest of his face. "I love you and you love me, it's what you said."

"Well, I don't know *exactly* what I said . . . dear."

"What?" he said. "What?"

That was when Stella remembered that she had an audience, and looked around at the rest of the orphan girls. Her face was tight and pinched and scared, her eyes huge as Bambi's. She wanted them to help her, and maybe they even wanted to, at least at that very moment.

The soldier snapped the box shut. "Say my name."

Stella looked back at him. "Excuse me?"

"Say it, say my name."

"I don't . . . I don't know what you want me to—"

"My name!" the soldier shouted. "Say it!"

Sister Cornelius woke up from her trance. "Young man," she said, now gentle, so gentle. "I'm afraid that visiting Sunday is next weekend." She walked down the row where the soldier was still kneeling, grabbed him by the shoulders, and pulled him to his feet. "I'll show you where you can sign up, and you can come back."

The soldier blinked at her, staring at the wimple she wore, the big cross around her neck. He held out the box to her, like he would drop to his knees and propose to her too, if only he could remember how to get the box open again. "She doesn't know me," he said to Sister Cornelius. "She doesn't even know my name."

⚬⚬⚬

Names do have power. When Benno said my name, it sounded as if he had an actual pearl tucked beside his cheek, stowed beneath his tongue.

He rode his bicycle for miles across the city each day, delivering messages and packages. By the time he reached our door, his last stop, the hollow of his throat glistened, the white shirt nearly transparent across the small of his back. If no one but Cook was home, if there was no brother or mother or father there to judge, to spy, to cluck in horror and forbid, I brought him to the pump on the side of our house. I would pump the water myself and watch him splash his face, the water droplets jeweling his hair. Sometimes he sat and drank a glass of lemonade I'd fetched from the kitchen, and he would wince at the sweetness, though he would finish it all, down to the slurry of seeds at the bottom. Sometimes I brought him a slice of pie or some coffee cake. He did love the cake, the touch of salt and spice in a crumb so heavy that sometimes bits of it would pepper his lips. I had to sit on my hands so that I wouldn't reach for them.

I told him about my stuffy older brother, William, he of the thick glasses and the thicker head, and my younger brother, Frederick, of the quick smile and quicker fists. I read to him from my smuggled copies of *Detective Story*, acting out the most dramatic parts just to get him to smile. I told him about the woods where I could lose myself, and the lake where I could forget myself.

After he had been delivering messages for weeks and weeks, after I had given him many glasses of Cook's too-sweet lemonade, he came to the house with a cut across his forehead, a new bruise under one cheek. I asked him what happened, and he shook his head. Nothing that hadn't happened before, he said. Nothing new. But he let me sit him down on the stone bench in the yard, he let me dab the blood from his skin with the hem of my dress. At the sight of my knees and thighs, his eyes got wide and dark and deep. I dabbed longer than I had to.

The next time he came to deliver a message, while he was splashing at the pump, I ran straight for the woods, leaves churning up around my legs. He caught me by an old oak tree, the softest patch of the greenest moss underneath, a pillow for my head. Yes? he asked me. Yes, I said. Yes and yes and yes and yes. Hungry hands and mouths, a hunger like I'd never felt—pitiless, animal, claws and teeth. I was no lady, nothing more than a character in one of William's filthy postcards, but I couldn't bring myself to care. I couldn't make myself. Even when the fury of it had passed like a thunderstorm, and we lay panting in the pine needles, I didn't feel any shame, I wouldn't damn myself for it. Who wanted to be a girl in a box—a jewel, a stone? Who wouldn't want to feel that alive?

It didn't seem so much to ask. It didn't seem too much.

Mad Maureen said: It never does.

⸺∞⸺

Back in the cottage, in the dining room, the girls were supposed to be studying, but of course they were all whispering about Stella's marriage proposal. Stella herself sat alone at a table, sorting the letters from her soldiers. The radio played in the background.

"Do you think that all them other guys is going to come and propose to her?" Joanie McNally hissed.

"I hope they do," said Loretta. "Serves her right for lying to them all. How many boys does she write to, anyway? Fifty? A hundred? I can't even imagine what she's been telling them."

"I hope they don't come," Joanie said. "That was awful. Did you see his face? That scar and all?"

"He was in a war, chooch," Frankie said. "You think that nothing happens to people in a war?" She didn't want to be reminded about what happened to boys in the war.

"All right, all right. Keep your shirt on. I was just saying . . ."

"Yeah, well. Shut up," Frankie said.

"Richard!" Stella said, holding up a photograph of the wounded soldier, waving it like a flag. "It's Richard W.!"

Loretta's face was a mask of rage. She turned the page in her book so fast it ripped down the middle. "You're a little god-damned late."

BOMBARDMENT

LORETTA GOT A BEATING FOR swearing at Stella after Stella's marriage proposal, but she didn't regret it. Just like she hadn't regretted the beatings she got for asking why the orphanage didn't take in little black children. Or Mexican children. Or Jewish children—wasn't Christ a Jew? Anyway, Loretta did what she always did after a punishment: she simply read her books standing up, humming cheerfully as she did.

Stella, though . . . Stella had regrets. She regretted that Richard W. had been sent home so soon when his wounds weren't that bad, she regretted that she hadn't been prepared for his crazy proposal and his sad little ring, she regretted that everyone had witnessed it, she regretted that the nuns had taken away her cigar box full of names and photos and intercepted the new letters that came, she regretted that she was half starved and half loved when she was as radiant as any star, as worthy. Weren't all those letters proof?

What she most regretted, however, was the fact that she'd been caught, she'd been shamed for wickedness, when she was only *writing letters. She* was harmless. She regretted that she'd have to bear her shame alone.

So she did the only thing she could think of. She told Sister George that she could repent for her own sins, but she couldn't repent for the sins of others.

"What sins?" asked Sister George, just as Stella had known she would. "Which others?"

———— ✦ ————

Sister George found Frankie in class, conjugating German verbs. She hauled Frankie out by the hair, dragged her to her office, slammed the door behind them, the sound like a gunshot. She threw Frankie down across the desk. Though Frankie twisted and struggled, Sister yanked up Frankie's skirt. The strap whistled through the air, sang its own brutal song of cut and sting. Frankie steeled herself against the song, against the whip, telling herself that it would soon be over, telling herself that she could take the pain and the humiliation, that Sam—if this was about Sam—was worth any beating, and that what Sam was facing was so much worse. Again and again, Sister brought the strap down, ranting incomprehensibly the whole while, so hard and so much that Frankie's resolve collapsed and her prayers for this to be over turned to prayers for a shelling, because Sister was not going to stop until she'd torn Frankie to shreds and nothing short of a bomb would end it.

I jumped between them, threw myself over Frankie's body, but the strap whisked through me, singing all the way, no matter how loud I screamed for her to stop, just stop. STOP.

Frankie's screams went hoarse and raw, the blood trickled

down her legs, until she couldn't hear the strange and furious babbling of the nun over the thud of her own heart pounding in her ears, feel anything beyond the burning on her thighs, until the door burst open and Sister Bert flew in. She grabbed Sister George's arm, the strap held high.

"Nein, Georgina," Sister Bert said. "This isn't the way."

"Sie muss für ihre Sünden bestraft sein. Sie müssen alle bestraft sein."

"Can't you see she's bleeding? That's enough!"

"Sie muss lernen!"

"It's not her fault, Georgina," said Sister Bert.

"Sie lernen nie!" shrieked Sister George. "Warum lernen sie nie?"

"Blame Hitler!" said Sister Bert. "Blame the Nazis! Blame your brother for joining them!"

Storm eyed, habit askew, Sister George brought the strap down on Sister Bert instead. Frankie rolled off the desk to the floor. My vision went hazy and white. Wolf howled.

The glass in the window exploded as if a chair had been thrown through it.

I ran to the smashed window. On the cobbles below sprawled the girl with the broken face, blood snaking out from her hair. No, she said, through her ruined jaw. Please. Wait.

———— ∞ ————

Frankie woke up in the infirmary. She lay on her stomach, salved and bandaged by Nurse Frieda. Her aide, Beatriz, had left over-night, it seemed, some months before, Frankie didn't know why. Loretta did, but Loretta wouldn't tell, not yet. Loretta sat by Frankie's bed, held Frankie's hand, stroking the skin. She gave Frankie small sips of water and dried the tears that spilled over Frankie's cheeks.

Toni came too. She sat on the other side of the bed, not jiggling, not squirming, not teasing. She stared at the bandages, she stared at her own sister in wonder, in horror. Without saying a word, she left. She returned a half hour later, dragging Stella behind her like a reluctant puppy. She shoved Stella toward the bed.

"Toni, don't bother," said Loretta. "It's not worth it."

"Look!" said Toni, ignoring Loretta, pointing at the bandages that wrapped her sister's legs. "Look at what you did!"

"That wasn't me, that was Sister George," Stella said, trying to back away. "You can't blame me because Sister went crazy. It's not my fault."

Toni pulled her back, shoved her. "That was you! You caused this."

"She shouldn't have been messing with that boy!" said Stella.

"Look. At. Her."

"I was helping her. She can repent now."

"You did this. *You.*" Toni repeated the word you, you, you, you, you—an invocation, an incantation—until Stella cracked. And when Stella truly cried for the first time since her parents had died and left her a lovely, lonely orphan, there was no one to stroke her hand, no one to dry her tears.

⎯⎯∞∞∞⎯⎯

After Frankie's wounds had healed enough that she could rest on her side, Sister Bert came to visit, sitting stiffly in the chair that Loretta had vacated for her. "I'm so sorry, Francesca," she said, eyes roving over Frankie's drawn face. "This should never have happened."

Frankie thought that was too obvious a statement to comment on. She tried to turn away, but she was still too sore to move much.

"You wouldn't have known this, but Sister Georgina had an older brother. He lived in Berlin with her aunt and uncle. He was killed in action a few weeks ago. A bayonet. It's . . . a painful way to die."

Frankie pinned Sister with a hot glare, the hot glare that was becoming her signature. "I should feel sorry for him? I should feel sorry for *her*?" She'd meant for the words to cut, but her tone was dull as a butter knife.

"No," said Sister. "I don't expect any such thing. Not right now. Though you might be relieved to hear that she's been dismissed from her position and sent to live at a convent downstate."

"Nice job if you can get it," Frankie said.

Sister folded her hands on her lap. "I do hope you'll find it in your heart to forgive her one day. Not for her sake, but for yours."

That made no kind of sense to Frankie, so she didn't bother

245

responding to it. Instead, she said, "What made the window shatter like that?"

Sister said, "I'm not certain. Sister George must have hit the glass with the strap before I could stop her."

"I don't think so."

"What do you think happened?"

"I . . . I think someone heard me."

"*I* heard you, Frankie. God heard you."

Not God, Frankie thought. God was too busy sending quiet, gentle boys to fight in stupid wars. "An angel must have heard me."

"I suppose that could be true. The angels are all around us," said Sister.

Speaking of angels. "Where's Beatriz?" Frankie was sweaty and itchy inside her bandages.

"Beatriz took another position."

"You mean you sent her away too?" said Frankie.

As if this explained everything, Sister said, "She turned eighteen," and steepled her fingers under her chin. "She'll be doing very important work for the war effort."

"Oh. Where?"

"Overseas. Nurses are needed. She'll complete her nurse's training there."

"*Overseas?* Where overseas?"

"England," Sister said.

"England! But . . ." Frankie imagined Beatriz running through the streets of London as the Luftwaffe strafed the city, bombs everywhere. She pictured Beatriz ripping a gun from the belt of a felled soldier, taking aim at a passing plane, pulling the trigger till the bullets ran out. Then she imagined *herself* doing the same things—running, aiming, shooting. *Why not a woman?* she thought. *Why not?*

"Frankie? There's something else we need to talk about."

Frankie shook her visions away. "What?"

"Your friend."

"Which friend?"

"The young man. Samuel. Sam."

Frankie didn't want to talk to Sister about Sam. Sam was hers, not Sister's. "When can I go back to my cottage?"

Sister Bert tapped her lips with her steepled hands. "That's what I came to discuss with you, Frankie. Even though your punishment was severe, far too severe—"

"You mean wrong?"

"Severe. And even though Sister George won't be coming back, it's been decided—"

"It's been decided by who?"

"—that under the circumstances . . ."

Circumstances. Frankie waved a hand. Sister didn't want to talk about Sam, she wanted to talk about *sin*. A sin of the flesh.

"We were saying goodbye," Frankie said, too tired and sore to ask how Sister had found out, too tired and too sore and too sad to be embarrassed about it. Frankie had nothing she wanted to confess. Not to Father Paul, who she was sure had never said goodbye to anyone. Neither had Sister Bert, not outside of a book. If she had, she would understand.

Sister Bert leaned forward and took Frankie's hand the way Loretta had. "I'm glad you had the chance to say goodbye."

Frankie's hand was limp in Sister Bert's. Sister had never touched her like this before. "Don't you mean I'm going to hell?"

"Frankie," Sister Bert said. She cleared her throat. "Francesca."

The sound of her full name sent a dart of fear through Frankie's stomach. "What?"

"We got a telegram."

Frankie's thoughts skittered, darted into the darkest holes in her mind. *Oh no not Vito please don't say Vito don't say it.*

"Sam's plane was shot down over France."

"What?" said Frankie, almost laughing with the impossibility of it. "No. He just left. That can't be."

"He didn't make it."

"No."

"I'm sorry."

"You're wrong!"

"I wish I was. At least it was quick. You can be comforted by—"

Comforted? *Comforted?* "No!"

"Frankie," Sister began, but Frankie pulled her hand away and covered her ears.

"Stop talking!"

"I am so sorry," Sister said. "You don't know how sorry I am."

Frankie squeezed her eyes shut, trying to wall out the world again, but the world could not be denied. She felt Sam's hands on her skin, could summon his woodsy-earthy smell as if he were the one sitting by her bed, telling her he was sorry. Her body heaved, her stomach lurched, and she threw up all the water she'd managed to take in. Watching her struggle to catch her breath stole all of mine; though I didn't need to breathe, I clutched at my chest. Wolf whined and pawed at the floor.

All she'd asked for was a little bit of time. Not too much to ask, and far too much, as I could have told her, if only she could hear me.

<hr>

In her shock, she only lost more time. We both did, I think. I woke up on the floor of the infirmary. In Sister Bert's place, Toni sat, gnawing at a fingernail. In a chair on the other side of the bed, Loretta slumped with a book on her lap. The girl with the bloody hair and gaping mouth hovered by the window, but nobody saw her but Wolf and me.

"Frankie!" Toni said when Frankie's eyes fluttered open. "We thought you'd never wake up!"

Frankie's voice sounded like mine when she croaked, "I didn't want to."

Toni took one of Frankie's hands and Loretta took the other. Unlike with Sister Bert, this didn't feel strange to her.

"I wish I'd talked to your fella," Toni said. "I wish I'd known him."

"Yeah," Frankie said. "Me too."

Loretta said, "You only had to look at him to see how much he loved you."

Love, Sam, Love, Sam, Love, Sam.

"We were going to have a house and a garden," Frankie told them. "We were going to have flowers. We were going to grow our own vegetables. We were going to be happy."

"Of course you were," Loretta said. "Of course."

———∞———

After the nuns shooed Loretta and Toni away, Frankie took out a letter she had never finished, one she had started right after the service for the orphanage boys but couldn't get right. She took her black pastel to the pages.

~~Dear~~ *Sam:*

~~Today is a sad day because we had to go to a service for some orphanage boys. I'm not sure if you knew them. One of them named Clay. Stella had been writing to him for a while. She might a worn at the service, but when we asked her about Clay later, she looked at us through his letters ~~ *there is joy in everything, even* in sadness, ~~like Sister Bert always say. Remember Sister? She looked like a beautiful boy. Have you seen any nuns over there? I bet you don't miss them, even the ones who look like beautiful boys.~~

~~Do you miss me?~~ I miss you. I dream about the greenhouse. I dream about our garden, ~~the one we'll have together. We'll plant those tulips that you said were worth more than gold. The bees will visit us, or maybe we'll have a hive.~~ The bees ~~will never sting, and if they do it will feel more like a kiss. I'll make you any kind of cake you want with the~~ honey. ~~Or with eggs, we can get in. Or that dish your mother made, the frangy, no with the~~ apples ~~and the cabbage. Gumbo? Gumbo! Ham and collards so green they'll make your eyes hurt. Fluffy mashed potatoes. Real butter on everything. You can~~ play for me ~~while I cook, you can play for me always. As long as happy as we are, as we will be.~~

Till I see you again,

~~Your girl, Frankie~~

<hr>

The next morning, Sister Bert found Frankie asleep, fingers stained black.

<hr>

They let Frankie heal as best she could for a week. Then Toni and Loretta came to visit. "Are you feeling well enough to get out of bed?" Toni asked.

"Why? Do they need me in the kitchens?" Frankie said.

"Do I have to scrub floors or toilets for penance? Do they want to cut off my hair?"

Toni bit her lip and looked at Loretta. Loretta sighed and said, "They decided that it's disruptive to the other girls to let you and Toni stay."

Disruptive. "What does that mean?"

"You and Toni are leaving."

At this, Frankie laughed. You had to find reasons to laugh, she thought, especially when nothing was funny. "Are we being sent to a convent in the country?"

"No," Loretta said. "You're going back to your family."

"Family? What family?"

Toni said, "Daddy. We're being sent back to Daddy."

FOR I HAVE SINNED

FRANKIE'S FATHER, GASPARE MAZZA, sailed to America from Sicily in 1918, when he was twenty years old. After weeks spent crammed belowdecks with hundreds of stinking men, he'd emerged from the bowels of the boat like a moth from a cocoon, warming himself in the sun. From Ellis Island, he took a train to Chicago. He'd apprenticed with a shoemaker in the old country, and he did the same in his new one. In a rundown neighborhood on the South Side, Gaspare pieced leather in the dank basement of a shop owned by an old man from Napoli named Sesto.

Old men from Napoli were notoriously cranky, and Sesto was crankier than most. When he deemed Gaspare's work less than perfect, Sesto would deliver a sharp slap to the back of Gaspare's head. More than once, he kicked his apprentice down the stone stairs. When he decided that one of his female customers seemed more interested in the dark and handsome young man bringing the new shoes up from the basement than in the shoes themselves, Sesto waited until the woman left and then punched the boy in the stomach. Foul as he was, however, Sesto wasn't stupid. During the busy hours of the day, he began having Gaspare come up from the basement and put him to work behind the counter, where Gaspare could smile at the women who brought their shoes in for repair or ordered new ones. And, eventually, to help them try on the shoes.

Gaspare would sit a woman down on the small chair in the corner of the dark shop and kneel before her. He would gently, scandalously, tug the shoe from her foot, and then rest that foot on his own thigh, one hand on her calf as he fished for the new shoe. He would slip those new shoes onto the woman, and watch her shapely calves tense and her hips twitch as she paraded across the floor of the small shop to test his handiwork. He loved every woman who came into the shop—old or young, tall or short, fat or thin, brown or white, sweet or spiky, Italian or not. There was so much beauty in this world, so much beauty in these women, all of them so vulnerable in their stockinged feet.

One day a beautiful girl named Caterina brought in her shoes to be repaired. Gaspare liked the tone of her skin and her long curling hair, the cut of her nose and jawline, and could tell by her accent that she was Sicilian too. The skin of her calf was soft and pliant; she shuddered so prettily at his touch. Gaspare fell in love with her the way he fell in love with every woman: hard, and completely. With Caterina, however, he managed to *stay* in love, at least for a time. That was his problem, you see, staying in love. When you fall in love as quickly as Gaspare did, when you can be swayed by the merest hint of feeling, the merest hitch in the blood, you can fall *out* of love just as fast—with places, with jobs, with women. You might even trade in your own children, convinced you can start over, like exchanging a worn pair of shoes for new ones.

Frankie's father picked her and Toni up on a gray summer day, the air so swollen with rain that just breathing wore out their insides. Frankie waited for him to yell, to drench them in a flood of angry Italian, maybe even give them a smack or two, but it seemed he'd already yelled himself out that first visiting day after the letter from Sister Bert, and he wasn't going to yell anymore. He hugged them both as usual, and even carried their suitcases onto the streetcar. As they rode away from the orphanage in Rogers Park and toward their new life in West Town, Frankie tried to be hopeful. She closed her eyes and told herself that she was getting the thing that orphans wanted most in the world: a family. But it didn't feel that way. Vito was somewhere in North Africa. Sam, beautiful Sam, was gone. Toni curled herself into a ball on the seat next to her, and their father sat across the aisle, whistling a tune Frankie couldn't recognize.

Ada wasn't lying when she wrote and said that the apartment was small. Her lips were drawn up tight as a buttonhole as she led them from tiny room to tiny room, through one narrow doorway after another, to where they would be sleeping. "You'll have to share this room with Bernice and Cora. We only had room for one more bed, so you'll have to share that, too, if you can fit. If not, one of you can sleep on the couch in the living room. You can put your things in the two bottom drawers." She gave them one long look, like a woman eyeing the rabbits that ate up the carrots in her garden, before she shut the door. Frankie gingerly sat on the bed, her wounds still sore, as Toni unzipped her suitcase and began filling up one of those two drawers.

In her own suitcase, Frankie had the few items of clothing she owned, Sam's trumpet, her sketchbook and pastels, and her high school diploma. They had given her the diploma a whole year early because she had enough credits, but she wouldn't be allowed to march in the graduation ceremony later this month. She was the first girl in her family to ever finish high school, the first *person*, as much good as it did her. Loretta had bought her a nice frame to put the diploma in, which she gave to Frankie the night before they left. Though Frankie couldn't imagine that her new sisters would let her hang it here.

Frankie felt like someone had unzipped her skin and dumped her out of it, left her more naked than naked. One minute they were at the orphanage wishing someone would come take them away, and then they were here, wishing they could get back in. Their father was a stranger, and Ada . . . who knew what Ada was?

"Don't you want to unpack?" Toni asked. Frankie just shook her head and watched as Toni dragged her suitcase over and started unpacking for her, putting her clothes in the other drawer, placing her diploma in its frame and leaning it against the wall above the dresser. She took out Sam's trumpet and stood it next to the diploma. She tucked Frankie's sketchbook and pastels in the drawer and covered them up with a sweater.

Toni did things like that now, little things, kind things, to try to make up for the fact that Frankie had been beaten, that they were here, that Sam was gone. Frankie had gotten one letter after she learned he was dead, like a note from a ghost. It was V-mail, the print shrunk down so tiny it was difficult to read. It was full of blackouts.

I'm writing you from ▮▮▮▮▮▮▮▮▮▮▮ . *Yesterday, we went to* ▮▮▮▮▮▮▮ . *I miss your pretty cat eyes.*

She'd read it over and over until the paper felt as soft as tissue.

Toni finished unpacking and sat down on the bed they were supposed to share. "What do we do now?"

Frankie shrugged. "I don't know."

With her chin, Toni pointed at the door. "She hates us."

"You're right."

The door swung open, and Bernice walked in. She was tall but mousy looking, broad in the cheeks and in the hips. Her brown eyes were as flinty as Ada's.

"I was wondering when you two would show up," she said.

Frankie and Toni had never said more than three words to her before in their whole lives, so they didn't say anything as she pulled off her gloves one finger at a time and threw them on top of the dresser. "At least you managed to get your diploma," she said, nodding at Frankie. "You'll be able to earn your keep."

"Earn my keep?" Frankie said.

"Money don't grow on trees," said Bernice. "*Doesn't* grow on trees. We already got a lot of mouths to feed."

Frankie wondered what in the heck she was talking about, considering that all of them were living with *her* father right behind *her* father's shoe shop. She was about to say something else when Cora sauntered into the room like a saloon girl in a Western picture, loose-jointed and slippery.

"Well, look what the cat dragged in," she drawled. She was a lot prettier than Bernice, with perfect lips painted apple red, the same color as the dress she wore.

Toni didn't like the way they looked at Frankie, the way they were acting like they owned the place, because she said, "What are you talking about, *cats*? There ain't no cats here. Except maybe you two."

"Shut up, little girl," Cora snapped. "Or I'll shut your mouth for you."

Toni stood up, but Frankie grabbed her arm. They were in enough trouble without asking for more. If Ada threw them out, then they'd have nowhere to go.

Cora smiled in that way people do when they'd rather kick you but aren't sure that they can get away with it. "I hear you got an interview on Thursday."

"What? Where?" Frankie said.

"At Berman's. Our cousin works there, in the factory. But they need a girl for the typing pool, so Mother arranged it. You *can* type, can't you?"

Through clenched teeth Frankie said, "Yes."

"'That's good." Her eyes slid down Frankie's body. "I hope you have some decent dresses with you. That thing looks like it's been through a war."

Automatically, Frankie clutched the collar of her dress before she realized that that was what Cora had wanted her to do. To feel ashamed.

Frankie was done with shame. She let go of her collar and snatched up her diploma, rubbed her thumb over a nearly invisible nick in the frame. "I'm just going to hang this over the dresser." She didn't wait for permission.

<hr/>

Though I stayed with Frankie and Toni for a time in that cramped apartment, eventually I missed the orphanage too. In the middle of the night, I visited the babies in the baby house and the girls in the cottages. I talked to this girl and to that one, whispering feverishly in their ears while Wolf licked their feet. I stroked their hair and flicked their studded curlers, told them one day someone would run their fingers through that hair and they would wish that it would never stop, never stop, don't stop. I called for the ghost with the broken face, but she wasn't taking requests.

Then I sat at the foot of the angel, Wolf in my arms, and said that if I couldn't become an angel to leave this world, shouldn't I be able to have an effect on it? Did I burst the light bulbs in the library? Did I knock the photos from the table in the blue house? Could I do it again? Could I help Frankie? Could I help *anyone*? What use is a ghost who knows she's a ghost?

Why am I here?

Instead of answering my questions, the angel told me of the world. About the Fosse Ardeatine massacre in Rome that killed hundreds of Italians, including Jews and members of the Italian Resistance. The Slapton Sands tragedy: American soldiers killed in a training exercise in preparation for D-Day. D-Day itself, when thousands of troops landed at Normandy in France, and thousands were massacred so that the Allies could take the beach.

They too asked why, the angel said. But who can comprehend the will of God?

I resolved never to visit the angel again and went instead to my stretch of sand at Lake Michigan, to the library, and to the bar, where Mad Maureen plied me and Wolf with bourbon and her tattooed fish blew us kisses. Not-drunk on the not-bourbon, we sat in the atrium of the Rookery, blearily watching the shadows creep. Wolf pounced on the shadows as if they were burrowing chipmunks and the marble floor was snow.

I'd given up on searching for Marguerite, but I got so mad at the man who had taken her from me, the man who had rooked her, that I went to find him at his antiques shop. Where I should have looked in the first place. Where I should have been looking all along.

Marguerite was sitting at the big wooden desk, nose to nose with the man's little black cat. The man himself was nowhere to be found, though the photographs on his desk were jumbled, and one was on the floor. The one with the wide-eyed redhead, unassuming as milk.

How long have you been here? I asked her.

Weeks. Months. I don't know. I followed you that first time. I stayed and read. She waved a hand around. He has an edition by Frances Ellen Watkins Harper. *Iola Leroy, or Shadows Uplifted.*

Are you uplifted?

You're not as funny as you imagine, she said.

You didn't know he had this place? How could you not know?

I never looked for him, she said.

You never looked?

It's not what you think, Marguerite said. He didn't kill me.

Do you know who did?

He didn't. He . . . loved me.

Now who's lying to herself? I said.

What do you know about it? she said, suddenly furious. Those stories I told you? The stories my mother told me, and her mother before her? I wrote them down, I made them my own. He encouraged me to do that. I was going to be a writer, like Frances Harper. You don't know what that means, what that . . . meant to me.

Once there was a boy, I said.

A *boy*, she spat.

Listen: once there was a boy. There's no other word for him, because he wasn't a man yet. My family didn't approve. And I—

Did you love him?

I hesitated before answering. He consumed me, I said.

Did he love you?

I thought about the way he said my name, as if he had a pearl tucked under his tongue. I thought about the woods and the lake, his hands and the need in them. Was need love? Was hunger?

I said, I don't know.

Then it's not the same! she shouted.

Let me take you somewhere, let me show you something. I tried to take her hand, but of course I couldn't. Please, I said.

Reluctantly she got up from the desk. We left the bookshop and the fearless little cat behind, and we walked we ran we flew to the blue house in the sea of brick. Wolf beat us there, was already peering inside the back window.

What is this place? Marguerite asked.

I led her to the window where Wolf was propped up on his front paws. Inside, the man with the boxer's build was sitting on the edge of the bed, putting on his shoes. He wore a pair of trousers with suspenders, a sleeveless white undershirt.

Is that him? Marguerite said. Her eyes scoured his muscled shoulders, his smooth skin. It can't be, she said. He's much too young.

I put my not-hand on the glass when the glossy-haired, berry-lipped girl walked into the bedroom. We're not here for him, I said. We're here for her.

Why?

Just look.

Marguerite looked. Well, she's a pretty little thing, like you. Then Marguerite closed her eyes. A little thing *like you.*

She is, I said. Look again.

Marguerite pressed her face close to the glass, *through* the glass, dipping into as if it were water. She stepped back from the window, back from me and Wolf. Said, She looks white but . . .

That's why he wouldn't tell me his name, his real name, I said. He told me I'd ruin it even if I didn't want to. He said it would sound ugly coming from me and he didn't want his name to sound ugly. He didn't want *me* to sound ugly.

What are you saying?

He was Chinese. He delivered messages on his bicycle all around the city. I think his parents had a business somewhere in the city. A laundry or a grocery.

You . . . you . . . and this boy? She reached out, tried to take my arm, gripped nothing but air. Her not-hands knotted, worked.

Don't, I said.

A Chinese boy. A *white* girl. In 1918? You could have gotten him killed. Oh my lord. Did you? Did you get him killed?

No, he got . . . hurt, I said, remembering Frederick, remembering William. I died instead. I had her and I gave her up and then I got the flu and died instead.

Marguerite put her hand to her forehead, paced the tiny yard, Wolf at her heels.

I said, I think this is why I'm still here. I'm paying for what

I did. Or because I can't let go. Or something like that. But . . .

She came to a dead stop in front of me, her chest heaving as if she were trying to catch her breath. But?

But even with all of that. Even with—

What?

If I had the chance, I would do it all again.

Her not-hand lashed out to slap me but flew right through me like a wisp of smoke cut by a breeze, the way it did with the newspaper the very first time I'd seen her. She kept at it, slapping with her left hand and her right, as if she truly believed she could touch me. And after a while, I leaned into it, as if I truly believed I could feel her.

Later, we lay in the grass of the grubby yard, watching the clouds take shape overhead—a hawk, a fox, a bear, a wolf.

Marguerite said, My family loved me so much. And I loved them. But I destroyed them anyway, because I loved him too.

How do you know that?

I just know. I could bear my mother's anger, but I could never—can't—bear her disappointment. I can't bear her heartbreak.

But maybe she's not disappointed in you.

Of course she is! I destroyed myself! I destroyed everything! I never even showed her my stories. Her stories. I should have shown her. Why didn't I show her? Marguerite wiped not-tears from her not-eyes. I've asked for forgiveness so many times. I've prayed. But I don't think God hears the prayers of the dead. And I don't think he forgives me.

I could have talked about the angel, about the churning furnace of this world. I could have talked about the will of God and all His mystery. I could have said that there was no use in getting angry.

Instead I said, Tell me another story.

What kind of story?

About the redhead in his photograph. The one who looks as harmless as milk.

THE JEZEBEL

ONCE THERE WAS A BEAUTIFUL girl, the youngest daughter of a preacher man. Her eyes were like cornflowers, her hair was like fire, her skin—

Like cream? I asked.

Peaches and cream, said Marguerite. And she was desperately in love with the son of a scholar, a fine young man, tall and fair as a god in a painting. It seemed as if the match was made in heaven.

But then she came along.

She? I asked.

A temptress, dark and alluring. The scholar's son was smitten. Ensorceled. He told the preacher's daughter that he could not marry her, for he was in love with someone else. He said that the preacher's daughter deserved better than a man with designs on another.

The preacher's daughter could not believe the scholar's son could have been distracted so easily, could defy the wishes of his parents, of his *people*. She feared for his soul, feared that a devil had taken it. A filthy Jezebel. She was determined to save him. She enlisted her father, the preacher. They implored him to think of his family, to think of his community. Equality for all was a lofty goal, but this was too much to ask. This would tear the town apart. He had to leave the Jezebel. He had to. And finally, worn down by the entreaties of the preacher, he did.

But when he left the temptress, he also left his heart with her. And no matter how much the preacher's daughter tried, she couldn't make him love her instead. So she asked that the temptress come to their church after Sunday service. Just to talk, just to understand. Woman to woman.

The Jezebel dared to come, and the preacher's daughter was not afraid. She invited the woman into the meeting room for tea. It was a special sort of tea. The kind that made a person sleepy if you drank enough.

The women talked. The preacher's daughter begged the temptress to leave the scholar's son alone. You will ruin him, she said. It's an abomination, you're a churchgoing woman, surely you've read scripture. But the Jezebel claimed that the scholar's son was in love with her and she with him, that she never meant to hurt anyone. Here was the truth of it, the Jezebel said: they would be married one day, she was sure of it. Love was God's own creation. And so was she.

The preacher's daughter flew into a rage at such blasphemy, but she didn't show it. She waited until the Jezebel had finished her tea, waited until the cup slipped from her hand and smashed to the floor, waited until she was slumped in her chair. Then she took a pillow from the settee, placed it over the Jezebel's face, and held it. She was surprised at how easy it was to vanquish evil.

The preacher found her there, standing over the Jezebel. Together, they put the pillow into the hearth, where it burned, but they left the smashed teacup on the floor. They called for help. They claimed the Jezebel had collapsed, they didn't know why. One of God's mysteries. They would pray for her and her family.

The scholar's son was devastated, but the preacher's daughter comforted him. And even if the scholar's son wondered how the temptress had come to be in the church that Sunday, how a healthy young woman collapsed while drinking tea—even if he had poked at the remnants of a pillow burned in the hearth, even if he stayed up at night, not sleeping, looking down at the peaceful peaches-and-cream face of his lovely new wife, wondering who he had married—he said nothing.

He said nothing.

He said nothing.

⸎

Why does the world demand girls be beautiful, but when they are, punish them for it? Why does it punish girls either way? Why does the world want girls to be sorry, some even more than others? Sorry, sorrier, sorriest.

On the day of her job interview, Frankie woke up and brushed her hair in the mirror. It was long now, longer than it had been before Sister George had sheared it, longer even than she would have been allowed to keep it if she'd still been in the orphanage.

Pretty hair. Jezebel's hair. She wished that Sam were there to comb his hands through it and never stop.

She dressed in her best dress and gloves. Toni helped her draw a line up the back of her legs with a pen so that it looked as if she were wearing stockings. And then Toni perched the hat that Aunt Marion had given her so long ago on Frankie's freshly rolled curls.

"There," said Toni. "It's like you're a lady or something."

"Or something," said Dewey, Ada's youngest son, still a year from his enlistment date. He had eyes like sandpaper and stiff, white-blond hair that sprouted doll-like from his head. Dewey scoured Frankie and Toni both raw with his mustardy-brown eyes, his lopsided smirk, the way he had of eating with his mouth open, of spraying food half chewed. They stayed as far away from him as they could. Which wasn't far enough.

When Frankie went into the kitchen, only Ada and her father were there, looking like they'd been fighting and she'd just walked right into the middle of it. Her father told her that he'd be taking Frankie to catch the streetcar and got up to get his coat. Ada didn't offer any breakfast, which was just as well; Frankie was too nervous to eat. Ada stared at the hat on Frankie's head, frowning.

"Things will be okay, yes?" said Frankie's father. "You will be fine." Her father pulled some change from his pocket and counted out the fare. "You give this to driver and tell him

Berman's. Lots of girls work there, so they always stop."

"They always stop," Frankie said. "Sure."

She'd chased down streetcars before, of course, but this was different. If she got the job, she'd have to catch the streetcar every day and go to work, all by herself. With all those chores she'd had to do at the orphanage, she'd never had to do any of them all on her own, except as a punishment. What if she got lost? What if she couldn't figure out what she was supposed to do? What if the other typists hated her? The streets never looked so wide, and the streetcar never looked as big as when it pulled up in front of her.

"Dad?"

"Yes?"

"What if I don't get the job?"

He looked her up and down, nodded in approval. "I made you nice shoes. You will get the job," he said.

She felt as if she would be sick all over her tidy outfit. "But what if I don't get it? I mean, there'll be other jobs, right?"

"Your mother make this happen," her father said, frowning. "You have to get the job, yes?"

Frankie couldn't understand what he was talking about until she realized he meant Ada. He was saying that Ada was her mother.

Ada was not her mother. Ada would never be. And what kind of man was her father that he would say such a thing?

Her rage burned out quickly. Her bones felt like pudding as she said goodbye to her father and staggered up the stairs to the driver. She put the change in his palm and said, "Berman's."

"What?" he said. "Speak up, girlie!"

"Berman's," she said, a little louder.

"I can't hear you," he said, leaning his face in.

"Berman's!" she shouted.

He scowled. "Well, Berman's. You didn't have to shout."

She found a seat right up front and watched out the window. Her stomach was now hard as a cinder block. If Superman punched her there, she thought, he would break his hand.

The ride was only twenty-five minutes, but it felt like hours. Her eyes were hot and dry as she stepped off the streetcar and walked the one block to Berman's. At the front desk, a woman sat filing her long red nails. Frankie cleared her throat, hoping that she would notice Frankie standing there, but she didn't. She cleared it again, and still she didn't look up.

"Excuse me," Frankie said.

"Yeah?" she said, still filing.

"I have an appointment to see Mr. Gilhooly."

She put the file down. "You that new girl?"

"What?"

"You that new girl for the typing pool?"

"Yeah. I mean *yes*, I guess I am. I'm Frankie. Francesca. Mazza."

She scooped up a phone and called someone. "Yeah, it's me," she said. "New girl's here. Yeah. Yeah. Yeah." She put the phone down. "Wanda will be right out. She runs the typing pool."

"Okay," Frankie said. "Thank you." She sat in one of the chairs. She realized she was sitting with her legs far apart, so she crossed them like a lady. Then she crossed them the other way. She worried that crossing her legs would smear the lines Toni had drawn for her and uncrossed them again. She put her purse down in the seat next to her and then put it on her lap. She fixed her borrowed hat, pulling on the felt.

"You all right?" said the receptionist.

"Oh, yes. Fine."

"That's a swell dress."

Frankie clutched at her collar and glared but saw that the woman was smiling in a nice way. Maybe she really liked the dress. "Thank you," Frankie said.

"You don't talk much, do you?"

Frankie didn't know what to say to that, so she didn't say anything. She'd talked plenty in the orphanage. She didn't know how to talk out here in the world.

A door behind the big reception desk opened, and another woman stood there. "Francesca Mazza?"

"Yes."

"Follow me."

Frankie followed her into the back offices. The smell of smoke wafted in the air as the men inside the offices chomped on cigars and cigarettes while they yelled at people on the phone. "Salesmen," Wanda said, and twirled a finger around her ear. One of her eyes had a freckle right in her iris. Frankie wasn't sure where to look. It was as if she had a hole in her eye that Frankie could fall into and disappear.

She led Frankie to a typewriter and told her to roll up a piece of paper. Frankie started to take off her gloves, but Wanda stopped her. "Keep 'em on," she said. "I'm not hiring you until I know you can type. Last girl said she could type and her forms came back like a cat had jumped across the keys. Just type what I say. Ready? Dear Mr. Gilhooly, G-I-L-H-O-O-L-Y, I would like to order a set of screwdrivers and a set of nuts and some bolts. Please send me these items as soon as you can. . . ."

Wanda talked very fast, and Frankie had to concentrate to make sure her gloved fingers didn't slip off the keys. After a minute or two, Wanda stopped talking and whipped the page out of the typewriter to look at it. Frankie crossed her fingers under the desk.

"Hmmm . . . ," Wanda said, flipping the paper over. "All right. Gimme some shorthand. 'The rain in Spain falls slowly on the plain.' Wait, don't write that part. Write, 'The applicant was a good typist, but we don't know about her shorthand. If we hire her, we're going to need another typewriter, a desk, a chair, and more pens and pencils. Also, six reams of paper.'"

Frankie picked up the paper and showed her the shorthand. Wanda smiled at her and winked her freckled eye. "All righty. I think you've got yourself a job. Pays seventy-five cents an hour, not including lunch. Come back at nine a.m. sharp tomorrow."

Frankie walked out of the building in a daze. She got the job, which meant she would be making more than twenty-five dollars a week. What could she do with all that money? How many dresses could she buy? How many sacks of flour or pounds of rice? How many sketchbooks? Paints? For one bliss-ful moment, she forgot all her misery and confusion. She almost did a dance in the street.

A woman passing by smiled at her. "You look happy!"

Almost immediately, Frankie's blissful feelings faded. How dare she be happy when her brother was fighting a war? How dare she be happy when Sam was gone? Her eyes welled with tears.

The woman touched her arm. "You're allowed to be glad for a moment."

"You don't understand," Frankie began.

"I don't need to," the woman said. "We only get scraps in this lousy life. Take what you can get, do you hear me?"

"But—"

The woman drew Frankie into a brief but ferocious hug. "Take what you can get."

<hr />

When I visited the blue house in the sea of red brick, Marguerite came too. We watched the berry-lipped girl and her boxer man, though we chose what to witness. I liked having Marguerite with me, liked having Wolf at our feet. We were like some strange little family. If you didn't think about it too long. If you forgot that we were dead.

Afterward, we would stretch out on a roof downtown, on the deck of a boat in the middle of Lake Michigan, counting the stars, little doorways.

Marguerite said, You never told me her name. The baby's.

She's called something else now, I said. But when she was born, I called her Mercy.

THE CHURNING FURNACE

THE WAR IN EUROPE RAGED on, but Frankie's war had just begun.

Ada's eyes followed her everywhere. Every step she took, every bite of food she ate, every sip of water. The nicer Frankie tried to be, the smaller the portions of spaghetti and meatballs, the drier the toast, the more Ada watched. And the more Ada watched, the more Ada got from Frankie's father. Frankie's first payday, she handed the money over to her father, only to see him turn around and hand the crumpled bills to Ada. "For room and board, for you and your sister," she had said.

"Ada hates us," Frankie told Loretta the first visiting Sunday she could get away. "And so do Bernice and Cora."

"I could have told you that," Loretta said, pulling a wrapped meatball sandwich and a jar of leftover spaghetti from the bag Frankie had brought. Loretta unwrapped the sandwich, took a bite, chewed thoughtfully. "I remember Ada coming here to visit all those kids of hers, staring down her nose. She looked like a crow. No, that's not fair to crows. She looked like a vulture."

"Not fair to vultures," said Frankie. "At least I got my job, so I'm gone all day. You should see how they treat Toni, like some kind of Cinderella. She might as well be in here with you."

Loretta chewed, looking up out of the corners of her eyes the way she did when she was thinking. "How's your job?"

"Fine, I guess," Frankie said. The truth was that the job was so boring that it made her bones ache, and she got a terrible pain in her wrists, and the other girls scared her sometimes, made her feel tongue-tied and alien, but she felt spoiled rotten for even thinking that, with Loretta still scrubbing down floors. So Frankie said, "It's sort of dull to type all these forms all day, but it's better than washing dishes, so I shouldn't complain."

"No," Loretta said. "You shouldn't. How much do they pay you over there?"

"Seventy-five cents an hour."

"Seventy-five cents an hour!" Loretta said. "You *really* shouldn't complain! You're rich!"

"Yeah, well. I have to give it all to my father. To pay for me and Toni." She reached down and fixed the laces on her shoes so that Loretta couldn't see the resentment on her face. "They don't have much, and every penny counts. He gives me some for the streetcar."

"Well," she said. "It's good that you got the job, then."

"Yeah."

"And maybe when the war is over, your dad's business will pick up and you can keep a little more of that money. For this." She pulled a small piece of paper out of her pocket and handed it to Frankie. It was an ad. "I found it in a magazine that Sister Bert gave me."

CHICAGO PAINTING ACADEMY

Practical training in decorating, paperhanging, graining, marbling, sign and pictorial painting.

"What is this?"

"Art school, silly!" Loretta always got excited when she was talking about school. She was so strange, that she thought that everyone would want to go to school for as many years as possible.

Frankie studied the ad. "Painting I get. But what's graining? And marbling?"

"I have no idea, but they'd teach you. Isn't that a thrill?"

"I guess," Frankie said.

"Come on, Frankie. It would be fun! More fun than typing, don't you think? Somebody has to draw all those signs and billboards and stuff. Why couldn't it be you?"

The truth was, Frankie had asked her father about art school, not long after he'd brought them home. She'd said, "Maybe after I've worked for a while, I can go." He just laughed and laughed.

Frankie folded the ad into a tiny square. It felt as if she were folding herself up.

"I always loved your drawings," Loretta was saying. "I think you could make a lot of money. Or some money. Or at least you'd be happy." Loretta finished the meatball sandwich and licked her fingers. "Have you drawn anything lately?"

"No," Frankie said. "I have to work all the time. And I have chores when I get home, so . . ." She rubbed the grain of the wooden table. "Not much different than living here, I guess. It's just a lot harder to talk to people."

"Why? What do you mean?"

Loretta's question battered Frankie, made her burst like a dam. "They weren't raised in the orphanage. They don't know what it's like. And I don't know what anything else is like. I get confused when I'm sent to the grocer to buy something. All these red stamps and blue stamps, sugar stamps and shoe stamps. I'm not used to the cigarette lines, meat lines, and soap-flake lines. I can't talk about . . ." She swallowed. "Sam. I can't go to dances. Every time someone shuts a door, or opens one, I jump, because I keep thinking about Sister George, getting trapped somewhere with someone who wants to beat me for no reason, and it doesn't matter that I know they won't. I can't even keep the lines on my legs straight. I don't know how the other girls do all these things. I don't know how the other girls are girls. I don't know who I am anymore."

Loretta leaned back as if Frankie's torrent had washed her downstream. "Oh," she said. "Well."

Frankie flushed, embarrassed that she had said so much. "What about you?"

"What about me?"

"How are you? How is it here?"

"How do you think? Lots of scrubbing. And it's hot."

"You wouldn't be so hot if you took off that sweater."

"I can't," she said. She rolled up a sleeve, wincing as she did it. The inside of her forearm was red and blistered.

"Loretta! That's horrible! Did you get that in the laundry? Did you go to the infirmary?"

Loretta rolled down the sleeve. For her, there was no one to go to the infirmary *for*. "I'll be fine. It probably won't even scar much. And anyway, who cares?"

"I care!" Frankie said. "I'll bring you some cream next visiting Sunday."

"That's two weeks from now. It will already be healed."

She was right, of course. Frankie sighed, and tugged at the waves that were almost down to her shoulders. Sister Cornelius nodded at her from her desk at the front of the room. "It's strange to be here."

"You look like a different person," Loretta said. "Your hair is getting long."

"Finally."

"It's beautiful."

"That's what Dewey said."

"Who's Dewey?"

"Ada's younger son. He has a year before he goes into the service."

Loretta's eyes searched Frankie's face. "Ada's son said your hair was beautiful?"

"Yes."

Loretta frowned. "He's practically your brother."

"No, he isn't."

279

"Is he kind of creepy or something?"

"You could say that."

"I think maybe you should stay away from him."

"I think so too. I just don't know how I'm going to do it. The apartment is small, we're practically eating and sleeping and living on top of one another, no windows and too many open doorways and—"

Loretta picked up the fork Frankie'd brought for her and pressed it into her palm. "You might want to keep this handy."

Dear Frankie,

I can't believe it! I don't hear from you in weeks and weeks and then you tell me that you and Toni were booted from the orphanage and are living with Dad! It's like the war. You turn around for a few minutes and then everything changes.

And I really can't believe you got yourself a job that pays 75 cents an hour! You can't hear me, but I'm whistling right now! My sister, all grown up! What are you doing with all that money? Saving up for a baby Lincoln, I bet!

I can't wait to get home and get myself a new job too. All the fellows are so tired of being tired, if you know what I mean. We just want to get home, take a hot bath for about a thousand years, and eat until we bust. That's what I want to do, anyway, eat until I bust. Are you going to cook up some good Italian spaghetti for me? I hope so.

You hang in there until I come home. I know what you mean about Ada, but she's all bark and no bite. And Bernice and Cora

*are just like her, all talk. The only one who's a little strange is
Dewey, but he's probably grown out of the worst of it. Stay out
of his way as much as you can and you'll be fine. Anyway, a
nice-looking girl like you is sure to meet some nice fellow soon.
You'll be off and married in no time, and you won't have to
bother with Ada and her kids anymore if you don't feel like it.*

*Well, that's all for now. If all goes right, I'll be home in a
short time and I'll be looking for some spaghetti.*

Love,

Vito

"Whatcha got there?"

Dewey with his mustardy sandpaper eyes shambled into the
kitchen where Frankie was reading her letter at the table.

She put the letter in her pocket. "Nothing. A letter from my
brother."

"Your brother, huh?" he said. "What he have to say?"

"Not much. He wants to come home."

"Ummmm," Dewey said, not listening, just gaping. He
licked his thick lips.

Toni walked into the room, stopping dead when she saw
Dewey. He gave her one of his sick smiles and tipped his dirty hat.
"Hello there, Antonina. That's a very pretty dress you got on."

Toni didn't say anything, just crossed her arms over her
chest and stared at him until he shrugged. "You ladies have a
nice day," he said, and swept out of the room.

"Ew," Toni said after they heard the front door slam. "I

wouldn't trust him as far as I could throw him."

"I'll say." Frankie worried the corner of Vito's letter, then handed it to Toni. "You watch out for Dewey, all right? Don't get in his way."

"I'm trying not to, but he keeps popping up everywhere. He's like a roach, only bigger."

"Where's the roach?" Their father stood in the doorway holding a shoe that he was resoling. "I kill it."

Toni and Frankie looked at each other. "No, Dad," Frankie said. "There's no roach. Toni was just fooling around."

"Oh. Yes." Their father went over to the sink and got himself a glass of water.

Toni sat down at the kitchen table to read Vito's letter while Frankie watched their father's back. It was a big back, a strong one, and she knew just by looking at him that he was much stronger than Dewey. The thought didn't make her feel better. Sometimes when she talked to her father, he wasn't focused on her face, he was looking at her hair or her forehead or even somewhere behind her. And when they were all crowded around the kitchen table, eating dinner together, her father would say, "Pass the potatoes, cara mia," and "Bella, such a lady," but he only had eyes for Ada. Just like he only had money for her, space for her, room for her children.

A person figures out her place in the vast and churning world very quickly, and Frankie's was right in Ada's shadow.

───※───

We were shadows, Marguerite and Wolf and I, but that didn't mean we couldn't live it up a little, so to speak.

At the bar, I introduced Mad Maureen to Marguerite.

This is Miss Marguerite Irene Knowles, I said. Miss Marguerite was murdered by a preacher's daughter with a cup of poisoned tea and a pillow.

I'd say that calls for a bourbon, said Mad Maureen, flexing her fox for the fox.

I've never had spirits before, said Marguerite.

Spirits for the spirits, I said.

I grew up during prohibition, Marguerite said. Oh, people made bathtub gin or bought bootleg, but the only spirits my family used were the kind we put in cough syrup. She took a sip of the bourbon, winced. How is it that I can taste this?

The glories of God? I said.

The glories of bourbon, said Mad Maureen. Hey! What do you two geniuses think you're doing? she shouted at two men rolling like wrestlers on the floor. They didn't hear her, or they didn't care. One broke a bottle over the other's head, the other pulled a knife. They would die on the floor of the bar, get up, and do it all over again. Mad Maureen would shout, and they would ignore her. The bartender—the living one—would march back and forth behind the bar, walk right through Mad Maureen. She would stiffen and yell, Kiss me where I sat on Saturday! and the bartender would pour a drunk another beer.

Marguerite pointed at the rows of bottles behind the bar. Why don't you try and knock one of those off the shelf?

I swallowed the bourbon, coughed. Why don't you?

I asked you first.

I can't, I said.

You can, you've done it before. The light at the library.

I didn't do that.

Yes, you did. So practice. The more you practice, the better you'll get.

And what good will that do?

People will see it. Maybe they won't see *you*, but they'll see what you've done. Your effect on the world. That's something.

I don't think so.

It's more than those two gentlemen can do, she said, toasting the men wrestling on the floor. It's more than they know.

I remembered Marguerite casually poking books off the library shelves, I remembered the picture on the floor of the bookshop. I had done things like that too—I had poked the feet of children, tugged at their blankets, crooned till they heard me—without understanding how it worked, or why. And maybe I had burst the light fixture, maybe I had knocked the photographs off Mercy's coffee table. But it all seemed so accidental. Like catching the flu.

Well, how did *you* do it? I said, turning to Marguerite. When you made that newspaper fly?

You were annoying me.

So I just need to get angry?

No, said Mad Maureen, wiping down the bar. You have to focus and you have to let go at the same time.

What does that mean? Marguerite asked.

Mad Maureen said, What happened when you died? When you first came back?

I said, Everything was hazy. Bright and dark. Blurred. Like seeing through tears.

Mad Maureen said, And you had to learn to gather yourself, redraw the lines of yourself?

Marguerite nodded. Yes.

And the more you gathered, the more you drew, the more real you felt?

Yes, I said.

Well, said Mad Maureen, you need to let that go. Let yourself disperse through the air like a mist over the lake. But at the same time, as you take your focus off yourself, you focus instead on what you want to do. You draw the lines of the act itself, get me? A book falling from a shelf. The window smashing. The light bulb bursting. A tattoo drifting across a sea of skin.

Marguerite said, Wait, you . . . tell yourself a story?

Mad Maureen smiled. Yes. You tell yourself the story of what happened. And then it happens. Try it.

We did. Marguerite closed her not-eyes and I closed mine. I undrew the lines of myself, let them go hazy and slack.

A strange fluttering filled my not-chest, a panicked scrabbling, like claws against a locked door. My not-eyes shot open.

What? said Mad Maureen.

I don't like how it feels.

You have to let go of yourself when you move through a door or a wall.

Yes, but that's when I'm *moving*. It's quick. I don't have to think about it. This feels awful.

Like dying? You've died before, Mad Maureen said. What's one more time?

Again, we closed our eyes. Again the strange fluttering, the panicked scrabbling, my not-heart throbbing in my not-throat. My not-skin pricked by a thousand needles. Not-lungs burning.

I gasped and coughed some more. I can't do it, I said.

Marguerite said, I can't either.

Yes, you can, said Mad Maureen. You have gathered yourself before, you will gather yourself again. You're spirit, not flesh, and your spirit is strong.

But—

How do you think you're here, talking to me? Mad Maureen said. How can you taste the liquor? Feel the fur of that little fox in your fingers? How do you keep finding each other? That's how powerful you are. Let yourself feel it.

I took Marguerite's hand. I could almost feel, *did* feel, her slim fingers in mine. I could almost feel, *did* feel, her gentle squeeze in response.

Again, we closed our eyes. Again, we undrew the lines of ourselves. Hot sparks of pain coursed through me. The fluttering and scrabbling was replaced by a feeling of weightlessness, of recklessness, of *wildness*. What was death to us? Death was nothing! Nothing! We released the spirits of ourselves into the smoky bar all around. As my thoughts went white and dark and bright at the same time, as I was on the verge of losing all sense of myself, I told myself a story. The story of a bottle.

Once upon a time, a bottle of vodka, the most expensive bottle on the shelf, teetered, then fell.

A thud and a crash. First the bottle, and then me back into myself.

"Shit!" said the bartender.

Mad Maureen clapped. That will teach you, you nasty oaf.

Another man's beer stein shot all the way down the bar and off the counter, smashing against the wall.

Marguerite, beautiful Marguerite, sat grinning at me. I grinned back.

And there you go, said Marguerite.

And here we are, I said.

We practiced again and again, until the bartender was charging like a bear around the bar, accusing people of playing tricks on him, shooing everyone out. Until Mad Maureen said that we'd had enough fun for one day and we had to leave something for tomorrow.

You have to confront her, I told Marguerite.

Who? Maureen?

Stop that. You know who. The preacher's daughter.

Marguerite took another sip of her drink, made a face, set the drink down. There's no point, she said. She's dead. Peacefully. In her sleep. Something about a blood vessel.

Then you know what you have to do.

He wasn't the one who killed me.

He left you! He *married* the woman who murdered you, knowing that she did it! He let her get away with it!

Why are you so angry?

Why *aren't* you? I said.

What would you have me do? Knock over more photographs? Push books off the shelves? Haunt his cat?

He can see you, Marguerite. Show yourself to him. Make him repent.

I'm not God, she said.

You're a child of God.

So are you.

I died of the flu. I can't punish anyone for it. I can't get justice. But you can.

She holds the glass in both hands as if to warm it. What if he doesn't repent? What if he tells me that even with everything that happened, he would do it all again?

Love you?

Hurt me.

I took the bourbon from her hands, drained it, turned the glass over, and slapped it down on the bar.

Then, I said, we kill him.

THE DRAGON KING

MARGUERITE VANISHED AGAIN, as was her way, though this time I was sure she would be back. But we missed her at the little blue house in the sea of brick, missed her at the lake, missed her at the bar, missed her at the library. The blond man had stopped coming to read *The Hobbit*, but that was no problem, not anymore. I found the book on the shelves, told myself the story of a book falling, a book opening to just the right chapter, just where we left off. I read chapter ten to Wolf, I told him about the hobbits and the thirteen dwarves stuffed inside barrels, floating down the river and out of Mirkwood forest. Bilbo sees the Lonely Mountain, where they'd really like to go, but instead, the river takes them toward Lake Town. At Lake Town, Bilbo frees the dwarves from the barrels. Thorin marches to the town hall and declares that he, a descendant of the King under the Mountain, has returned to claim himself king. The people of Lake Town have heard the stories of how gold flowed down the river when the King under the Mountain reigned before Smaug the dragon came. The people rejoiced.

Inside Berman's, though, there was no rejoicing, only typing, typing, and more typing. When Frankie went to sleep at night, she heard the clackety-clack of the typewriters snapping in her ears. Her wrists and back ached, and her vision was blurry. She liked the money (though she didn't get to keep much of it), but she had to wonder if her brain was drying up like an old sponge.

One day Mr. Gilhooly poked his bald head out of his office. Frankie thought he was going to call for Wanda the way he always did, but this time he barked, "Which one of you is Mazza?"

Frankie was so startled, she didn't answer. She'd been working there for months, and no one but Wanda had ever said her last name before. The other girls already had their friends, and Frankie didn't know what to say to them anyway. She tried to deal as best she could, but every time she got tongue-tied and shy with people who weren't orphans, people who had never been beaten or shorn, people who came and went as they pleased and always had, people who were free, she got angry all over again. Then scared that she would never be able to manage in this world. That it was far too big and far too small at the same time, and she'd always be scrabbling for a doorknob, searching for a way out.

Mr. Gilhooly's bald head went pink. "Mazza!"

"That's me," Frankie squeaked.

He peered at her through his thick glasses. "I lost my girl last week. Got married when her soldier came home. Wanda says you take shorthand."

"Y-yeah," Frankie stammered. "Yes, sir."

"Why don't you come in here and we'll give it a shot, what do you say?"

The light shone off his pink scalp as she tried to figure out what he meant. Would she be his secretary? Would she start now?

"Well!" he said.

"Uh . . . yes," she stammered.

"Get your steno pad, then, and hop to it." He disappeared into his office. Frankie searched her desk for a steno pad and a pen and started to walk to Mr. Gilhooly's office. Her insides twisted tighter and tighter with every step she took. She was okay in the typing pool, she was a good typist and no one paid much attention to her, which was the way she liked it. What if Mr. Gilhooly was a hothead? What if he was like Dewey, with his mustardy sandpaper eyes? What if he got mad like Sister George? What if she had to work there with him, all day, in his small office, trapped and terrified like some feral cat?

By the time she reached Mr. Gilhooly's office and knocked on the side of the door, her knees were knocking loud as type-writers. Her throat dried up tight. Mr. Gilhooly shuffled papers across his desk and scratched at his head. He looked mad.

He waved at Frankie. "Come in, come in!"

She walked inside the office and in a few steps she was standing in front of his desk. "Well," he said. "Are you going to sit?"

She sat.

"Are you ready?"

She swallowed hard and showed him her pen.

"Swell," he said to the papers on his desk. "Swell. Let me just find . . . ah, here it is." He found the paper he was looking for and held it up. Even in Mr. Gilhooly's office, Frankie could hear the loud clacking of the typewriters. He could too. "A man can't hear himself think!" he said. "Can you get the door?"

"What?" Frankie said.

"The door," he said again, eyebrows raised if she was deaf. "Close the door."

"Oh. Right." She put her pad and pen on the chair and walked over to the door. She grabbed the knob and pushed, but it wouldn't shut all the way. Why did he need her to shut the door? Her feet itched in her good shoes, telling her to run while she still could.

"You have to lean on it," Mr. Gilhooly said.

She didn't want to lean on it, she didn't want to close it, why did he need her to close it? She pushed harder, but the door still wouldn't shut. Her mouth felt like a desert, her heart banged in her chest.

"No, you have to really lean on it. The wood swells in this heat."

She pressed her body up against the door and pushed as hard as she could. With her nose right up on the wood, she could smell its door smell, like pencils and something else too. Smoke, the pine-scented cleaner they used on the windows, the salt and sweat of a thousand hands. Her head swam with memories: sitting in the bath while Aunt Marion scrubbed her back, the sound of a gunshot echoing through a tiny Chicago apartment, then crawling to the bedroom door, kissing Sam in the greenhouse thinking they were safe enough to do it, praying that Chicago would be hit by bombs just so that Sister George couldn't beat her anymore. Every closed door was a test, every open one was a trap. And now she was going to shut this door and no one would be able to hear her scream over the sound of the typewriters.

A sob caught in her throat.

"Did you shut it? Do you need me to do it?"

Nothing's going to happen, everything is all right, he's fine, he just wants a letter, just a letter, she told herself. Her body didn't believe it, though. It banged and shuddered and watered and itched. She turned her face toward the door so that he wouldn't see the tears that suddenly spilled all over her cheeks.

"Hey, what's wrong? Are you okay over there?" In that moment he sounded kind, and that was all it took. She put her head in her hands and wept like a baby.

———✥———

Mr. Gilhooly called Wanda and she took Frankie to the ladies' room and got her a glass of water. Wanda said that Mr. Gilhooly thought Frankie was having "woman problems" and that she'd scared him so bad that Frankie would never have to take dictation again, ever, if she didn't want to.

Wanda let Frankie go home early, but when Frankie thought about "home"—the cramped collection of rooms, her there-but-not-there father, creepy Dewey, broad-faced Bernice and slinky Cora—she decided to duck into a coffee shop instead.

She took a seat at the counter and the waitress came over to pour her some coffee.

"If you don't mind my saying," said the waitress, smiling, "you don't look so hot."

"Thanks," Frankie said.

"Don't mention it." She plunked down a little pitcher of cream. "Bad day?"

"Yeah," she said. She didn't explain.

The waitress didn't care. "No sugar. Ran out yesterday."

"That's all right, I don't need it. I'd like some toast, please. With oleo."

"Coming up."

She walked over to the window and told the cook, who glanced in Frankie's direction and then popped some slices into the toaster.

She sipped the coffee. She liked the smells in here, all the food smells . . . the gravy and the meat and the cream and the pie. Even though it was hot outside, she liked the warmth of the coffee shop. She liked how people seemed content and happy munching on their sandwiches. Nobody clacking on a clackety typewriter, no one asking you to take a letter and then trying to trap you behind a closed door.

The waitress slid the plate of toast in front of her. "Eat it while it's hot." She was white with curly red hair, friendly sort of hair, and big gray eyes round as quarters.

"Do you like your job?" Frankie asked her.

"Why? You looking?"

"Just curious."

"I like it fine. Harvey over there gives me lunch." She tilted her head at the cook. "I like lunch."

Frankie smiled. "So do I." Frankie looked down at the waitress's hands, but she wore no ring. "Are you married?"

"Say, you *are* curious. Harvey, this little girl wants to know if I'm married."

Harvey chuckled, wiping his hands on his white shirt.

The waitress, whose name tag said Nancy, said, "I live by myself. I have a room over the hardware store next door."

"A room?"

"Yeah, a room. You know, with a bed and a dresser. Have to share a bathroom, but that's all right. It's cheap."

A room. "But it's your own room?"

The waitress laughed. "Well, who else's would it be? Winston Churchill's?"

"Winston Churchill," Harvey repeated, chuckling again.

All the way home that afternoon, Frankie thought about Nancy's room. A room she had all on her own, and all to herself. Why couldn't she have something like that? She didn't like the job, and she didn't want to take dictation again, ever, but she worked hard, she made money. And the apartment was too small for all of them anyway.

But she couldn't leave Toni. She wanted a room of her own so badly she could taste it, but she wouldn't leave Toni in the same house with Bernice and Cora, in the same house with Dewey.

She found her father in the shoe shop, putting new heels on some old boots. He smiled at her in his there-but-not-there way and went back to his boots. He used a small hammer to pound tiny nails into the wood.

"Dad," Frankie said. "What do you think of me and Toni getting a room?"

He pulled the nails from between his teeth. "Eh? What are you saying? What kind of *room*?"

His expression said she should stop talking, but she didn't stop, wouldn't stop. "Well, it's pretty crowded here. I thought that maybe I could take some of the money I'm making and rent a room for Toni and me. To make more space for the rest of you. I know that Ada doesn't—"

"Ada makes beautiful home, beautiful home," he said. "What are you saying? Are you crazy?"

"I was just thinking that—"

He pounded on the work bench. "No. No girls of mine get *rooms*."

"Dad, if you just think about it—"

He picked up the boot and shook it at her, his face red. "Don't *you* think about it, okay? Don't you talk about it. I send you back. To orphanage."

He wasn't making any sense. He'd *left* them at the orphanage for years. And he didn't take them back until he'd been forced to. "They threw us out of there. You can't send us back. They won't take us."

"Don't you tell me what to do!" he yelled. "Maybe I call different place, I don't know. Maybe I call the police. You're not all grown up. You can't do things you please." He shook his head. "You stay here, you work. Or I find somewhere else to send you, yes?" He didn't wait for her to answer. He put the tiny nails back between his teeth, nodding yes, yes, yes, like a man reassuring himself of his own power, like a mad and fickle king.

THE MAGIC WORDS

PERHAPS I GOT RECKLESS. Perhaps I went a little mad myself. I flipped the hats off strangers in the street, I tickled babies in their cribs, I turned the lights on and off and on again. I sat with Stella as she slept and told her the story of the girl with the golden arm. She woke up rubbing her own left arm and starting at every little noise. When I visited her in the shower, when I knocked the soap from her hands again and again, she screamed. Sister Bert hauled her wet and gave her extra lessons for making such a spectacle.

Mad Maureen had forbidden me to knock any more bottles off the shelf, but I could drink as much bourbon as I wanted, though I didn't really want it. I was sitting there, at the bar, trying to figure out a way around Mad Maureen's rules, a way to entertain myself, when Marguerite appeared next to me. Wolf licked her not-hand with his not-tongue, and she patted his not-head, scratched his not-ears.

Where have you been? I asked her.

Praying, she said.

I missed you.

I missed you too, she said. But her not-eyes had a faraway look, as if she were already redrawing the lines of herself, ungathering.

Are you ready now? I asked her.

She dragged her eyes back to me, her attention. She said, No one is ever ready for something like this. You don't do it because you're ready. You do it because you're weary. And I am weary. I have been weary for too long.

So we went back to the antiques shop, Marguerite, Wolf, and I. When the little black cat saw us, she gave a soft chirp of recognition. She leaped from a chair to a table to the top of the highest cabinet, as if she knew what was coming, as if she was choosing what to witness, and this was the best spot from which to watch.

Do you think he'll see you again? I asked. Really see you?

She thought about this for a moment. Yes, she said. Because he still wants to.

At the front of the shop, Marguerite hesitated, as if waiting for him the way she always had. But then she closed her eyes and put her palms together, praying for something only she understood. Her yellow dress billowed, the soft curls on the back of her neck stirred. The lines of her blurred, as if I was seeing her through a wash of tears. Marguerite lifted her feet from the floor, floated wafted glided to the desk in the back of the shop. The man sat behind the desk, holding something in his hand. He glanced up. Froze.

"You," he breathed. "You're here."

I am, she said. The spirit was spiraling off her in sparks and ash, golden and bright.

"You're beautiful. More beautiful than . . ."

Than when I was alive? Than when you let me die?

At the sound of these words, a tear streaked his skin. He got up from the desk, using one hand to brace himself as he made his way around it. He willed himself forward, dropped to his knees in front of her.

"I've waited for you."

She said nothing.

"It's all right. I want you to do it."

Her fire only burned brighter. Do what? she asked.

"Do what you came to do. Punish me. That's what I deserve."

Is it? she said. Tell me why.

"I love you," he said. "I always have. I never stopped. It's tortured me."

Marguerite closed her eyes, her chest rising and falling, as if she were breathing still. How? she asked him. How have you been tortured? How have you hurt? How have you suffered?

"I thought about you all the time. You haunted—" He cut himself off. "I dreamed about you. I dreamed that I confronted her about what she did, that I turned her in for it. I dreamed I kept my promises to you and to myself."

You dreamed you were a better man, Marguerite said.

"I . . . I . . ." But he couldn't say it. Couldn't say yes.

Marguerite's face smoldered, the sparks around her lengthening and deepening into ribbons of burnt umber. So, she said, those were only dreams.

300

"After . . . after she died, her father caught me with this." He held up a pocket watch, open so that Marguerite could see the picture of herself tucked inside it. "I'd never replaced it. He took the children. They haven't spoken to me since. I've had no life at all, not really. And I'm done with what's left of it. So please. I beg you. Do what you came to do."

He bowed his head. He no longer looked beautiful to me, like a man carved from marble. He looked like a mewling, self-ish, broken thing.

To Marguerite, I said, Do it. He wants you to.

The man didn't seem to hear me. He kept his eyes on the shining sun that was Marguerite unwinding.

No, she said.

No? I said.

"But isn't that why you've come?" he asked.

From the surface of the desk, a book floated into the air, beating its leaves like wings. Another book did the same, and another, and another until the books twirled and flocked like birds.

No, Marguerite said. I didn't come to punish you.

Yes, you did, I said. I swept all the papers off a table. I tipped over a chair. The man looked frightened, and relieved.

Marguerite said to me, to both of us, Don't.

"Don't what?" said the man.

This isn't the way, she said.

"What isn't?"

The way to forgiveness.

"Do you forgive me?" he said.

No, she said. Her fine brows furrowed, then smoothed out again. The ribbons of umber brightened again, bronzed and brassed.

"What?"

She smiled, a smile so sudden that it cast its own beam of light. No, I don't forgive you.

He blinked, confused.

Once upon a time, she said, a girl fell in love with a man so small and weak and easily led, she died for it. She kept asking for forgiveness from the earth and stars, from God and from ghosts, but though forgiveness was offered, she never felt it, it could not touch her, it could not free her. Until she forgave herself.

Marguerite laughed, the sound like a choir. The book birds whirled in a frenzy.

She said, I do *not* forgive you.

Then she said: This is not where I need to be.

All the books dropped to the floor.

She turned and flew out the door of the shop, leaving the man on his knees behind her. Wolf and I ran rushed flew after her, the houses and the shops and the buildings a blur all around us. I couldn't understand where she was going, where she was taking us, until we reached a neighborhood on the South Side of Chicago, bustling with music and with the friendly chatter of people on porches and stoops, toasting a fine evening with finer company.

She stopped at a tidy brick house, the windows aglow with soft light. She pressed through the wall and I did too, Wolf alongside me. In the house, a family gathered around a dinner table. In the skin and in the bones of the faces of these men and these women, these children, I could see Marguerite's skin and bones, her history and her future. A regal woman sat at the head of the table, salt and pepper hair piled high on her head. She glanced up from her food, inhaled, shivered. She laid her fork and knife carefully on the edge of her plate.

"Baby?" she said.

"What is it, Mama?" said the mustachioed man next to her. "Can I get you something?"

"Margie," the woman said.

The other people around the table stopped eating, forks and knives hovering. The man took his mother's hand. "What about Margie, Mama?"

The woman didn't smile exactly, but the corners of her mouth curved gently upward, sinking into her brown skin, into the faint lines anticipating it. "She's here."

The man exchanged glances with a woman across the table, who scooped up a small boy and hugged him hard, though the boy wriggled like a puppy.

"What was that, Mama? Who's here?"

"I can't see her, but she's here. Aren't you, baby?"

Yes, Mama, Marguerite said.

The others in the room didn't seem to see or hear Marguerite, but the regal woman said, "I smelled the sweetness in the air. Like perfume, the way your hair used to smell when you were just a little one. And look at you. Shining like your own sun." The woman put a fist to her heart.

Tears spilled down Marguerite's golden cheeks. Yes, Mama. I wasn't sure you'd still be in the same house after all this time.

"I've been waiting for you. It took you long enough."

I know, Mama. I'm so sorry. I had . . . I had things to do. Things to work out. I'm so sorry. There are so many things I should have told you. There are so many things I should have done. Please forgive me.

"My beautiful girl, I loved you all your life, and I've loved you all this time." The woman got up from her chair and went to a small desk in the corner of the room. She pulled out a leather-bound book. When she saw the book, Marguerite's body shook as with tears, sobs.

"I kept your stories. I read them to the children." She gestured to the table full of people, who were staring in incomprehension and concern. "There's nothing for me to forgive," Marguerite's mother said. "God has forgiven you long ago. You have to forgive *yourself*. Can you do that? Will you?"

Yes, Marguerite said. Yes, I think I can do that now.

"You have somewhere to go, don't you?"

I don't want to leave you. I never want to leave you again.

"You will always be with me, but you know what you have to do. Your daddy's there. I won't be long."

I love you, Mama. I love you.

"I love you too, baby. Carry it with you."

Marguerite's skin shone with tears, shone with blazing golden light. She threw back her head and cried out, not in pain, but in sheer joy, the way a bird cries midflight. Wings so black and so bright they shorted out my vision sprouted from her back, wide as the room, wide as the city. The house fell away and there was only Marguerite, burning in her own lovely fire, her lips moving, silently telling herself the story of herself, the magic words, unwinding, then raveling into a whole new form. I dropped to my knees like that man at the bookshop, just another sinner, just another supplicant. Don't go, I shouted, take me with you, but she couldn't, I was her friend but I was not of her people, she couldn't teach me the words and I didn't have the power to learn them. Her history wasn't mine, her story wasn't mine. One last glance, one last beatific smile; she rose up into the air. She flew higher and higher into the plush and generous darkness, the long forgiving night, until she slipped through a star, a doorway, and heaven welcomed her in.

TOOTH AND CLAW

I DID NOT HAVE WINGS, so I could not fly away. I would have to run. Or claw.

I went back to the antiques shop with Wolf. We wrecked the place. Knocked over shelves, tore up books, smashed the pretty lamps, overturned the tables. We left the photograph of the redhead, unassuming as milk, in the middle of the room, untouched.

The man couldn't see us, but he could see what we were doing, what we did, the effect we had on his world. But I didn't kill him. He was too weak, too pathetic, and Marguerite wouldn't have wanted me to; she wanted him to live with it. And live with it he would. As he sat in the ruin of his shop, the ruins of his life, weeping, the little black cat curled on his lap, I bent and whispered in his ear:

Even the cat deserves better.

1945

DOORWAYS

THE QUEEN IN THE ToWER

AFTER MARGUERITE FLEW AWAY and we left the man's shop behind, I lost myself. I could not tell you where. If Wolf remembered, he kept it secret. I woke up in the cemetery by the orphanage, leaning against a headstone so old the name had worn away. Hello, ladies, hello, gentlemen, I said, but my heart wasn't in it.

Who was I kidding? I had no heart, not anymore. Perhaps I never did.

I went to see Frankie. All winter, she went to work, she went home, she went to work, she went home, she went to work, she went to the diner, her own little loop. In February, she turned eighteen, expecting to feel like an adult, expecting to belong to herself, but she felt trapped as ever. April came and President Roosevelt died suddenly, but the war rolled on without him as if nothing at all had changed. At night, she'd tried to get comfortable beside her sister on the lumpy old bed, turning over and over, but she'd once woken up when she heard someone—or some*thing*—scratching on the bedroom door. Scritch, scritch, scritch. She took to sleeping on the living room couch, with a fork under her pillow, just in case.

By May, Frankie was going to the diner every morning before work, just to get out of the house first thing. Sometimes she even stopped off for dinner, if she could spare the change. It usually meant that she had to walk home, but that wasn't so bad.

"Look, Harvey, there she is, our little party girl. Stay up late again, Frankie?" Nancy said one morning as she poured Frankie a cup of coffee and Harvey popped two slices of toast into the toaster.

"Sure I stayed up late," Frankie told Nancy. "But it's not why you think."

Frankie hadn't been able to sleep; so she'd been in the living room reading a book Loretta had sent, *A Tree Grows in Brooklyn*. Dewey had stumbled in, stinking of liquor, and sat on her as if he didn't know she was there. She kicked him off and he left, but she worried the whole night that he'd come back, that he'd sneak into her room and—

"Hey, Harvey, she says it's not what I think! What do I think, Frankie?" Nancy put both elbows on the counter and rubbed her chin. "I think that you got yourself a new boyfriend and the two of you were out dancing."

"Ha!" Frankie said. "You could not be more wrong."

"Okay," she said. "The two of you were out *necking*."

Frankie nearly spat out her coffee, and Harvey started to chuckle as he plated up her toast. "Nancy!"

Frankie looked around and then lowered her voice. "You shouldn't say things like that."

"Why not? Pretty girl like you probably has a parade of fellas following you around. Am I right, Harvey, or am I right?" She put the usual plate of toast in front of Frankie.

Frankie said, "No. No fellas for me."

"Aw, go on!"

"It's true. I had a fella once, but . . ." She trailed off.

"But?"

Frankie peeled the crust away from her bread. "But I don't think my father would appreciate me hanging out with a lot of fellas."

"He's strict, is he?"

"He's old-fashioned," Frankie said.

"I know the type, believe me," Nancy said, picking up a rag and wiping down the counter. "Wants his girl to get married but doesn't want her to go and meet the fella she's supposed to marry. It's a little mixed-up, wouldn't you say?"

"I guess."

"I don't guess. I *know*, don't I, Harvey?" Nancy finished wiping down the counter, dropped the rag into the sink, and put her hands on her hips. "You want to know what else I know?"

"What's that?"

"Your dance partner is right around the corner," she said, wagging her finger at Frankie. "You take my word."

Frankie left the diner, thinking about Sam, thinking about dance partners, when she noticed that people were already dancing. Lots of them, men and women both. Whooping and shouting and kissing one another. Before Frankie knew what was happening, a girl in a polka-dotted dress ran up to her. "Isn't it wonderful?" she said.

"Yes!" Frankie said. "What's wonderful?"

"Don't you know?" she said.

"Know what?"

The girl jumped up and down like a marionette. "Germany surrendered! The war is over!"

———

Frankie walked home through impromptu celebrations—people kissing and laughing, waltzing and hugging—her emotions seesawing between happiness and grief. Happiness that Vito would come home soon, and grief that it was too late for Sam, too late for so many others. Before she opened the door to the apartment behind the shoe store, she wiped all the happy/sad tears from her face, because she didn't want to have to explain them to Cora or Bernice or Ada or anyone. But she needn't have bothered. She was lucky to find the apartment empty for once, except for the envelope addressed to her on the kitchen table.

Dear Frankie,

I have someone you and your sister need to meet. I will pick you up next Saturday at noon and we'll all go together. You need to know.

Don't tell your father.

Love,

Aunt Marion

Go? Go where? Frankie thought. She hadn't seen Aunt Marion since that day at the orphanage. And meet who? Know what? Though she couldn't say exactly why, dread weighed her down, made her steps slow and heavy, welded her jaws shut. All week, the girls at the office chattered about the end of the war, about all the boyfriends and husbands who would come back, about the taste of sugar and real butter and steak, and she could barely bring herself to reply. Nancy served her toast, and she bit into it without tasting it, her mouth so dry that she couldn't distinguish the bread from her tongue.

Saturday came, and so did Aunt Marion, sturdy as ever, with her giant pocketbook. Aunt Marion told Ada that she had arrived to take her nieces out to lunch.

"How . . . nice," said Ada, her lips tightening into something that might have resembled a smile, if Ada's mouth and muscles remembered how to smile, if Ada had ever been happy enough or pleased enough or even polite enough. "Well, I'm *sure* they deserve it."

They did not get lunch. Instead, Aunt Marion marched Frankie and Toni onto a streetcar. Silently, they rode west for nearly a half hour through Chicago neighborhoods that Frankie had never seen before. When they reached Narragansett and Montrose, they got off the streetcar and walked. It was only when they reached the huge complex of buildings, buildings that looked to Frankie like something out of medieval times, England or somewhere, a place with courtiers and jousters and queens imprisoned in towers, that Aunt Marion said, "You're going to have to be strong, girls. Both of you."

"Strong about what? What is this place?" Toni wanted to know.

"It's a hospital," said Aunt Marion.

Toni shook her head, the feathers on her hat twitching. "But who's sick?"

Everyone, I whispered, my not-mouth dry, my not-throat tight. Everyone here is sick.

Even the dead. Especially the dead. The grounds were thick with them, restless and dreadful. A Civil War soldier took a sword to the gut, staggered, and fell. Victims of the Great Chicago Fire crawled on charred forearms, blackened knees. A man strangled a woman, while nine others waited their turn in line behind her. Another man cut off his left hand and declared to everyone, to no one, I think it will grow again. And because he was a ghost, it did.

Though Frankie couldn't see the ghosts, in some deep and wordless place she sensed their disembodied pain, their anxious agitation. She stopped walking before they reached the entrance, grabbed Aunt Marion's elbow. The giant purse swung on Marion's wrist like a pendulum.

"I'm not going in until you tell us what's going on," Frankie said.

"Like I said, this is a hospital. The state hospital."

"So?"

"People call this place by another name, Frankie. Dunning."

Toni scrunched up her face in confusion. "The *asylum*? But—"

"Why are we here?" Frankie's voice was high and shrill, an alarm.

Aunt Marion pulled her arm and Frankie's hand tight to her body, stilled the swinging of the purse. "We're here to see your mother."

—◦◦◦—

What Frankie knew about her mother: Her name was Caterina Costa. She came to America on a boat from Sicily in 1918. She was beautiful, with long, dark curling hair. Big chocolate eyes. Sun-kissed skin. She didn't know a word of English, but she met Frankie's father the shoemaker, and she married him. They lived in an apartment behind the shoe shop. She had three children, Vittorio, Francesca, and Antonina. They made her so happy. That was why everyone was shocked when Frankie's mother took the gun from the drawer in the shoe shop. But she only wanted to see what it felt like to pull the trigger, she would never try to hurt anyone, she would never commit such a sin. Frankie's father threw out the gun and put the children in an orphanage so their mother could rest. After a while, she was okay again. Everyone came out of the orphanage. She and Frankie's father tried to have another baby, but Frankie's mother died, and so did the baby.

Frankie's mother died. Frankie's mother was dead.

But she wasn't.

She wasn't.

She—

"—always had a sadness," Aunt Marion was saying. "It was hard for her to take care of you. That's why you were sent to the orphanage the first time. After you got out, she lost a baby, and the sadness got so deep she couldn't crawl out of it. She found the gun and tried to kill herself. They wrestled for it, and she ended up shooting your father by accident. She didn't mean to. He wasn't hurt badly. But she was sent here. And you were sent to the orphanage again. I agreed not to tell you then because you were too young, but now . . . you're a woman yourself. The both of you are. You have a right to know."

How had *I* not known? How had I not thought to sift through Aunt Marion's thoughts to see the truth?

A nurse led them through the women's wing. Frankie and Toni covered their noses and mouths against the smell, but they couldn't cover their ears, which were filled with the sounds of huffing and panting, ranting and weeping. The halls and the rooms were so packed with people that it was difficult to tell the cries of the dead from the cries of the living. "I am Jesus Christ returned," said an emaciated woman shuffling in mismatched house slippers. "Someday my prince will come and you'll be sorry when he does," said a naked one dancing atop her bed, "This food is poisoned and I won't eat it!" screamed another woman, throwing a tray against a wall. "The spirits are after me," said a girl crouching in the hallway, "and their purpose is doom, doom, doom."

"Sorry about the noise!" the nurse said cheerfully. "They're not normally so riled up."

Worse than the angry and unsettled ones were the silent ones drugged into slack-jawed oblivion, heads lolling in their wheelchairs. There were so many more of those—empty eyes, strings of drool dangling. I touched my not-lips with my not-fingers and could have sworn I felt the wetness there, a ghostly string tying me to—

Frankie's mother slept in a room with eight beds, though she was the only one there now, sitting in a chair by the small barred window. If she'd been beautiful at one time, if she'd had long dark curling hair and chocolate eyes, she didn't anymore. Her hair was thin and greasy and grayish brown, her expression blank and dull. She blinked as Aunt Marion pushed Frankie and Toni forward.

"Hello, Caterina. This is Francesca and Antonina. Remember I said I would bring them?"

"Happy birthday," her mother said, low and scratchy, the accent thick.

"It's not my birthday," said Toni.

"It was," said her mother. She held out a pack of cigarettes. "Here."

Toni held out a wary hand for the cigarettes, confused.

Frankie nudged her. "Say thank you, Toni."

"Thank you?" Toni said.

"Big," said her mother, looking at Frankie.

"What?"

Her mother held her palm flat over her head. "Big girl."

"I'm eighteen," said Frankie.

"Eighteen," her mother repeated. "I was sixteen."

Toni clutched the cigarettes, blurted, "Dad said you were dead."

Marion sucked a breath through her teeth. "Toni."

"Is it because you took the gun?" Toni said. "Is that why he put you here?"

"Toni!"

"Gun?" her mother said.

"Toni!"

"The gun. You wanted to kill yourself."

"Antonina, that's enough," said Aunt Marion. But her mother didn't have a reaction to what they were saying, not one Frankie could see. Frankie didn't know what to say. She didn't know what to *do*. What do you do when everyone has been lying to you for years? What do you do when your mother has been brought back from the dead, but only part of the way? What do you do when the story you've been telling yourself about yourself is a lie? When your heart has been broken so many times and so fast it feels like little chewed bits of it are traveling the length of your body, beating all over?

I felt like chewed bits. Where had I seen Caterina before?

"He had the gun," said Frankie's mother, after a while.

"What?"

"I was too sad for him. He loved someone else. Adele? Adeline?"

"Ada?" said Frankie.

Her mother nodded. "Yes. Her. He said he would shoot

himself if he couldn't have her. I tried to take the gun. It went off. Boom."

Aunt Marion yanked the handle of the big pocketbook higher on her arm. "Now you know that's not true, Caterina."

Frankie's mother shrugged, as if it didn't really matter one way or the other. She reached down and scratched at bare dirty toes.

It was Sesto's shoe shop, where my fancy shoes had been made. I could picture them so clearly now, Gaspare and Caterina, her tiny foot resting on his thigh. Both of them so young and beautiful that no one could have recognized them.

Frankie's mother said, "Do you remember Esta?"

"Who's Esta?"

"That is her name. It means 'from the east.' I came from the east too. At first I was happy. Mostly I was not."

"You mean Sicily?" Frankie asked.

"My mother died. My father said I needed to go across the sea to find a husband." One corner of her mouth quirked up, as if some small, deep part of her thought this was funny.

"Vito is across the sea now," Toni offered. "He'll be back soon, though."

"Vito?"

"My brother. Our brother."

"Your son," said Aunt Marion.

"Oh. He's big?"

"Yes. Bigger than I am," said Toni.

"Antonina." Frankie's mother tested the name on her

tongue, syllable by syllable. *An-to-ni-na.* "Just a baby, too."

"Yes, she was," Aunt Marion agreed. "A beautiful baby."

"I'm not a baby anymore," Toni said.

"Esta was my baby. You didn't see her?" Frankie's mother made a cradle with her arms, rocked them. "So tiny."

Frankie, Toni, and Aunt Marion watched her rock her empty arms, faces collapsing in pity and confusion and sadness. I watched her, too, and as I watched her, I found myself making the same motion, rocking an invisible baby in my not-arms. It looked so familiar. It *felt* so familiar.

I had seen this before. I had *done* this. I had slumped in a chair with my head lolling and rocked my empty arms in a place like this.

In a place like this.

In *this* place.

Right here.

More than ten years before Caterina was.

The lights went out, then quickly came back on. My not-fingers tingled and sparked. I wasn't even trying to do it, and yet I felt myself unstitching, little spirals of silver spitting. My own fraying moon.

"What was that?" Aunt Marion said.

"The ghosts are ghostful," said Frankie's mother. "Hello, ghost!"

It was as if she'd given me permission, permission to see my own truth, the truth I had kept from myself. My vision blurred, doubled, showing me two eras at once, two versions of me. I was dead, witnessing Frankie's first glimpse of her mother in

more than a decade, and at the same time, I was alive, looking down at my own empty arms, my head a murky swamp of
Veronal. All around me were other girls, other sick ones who
heard voices or had visions, sad ones who had wasted with
despair, battered ones with broken wrists and broken ribs, poor
ones with nowhere else to go, brown ones whose skin or tongue
had damned them. There were girls who had worked too hard
or loved God too much, girls who'd been caught with pillows
clutched between their thighs, girls who had just been caught—
with boys, with girls, with babies, with drink, with ideas, with
a temper, with a plan.

But how had I been caught? I searched my not-brain for
any memory, anything real and true. I had had no plan after my
brothers took Benno and the nuns took Mercy, but my parents
did. Charles Kent agreed to marry me anyway, make a ruined
girl respectable, make my father rich. I was still beautiful, and
that was precious enough. The world had taught him he was
owed a girl, and I was his to do with what he liked. He told me
what he liked. I had whored for *that boy* and now I would whore
for a man. He tore the dress from my back, he would take what
he wanted and keep taking. I would wear his ring and he would
wear me like a puppet. So I hit him with the poker, once, twice.
He bled, he cried, I remembered that. I'd told Marguerite.

But then more memories lurched up like a body long sub-
merged, bloated and blue.

What he did after.

He'd staggered to his feet. He picked up the telephone. Four
men came. He said, "She broke into the house and attacked me,

she's deranged and hysterical, I have no idea who she is, she's a stranger to us all." The men wrapped me in a sheet, drove me out here to Dunning in a stinking, rumbling automobile, held me down while the doctors plunged the first needle in. It took my parents weeks to find me. And by the time they did—

How had I forgotten this, how had I lied to myself for so long? Time collapsed, the room spun and melted through the middle like film burned in a projector. I reached for Frankie as if she could anchor me, but she was alive and I was not and there were no anchors anywhere. Here I was, in a crowded corridor with the slumped and drooling patients, here I was on the Dunning grounds with the crawling, feverish dead, here I was at the top of a winding staircase, running down and down and down, trying to get back to the earth as if I'd never left it. Sunlight beamed all around and I looked up into a wide sky made of birds and glass. My father's voice boomed: "With all these crows roosting here, this building is nothing but a rookery." I was floating on the ceiling of the glass atrium with the birds that had found their way in. They cawed at me and I cooed—

—at the babies in their cribs, lined up like gravestones, which was probably why I was drawn to them, little cradles of life. Hello, you baby, I said. Good morning, cupcake. Sometimes they heard me, sometimes—

they

didn't

Running again, through the halls of the orphanage. Something was chasing me, something had come up from the catacombs beneath the building, lurching and shuffling and moaning. I tried to breathe, but I couldn't breathe, my dead lungs heaved and spasmed. I made for the window. A girl whose hair was ropy with blood unhinged her jaw to gulp me down. But I was already shattered, already gone.

HUNGER

I CAME BACK TO MYSELF on the shores of Lake Michigan, the water lunging at my feet. The elegant black man in the pin-striped suit and a knife sticking out of his neck spun a cane this way and that. He said I was the whitest girl he'd ever seen, he asked me the name of my wily red fox, he said we looked like we'd stepped out of a fairy tale, "The Girl and the Wolf." He wondered if I'd ever eaten anything that lit me up from the inside, set me aflame.

I said: I know hunger. I know how it hurts.

He said: Do tell.

BLESS ME

FRANKIE AFLAME: HER GLARE HOT, so hot.

"What are you staring at?" Bernice snapped over her morning oatmeal.

"Yeah," said Cora. "What are you staring at?"

Frankie's lids dropped to half-mast, but the heat in her gaze didn't fade. Did Vito know about their mother? Did Bernice know? Did Cora?

Ada knew. Ada scrubbed pots in the sink, her traitor's back to Frankie. Ada should leave the pots and scrub herself inside and out, she should reach under her own house dress, she should swallow the steel wool.

"What's *wrong* with you?" Bernice said.

"Do you hear that?" Frankie asked.

"Hear what, you loony tune?"

Frankie's father cobbled shoes in the shop and his hammer said liar, liar, liar. He thought he could lock her mother away, he thought he could pitch his own daughters. He thought they were all his to shut in a tower. Or turn out the door, leave for the animals.

Frankie stood, pulled on her gloves.

Bernice dropped the spoon into her bowl with a thud. "Where do you think you're going?"

"Church," said Frankie.

At this, Ada turned around. "We just went this morning."

"Are you telling me I can't go?"

"There's washing to do around here. And I thought I told you to wake your sister up. She needs to pull her weight."

"She needs to *lose* some weight," said Bernice.

"So do you," said Cora.

"Shut your ugly mug," said Bernice.

"Hey, I know!" said Cora, through a mouthful of oatmeal. "Why don't Frankie and Toni join a convent! That's what girls like them do anyway. I mean, what man would want to—"

"Learn some new insults, why don't you?" Frankie said. "You're both boring the crap out of me."

Cora's mouth dropped open in shock. "What did you just say?"

"Hush," Ada said to Cora and Bernice. To Frankie, she said, "You can go to mass tomorrow. We have the sheets to do, and the floors. The rugs need beating. Your father's shop needs to be dusted."

"I'm going to confession."

"Oh, what do *you* have to confess?" Cora said.

"Mother, you can't let her get out of doing her chores," Bernice whined.

Frankie ignored them both, kept that hot glare on Ada.

"Confession is good for the soul, wouldn't you say, Stepmother?"

Ada put her hands on her hips, the soapy water from the Brillo soaking into her dress. "I don't think I like that snotty tone."

Frankie straightened her hat. "Looks like I have something to confess after all."

—∞—

She took the streetcar to the Guardians. She slipped into the church, and then inside the confession booth. She waited for the shadow of Father Paul to appear behind the screen.

When he was settled, she said, "Bless me, Father, for he has sinned."

Father Paul said, "Don't you mean that *you* have sinned?"

"I said what I said."

"All right, Frankie. I'll bite. Who are we talking about?"

"He lied to me. He lied for fourteen years. My mother isn't dead after all. She's at Dunning. She's been there the whole time. My whole life."

Father shifted, the bench beneath him creaking. In that creak, Frankie heard another truth. "You *knew*?" But of course he did. There were nine hundred orphans at the Guardians, and he seemed to know them all, even the ones who had left. Even the ones who had been thrown away.

Frankie's nails bit into her palms. "Who else knew? The sisters? The orphans? Everyone but me?"

"Frankie, sometimes the adults in your life keep things

from you to spare you, to protect you."

"You think that he protected me? That he ever has? That he's doing it now?"

"You feel anger in your heart."

"I feel anger everywhere," she said. "I feel it in my toes."

"Fools give full vent to their rage, the wise bring calm in the end."

"I'm a fool then," said Frankie.

"You don't have to be. You can repent, and God will forgive you."

"What if I don't want to be forgiven?"

"Oh, Frankie. I am sorry for you. I am. For everything that's happened." He sounded sorry. And that was something. "But," he said, "anger only lets the devil get a foothold. Anger gets us that much closer to hell."

"And hell is where you burn."

"That's right."

But it wasn't true, Frankie understood that now. Hell wasn't fire and brimstone. Hell didn't burn. And the only devils to be found were the ones you find on earth, and there were too many of those, and they looked like everybody else.

Hell, though. Hell was empty. Hell was nowhere. A dead silent plain of echoes and dust and empty arms rocking. Of dead boys shot down over vast, cold oceans. Where people didn't even care enough about you to hate you. Where the people who'd promised to love you forgot your name.

Hell was cold. The coldest place in the universe.

"Frankie?"

"Bless me, Father, for I have sinned," she said.

Because if she hadn't yet, she would.

———⚬∞⚬———

Though I had promised that I would never again sit with the angel in the courtyard, I did, slumping at her feet, Wolf slumped along with me. The angel told me of the ruthless furnace of the world, the endless suffering that was its fuel. She spoke of Hitler's suicide in his underground bunker, how he tested the cyanide on his favorite dog, Blondi, before he and his wife swallowed the capsules themselves, leaving the Allies with only his minions to punish. She told me of the Russian sharpshooter, a woman with hundreds of kills to her name, who shot three drunk American soldiers because they wouldn't stop laughing about all the girls that they had raped, their plans to find more. She told me of Anne Frank and her sister, who died of typhus in Bergen-Belsen just months before it was liberated by British troops. She told me of the most powerful bombs the world had ever seen, the plan to unleash them, the mushroom clouds, the radiation, the unspeakable, unfathomable tragedy of it all.

I had the same questions I always had: Why was I going in circles, what were the magic words, why did the world spasm with such horrific pain, why, why, WHY? She had the same answers. I left in the same fury when Frankie pushed out of the church.

And then Frankie stopped short. Turned, stared up at the window of Sister George's old office. The ghost with the broken face burst from it, fell to the cobbles. Frankie didn't see her, couldn't hear her, but sensed . . . something, someone, writhing on the stones, hair ropy with blood. Frankie bent, squinted, trying to sort the shadows from the light. The ghost peeled herself up from the ground, drifted back from where she came, dispersing through Frankie as she did. Frankie gasped, shuddering with sudden cold.

The ghost floated back to the building, and Frankie followed the trail of her chill, rode along that icy eddy. The ghost slipped through the wall, Frankie sneaked through the door into a silent hallway. No voices, no nuns, no orphans riding a gig. She followed the breeze past door after door until she reached the end of the hallway, the darkened door at the end. The ghost disappeared behind it, but Frankie hesitated. This was the door to the basement, the catacombs, the tunnels beneath the orphanage, where everyone feared to go. The nuns only occasionally locked the door; the stories—and the fear of the strap—kept the children out.

But Frankie was hot, so hot—cracked and raw, determined to turn over every rock, to follow the ghosts of sadness and pain and truth that she had felt at the hospital, that she had felt outside. She gripped the freezing knob, twisted it ever so slowly, pushed it open. It creaked on rusty hinges. Behind the door was a small landing, then a set of stairs that disappeared into the darkness. The ghost girl's chill still lingered, the smell of ash in a spent hearth. Frankie walked slowly down the steps and into the corridor below.

It was dark but not dead, the air electric, like a struck match before the flame. Goose bumps cascaded along Frankie's skin from her fingers to her shoulders, her hair prickled.

"Hello?" she said.

The darkness beckoned, gathering itself, luring her deeper. She found a light switch on the wall and could now see there were doorways here, too, on either side of her. She peered into the small rooms as she went. In each one was a narrow bed and a dresser. She counted twelve rooms before she entered the next, laying a palm on the cool surface of the mattress. But the bed was not an ordinary one. It had stirrups at the foot of it, straps at the top. Confused, Frankie fingered the stirrups, stared at a tiny red stain on the fabric of the bed. She didn't see the ghost in the corner, hair ropy with blood, she didn't hear her plaintive keening. But she had a vision nonetheless, of a girl in the bed, feet in the stirrups, arms pinned, beseeching the nun who was walking away with her baby, "No, please, wait."

The pain of it punched her in the chest, and she closed her eyes against it. Maybe some girls were relieved, maybe some girls hoped the babies would be taken in by loving parents, that this was for the best, that they would all have a better life. But the feeling was the same. No matter what you hoped for, hope could break your heart.

She backed out of the room and out into the hallway, instinctively cradling her arms in the pulsing dark just the way her own mother had back at Dunning. Girls were punished so hard for their love, so hard, hard enough to break them.

Frankie tightened her arms, cradling herself.

But maybe, once upon a time, her mother had loved her that hard too.

She didn't bother with the streetcar. She ran the whole way home, every step a Hail Mary, every breath an Our Father.

MERCY

"WHERE HAVE YOU BEEN?" Toni said when Frankie walked in the door. "Why are you so sweaty?"

Frankie took off her hat. "Where is everybody?"

"They worked me like a dog all day, and then they all went out," Toni said, plopping herself into a kitchen chair. "Dad took Ada to see her mother. Cora and Bernice got all dolled up and went down to the Servicemen's Center. And Dewey . . . well"—Toni hugged herself, her eyes focused on the scratched surface of the table—"I don't know where Dewey is and don't care."

Frankie sat down next to her. "What about Dewey?"

"Don't worry about it."

"Toni, did something happen? Did he do something?"

Toni rubbed her finger against one of the scratches. "I was washing up in the bathroom and he walked in. He said it was an accident."

"It wasn't," Frankie said. "That piece of trash." She jumped out of the chair and stalked around the room, her agitation propelling her from the inside.

"He didn't touch me or anything."

"Goddamn it," Frankie said.

Toni tipped her head and considered her sister. "Did something happen to you?"

"No. I'm fine."

Toni waited for Frankie to say something else. When she didn't, Toni said, "Okay, if that's the way you want it. There's some ham salad in the icebox. It's terrible, you know Ada can't cook worth a darn, but it will fill you up."

Frankie sat back down at the table and pulled off her gloves. "I'm not hungry."

"You're never hungry. You're wasting away to nothing. You're like a little doll."

"I ain't no doll."

"Oooh! Listen to you, 'ain't no doll.'" Toni clapped her hands. "I like it when you talk like that."

"Like what?"

"Like a regular gal. One that don't—excuse me—one that *doesn't* work in an office." She tapped her fingers on the table. "So are you going to tell me what happened to you today, or not?"

Frankie couldn't. She wanted to, but she couldn't. Toni had come to Dunning, but she hadn't had the same reaction, didn't feel the same outrage. Maybe she'd been too young when their mother left. Maybe she was just a different kind of girl. Either way, Frankie didn't know how to explain the feeling she had when she visited the orphanage, the feeling she had when she was down in the catacombs—the sense that she hadn't been alone.

"Nothing happened," Frankie said.

Toni threw up her hands in surrender. "Fine. Don't tell me, I'll tell you. I got a job today."

"Where? Doing what?"

"Checker at the grocery. I start day after next."

"Wow. What made you do that?"

"Are you kidding? I'm tired of hanging around here, taking orders. Dad bosses me around the shoe store, Ada bosses me around here, her stupid kids boss me around, I hate it." The smile dropped off her face. "I don't like it here, Frankie. I thought I would. I thought it would be . . . oh, I don't know what I was thinking. Dumb stuff." She curled her hands into fists. "Guy came by to call and Dad wouldn't even let me see him! He said I'm not old enough. But Dewey . . . if that Dewey gets near me again, breathing on me or trying to touch me, I'll . . . I'll . . . I don't know what I'll do."

"Stab him with a fork?"

"Now there's an idea."

Something burned in Frankie's head, not the rage she'd felt before, but a thought that made her open her eyes so wide she felt the skin around them twitch. She put her palms on the table. "I've got a better idea."

"Oh, yeah? What is it?"

"I'm gonna get us out of here."

—⚬∞⚬—

Every morning for the rest of the summer and into the fall, Frankie got up, she put on a nice dress and shoes, hat and gloves, grabbed her handbag, and walked out the door to catch the streetcar, like she'd been doing since she moved in with her father and Ada. Only she didn't go to Berman's. She went to the coffee shop instead. In the ladies' room, she took off her nice dress and changed into the pink uniform and apron and hustled all day for tips. On weekends, she'd say that she was going out to church or to see Loretta, but instead she'd squeeze in a lunch or dinner shift, when the tips were best. She had to give her father the same amount of money she'd always given him, but now she had money to spare, and she saved every penny. It was her escape money, hers and Toni's.

At first she was so scared all the time that she could hardly breathe. She kept thinking that someone would find her out, that Cora and Bernice's cousin would have to go to talk to Mr. Gilhooly about some such thing and that he'd tell her that Frankie had had too many woman troubles and had to quit. But after a month went by, her father counting out the dollar bills and handing them to Ada the way he always had, and Cora and Bernice making fun of her dresses and how she should really go join the convent if she was going to spend that much time in church, she settled down.

"More coffee, sir?" She held up the pot.

"That's mighty kind of you," said the skinny young man sitting at the counter. He said "mighty" like some kind of southern boy, but Frankie could tell from his accent that he was Chicago born and bred. She topped off his cup and filled up the milk pitcher.

"Do you need anything else?" she asked him.

"A little dog soup would be nice." His eyes were green and twinkly.

She got him a glass of water and put it next to the coffee. "Thank you from the bottom of my heart," he said, holding the glass up before taking a sip. He was just a few years older than Frankie herself. She wondered if he'd been a soldier, if he'd known Sam. That was silly, there were millions of soldiers spread all over the world. Still, she wanted to ask him. She wanted to tell him of a dream she had in which Sam was playing a sad-happy tune on his trumpet, and when she'd asked him in the dream the name of the song, he'd said, "It's called 'The Goodbye Song.' Bye, Frankie. The boys are calling, I've got to go."

But she didn't say any of this. She said, "I haven't seen you here before."

"Nope, you sure haven't," he said. He held out his hand. "The name's Ray. As in ray of sunshine."

That made Frankie laugh. "Well, hello there, Ray of Sunshine."

"You can just call me Sunshine, if you want," he told her. "I'm waiting for you to shake my hand."

"You'll be waiting a long time," she said. She grabbed the coffee pot and made sure all her customers had a full cup. Frankie liked this job. She knew food, she knew hunger. She never had to worry about what to say to this one, or what to say to that one. All she had to say was, "What'll it be?" All she had to do was hold up the coffeepot.

When she made it back behind the counter, Ray of Sunshine was pulling out his wallet so that he could pay his bill. "Well, Miss Frankie," he said, reading the name on her uniform, "I don't suppose a beautiful young lady like yourself is in need of a dance partner."

She could say yes. She was old enough. But her father wouldn't agree. And she couldn't jeopardize her plans. She grabbed a rag and wiped down the salt and pepper shakers. "I'm too young to go out dancing."

He took a step back and clutched at his chest. "Oh, no, go easy on me. I've got a weak heart."

"Well, I won't be too young forever," Frankie said. She would be a woman in no time, a woman who could do what she pleased and work where she pleased and live where she wanted to. "I might just be in the market for a dance partner soon."

He fished around in his front shirt pocket and pulled out a shell, which he laid carefully on the countertop next to the quarter he'd already set there.

"What's that?" she asked, tapping the shell.

"It came all the way from an island they call Okinawa. The only thing I kept from my . . . travels."

"I can't take that from you," Frankie said.

"You can give it back to me when we go out dancing," he said. "I'll be counting the days."

She thought about the money stuffed in her mattress, the ad for a room to let burning a hole in her handbag. "I'll be counting them too."

———◆◆◆———

Frankie got home from her lunch shift, her feet tired, but her cheeks flushed. As soon as she opened the kitchen door, Ada barked, "I thought you were going to be home hours ago. Your father needs help in the shop."

"Why doesn't Dewey help him?"

Ada's eyes flashed. "I asked *you* to do it."

In the shop, her father was kneeling on the floor sliding a shoe onto the foot of a handsome woman with red lipstick on her lips and dark circles under her eyes. Frankie's father said nothing to Frankie, only indicated a broom in the corner with the slightest jerk of his head. Then he turned back to his customer.

"You like?" he said.

The woman stood up, walked the length of the store in the sleek black leather shoes. "Yes. These will do very nicely."

She sat, and Frankie's father removed the shoes. She slid into brown shoes that matched her suit and came up to the counter to pay. Frankie was sweeping behind the counter when the woman signed her bill. Frankie noticed the bracelet of faint purple bruises around one delicate wrist. I noticed her name.

Mrs. Charles Kent.

———◆◆◆———

The Kents lived in a sprawling mansion on the far north side of the city, miles from the house in which I had first laid eyes on him. In the cavernous foyer, Mrs. Charles Kent handed her parcels and her hat to the maid, asked for a cup of tea in the parlor. The maid told her that Mr. Kent was upstairs, but that he expected dinner promptly at six p.m. Mrs. Kent nodded, did not remind her maid that Mr. Kent always expected dinner promptly at six p.m., did not tell her maid what other kinds of things Mr. Kent expected. Perhaps the maid, like the rest of us, already understood his expectations.

Mrs. Kent repaired to the parlor while Wolf and I stole up the stairs. Charles Kent had his own suite of rooms that faced the back of the property, a bedroom and a sitting room both painted in hunter green, both with enormous windows that looked out on sweeping lawns and great shaggy oaks. An enormous portrait of Charles Kent with two hounds hung over the bed, the head of a deer glared at me from the wall in the sitting room, an enormous taxidermied bear lurked in the corner. Hello, deer, hello, bear, I said. There were no pictures of Mrs. Kent anywhere.

I found him in the bath, languishing in bubbles and steam. The skin around his watery eyes was creased, his dark blond hair streaked with gray. But he wore that hair in the same style he always had, slicked straight back. His downturned pouting mouth had the same too-pink cast, as if his lips were chafed, or stained. And his body was soft and grub white, little bits floating like sea creatures.

Mrs. Kent wouldn't miss him.

I sprang at him like the wild thing I was, and pushed his head down into the water. He thrashed and kicked at my not-hands, yanked at my not-arms, his nose and lungs stinging, filling. But as he bucked and gurgled, I felt the pressure in my own nose, my own lungs, the shuddering of my own death. The flu had drowned me too, asphyxiated me with my own toxic fluids, my own blood, and his drowning echoed my drowning. Gasping and coughing, I fought to keep hold of him, fought to punish him, make him pay like I had paid. But my hands on Charles's throat didn't look like my hands and the water didn't look like bathwater. I felt as if I were dispersing, dissolving, little shards of myself wafting away, then coming back to me in the right order.

The flu, the sickness, had come *before* Benno, *before* Mercy, *before*, not after, and I . . . I . . .

I had survived it? I had survived it.

What killed me? *Who* killed me? My fingers tightened around Charles Kent's throat. Was it you?

Charles Kent splashed and kicked the memories back to me, almost knocking me off my not-feet. After Benno was sent away, after Mercy was stolen, after Dunning, my family brought me home. The weeks of drugs had made my head lurch, had thinned the skin of the world so I could see beyond it. Wolves in the woods, mermaids in the water, ghosts everywhere. I saw my long-dead grandmother standing at the foot of my bed in the middle of the night, scolding me in her British accent. In the yard, in the middle of the day, I saw men wearing outfits of fur and skin who babbled at me in French. A little girl, no more than six, liked to ride with me in the back of our auto, giggling when we took sharp turns and slid across the leather seats, and when she slid through me. When I giggled along with her, when I pointed out my grandmother or the mermaids, my father's frown got that much deeper, my mother's sutures pulled that much tighter.

In moments of clarity, I tried to explain: "I loved him." Or, "Her name is Mercy." Or, "Charles tried to hurt me." Or, "Am I dead? When did that happen?"

Still, I ran in the woods, I swam in the lake, I came home disheveled and damp. The last time, during a party at our house, I slipped away and went to the water, not even bothering to take off the dress and shoes my parents had bought on credit. The water was freezing, cold enough to clear my head some, cold enough to slow my blood. When I couldn't feel my limbs, I crawled to shore to find William waiting for me in the sand.

"What in the bloody hell are you doing, Pearl?" he bellowed. "Haven't you done enough?"

Frederick swayed behind him, a bottle in his hand. "Shhh, Willy. Someone will hear you."

"I asked you a question, Pearl. Haven't you done enough?"

"His name wasn't really Benno," I said. "He wouldn't tell me what it was because he was afraid it would sound ugly coming out of my mouth."

William kicked me over to my side, as if he were trying to flip a bug. "You *are* ugly. You're disgusting." He stared down at me, his teeth bared like no animal I'd ever seen. "I can hardly stand to look at you."

"You didn't have to hit him like that. You hurt him."

He kicked me again. "Shut up. We could have killed him and no one would have blamed us."

"I would have. I do."

"You're a whore. A crazy whore."

"And you're cruel. Stupid and cruel. I'd rather be a whore."

"You're not even good for that," he said.

I made an angel in the sand. "You're just proving my point."

"Don't make it worse, Pearl," Frederick slurred, staggered. "Father had to pay so Charles's family wouldn't sue us."

"He hurt me! He sent me to that place!"

"Father's investors walked away. No one else will come near us. We're already ruined because of you, do you understand? Do you want us to lose everything?"

"Maybe you ruined yourselves. Maybe we all do that."

Frederick threw the bottle at me, but missed. William kicked me, and didn't.

"You never think of anyone but yourself. You never *think*. We should send you back to Dunning."

"They were a lot nicer there," I said, clutching my ribs. "They smelled better, too."

"Jesus, Pearl," said Frederick.

"I can't see him. But I can see the mermaids now."

"Shut up about the mermaids!" said William. "Do you hear yourself?"

"Why don't you try, William? Look!" I pointed at the water. "They're right there. And there. And there."

William's hands flew to his hair, grabbed handfuls on each

side. *"Will you shut up?"*

"No, I won't," I sang. "And you can't make me."

Once upon a time, a girl got in trouble and then went on to make some more. One brother was too drunk to punish her, but the other brother was willing.

William took hold of one arm and dragged me back toward the water. I fought with everything I had, but in the end, what did I have left to give?

At least the mermaids were there to keep me company.

I had mercy, I let Charles go. He fell from the tub, vomited on the tile, looked up. Just for a moment, in the slanting blue light of the late afternoon, he saw my face, and screamed.

That would do.

For now.

NO MEMORIES BUT ONE

WHAT I KNEW ABOUT MY mother: Her skin was creamy white. She had perfect posture. Her hair had gone silver by the time she was twenty-five. When she was angry, her lips pulled tight like a row of sutures. Her most prized possession: the set of pearl and diamond wedding rings she wore on her left hand.

William had those rings now, tucked in the same box where he'd kept his French postcards. He was easy enough to find, so easy that it was a marvel that I'd never bothered to look. He and Frederick lived in the same house where we'd grown up. They'd inherited it after my parents died in an automobile wreck in 1937. My brothers were lucky that there was something left to inherit besides the wrecked automobile. The family had lost everything else in the stock market crash of '29.

Not that the house was much to be proud of. The brick was dull and dusty, mortar falling in gray fingers to the dirt. The shrubs and lawns were patchy and piebald and brown, the woods behind razed and sold off in lots. Other families had built their homes there and blocked the view. When William stood to look out the window of the grand parlor, he saw into the dining room of the house next door, another family laughing over dinner.

William and Frederick didn't laugh much. I sat with my brothers around the fireplace while Wolf sniffed at the stained rugs, the chipped furniture. William was fuming, Frederick was drunk; it seemed to be a common state of affairs. I remembered them so well when they were young, William of the thick glasses and thicker head, Frederick of the quick smile and quicker fists.

William still had the thick head, Frederick the quick fists. They used them on each other.

"They're the only things we have left," Frederick was saying, or trying to say, through a wine-thickened tongue.

"I'm not selling them. We'll sell something else."

"Maybe I could sell you, if you were good for anything," said Frederick.

"I need them. They're for my future wife," William said.

Frederick slapped his knee. "What future wife? No woman in her right mind would ever marry you. You repel them all like you always have."

"And no woman would ever *stay* with you," William said. "Where's your wife now? Where's your son? How long has it been since you've seen them?"

"Oh, go slobber over your postcards, you pathetic piece of—"

William pushed Frederick out of his chair; Frederick sprang up and punched William out of his shoes. The two of them rolled across the carpet like children, flailing flailing flailing.

The house was mortgaged to the hilt. When they died here, and they would, the house would be turned over to a bank and then to a builder, and the builder would knock it down, as if it had never been. As if they hadn't.

The area children called William and Frederick "the uncles." They said it in hushed tones, as if they were telling a ghost story.

We are all our own devils, and we make this world our hell. Oscar Wilde had said that.

I'd come back to punish them, but it seemed that someone already had.

—————⊶∞⊷—————

Still.

I took the rings. I left the postcards burning in a trash bin by the window. Maybe the curtains would catch. Maybe they wouldn't.

—————⊶∞⊷—————

I left the house behind and went to the lake, settled myself in a snowbank, Wolf at my feet. The mermaids bobbed in the distance. The sun was high and strong. When the birds cried overhead, I said Hello, I love you, hello, I miss you. You never know what shape an angel might take, and Marguerite would hear me.

But it didn't take long for him to appear, swinging his cane this way and that. When he reached me, he stopped short.

You're the whitest girl I've ever seen, he said.

I know.

You're so white you're almost blue.

You can call me Blue Girl, if you want.

He tapped the handle of the blade sticking out of his neck. That would be like you calling me Knife Man. But this is not all I am.

I thought about that. How I'd assumed he was a ghost like any ghost, no memories but one. How I'd assumed that I was so special, when I'd been playing my own death over and over just like everyone else. When I had hidden myself from myself because it hurt too much.

I thought he was a character in my story, but maybe I was a character in his.

You're right, I said. What shall I call you then?

The name's Horace Bordeaux, like a fine wine.

Only better, I said.

Now you've got it.

You can call me Pearl.

Well, Pearl. I was about to take myself out to dinner. Are you and your little friend hungry?

As it turned out, we were.

⌒⌒⌒⌒

Horace took me and Wolf to a Chinese restaurant all the way downtown, maybe the first one in Chicago. When we walked in the door, a man whose black hair was shot with silver glanced up from his work at the counter in the back. Even with the silver

348

threads in his hair, the lines etched on his face, even though he was a stranger now, I knew who it was. I knew.

Once upon a time, a boy chased a girl through the woods to their joy and their ruin. But the boy lived to be a man, lived to marry a lovely woman with strong hands and a delicate face. He had three more children with her, and they were lovely too. It was its own kind of fairy tale, its own kind of prayer.

Upstairs, in the bathroom of the restaurant, I turned on the hot water. In the fog on the mirror, I drew a picture of Mercy.

Then I sat with Horace over dinner. He asked me to tell him about myself.

I said: I was the wolf. And you?

He said: Let me tell you a story.

We spoke perfect Chinese. The food was hot and spicy and lit us up from the inside.

We ate our fill.

WITNESS

MUCH LATER, I WATCHED MERCY and her boxer man while they slept. I am here, I am here for you, I told her. One day she would wake up, one day she would see me, one day she would forgive me, one day I would forgive myself. And maybe, one day, she would see herself, know herself. I had transgressed, but she wasn't a transgression. She was everything good and beautiful in the world.

In the meantime, I slipped the pearl and diamond rings on her hand.

She could always sell them.

DOORWAYS

AS FOR FRANKIE, SHE TOO had already flown away.

Well, in her head she had.

In reality, she was still lying on the couch in her father's cramped apartment in the dark, waiting for Toni to creep out to the living room. She had her bag packed and tucked under Toni's bed; all Toni had to do was grab it along with her own. Every cent Frankie had saved was crammed in an old purse she hugged against her chest.

Also crammed into the purse: a pad of paper, her pastels, and two more letters.

Dear Frankie,

By the time you get this, I will probably be halfway across the ocean. I've left the orphanage. Sister Bert arranged for me to get my diploma a little early, just like she did for you. I just couldn't stand it there a minute longer, not one minute. Without you, and without Beatriz. Yes, the nurse's aide from the orphanage.

You asked me once if I always confessed everything to Father Paul. I'm confessing to you instead. I'm going to be with her. I don't care if we have to live in a pile of bomb-ridden rubble and eat dirt for breakfast for the next fifty years.

I know how much you loved Sam, how much you risked for him. That's how much I love her. I'm not going to ask for your forgiveness, because you only ask for that if you think you're doing something wrong. I don't care what anyone says, this isn't wrong. But I do hope you understand.

I know you didn't have much time with Sam. And it isn't fair. But that doesn't mean it was any less real. That's something to hold on to, so hold on to it.

I board the boat in a half an hour, so I have to go. I'll send my new address to Sister Bert, so you'll always know where to find me.

One more thing: be happy, Frankie, as happy as you can. And if you can't be happy, just live as much as you can. Be like Francie in A Tree Grows in Brooklyn, *be something every minute of every day, be sad, be cold, be warm, be hungry, be full, be ragged or well dressed, be truthful, be a liar and a sinner, only be something every blessed minute. Make art, make the most beautiful art you can, draw everything you see, everything you feel. And when you sleep, dream all the time so that not one little piece of living is lost.*

That's what I'm going to do.

Love,
Loretta

And:

Dear Frankie,

I didn't know about Mom. I swear to God, I didn't know.
You and Toni are my family.
You.

Vito

So many people were gone now—Sam, Loretta, even her own parents, in a way. Every little decision you made, every person you met could change your life, set it on a different course, or end it. At the diner, Ray of Sunshine told Frankie about the day he'd lined up at the recruitment office. Officers were counting off the boys one, two, three, four, and then circling back to one again. Ray realized that the numbers were for each branch of the military: army, navy, air force, marines. When he counted the boys on his own line for himself, he saw they'd mark him for the navy. He asked the boy in front of him to switch places so he could chat with another boy. "No way I was going to die on a boat, no way I was going to drown," Ray said.

"You didn't die at all," Frankie said, pouring him a fresh cup of coffee. "And you're here now."

He winked at her over the brimming cup. "So I got lucky twice."

I'd gotten lucky too, if that was the word for it. If I hadn't been watching Frankie at the orphanage, if I hadn't followed her for so long, maybe I would never have met Marguerite, maybe I never would have remembered myself, come back to myself, rewritten my own story. The door to heaven didn't open up for me, but not everyone was that kind of angel.

Some had wings, others had claws.

Now Frankie held the purse tighter. The old clock on the table ticked off the minutes, a countdown to midnight. The sky through the tiny windows seemed so black, blacker than black, like a great black hole, and she didn't know how she'd fling herself into it, set herself on a different course, make herself disappear.

Instead, she fell asleep.

Soldiers fell asleep with their stomachs rumbling, with the sound of guns booming, why not Frankie on the night of her greatest escape? Toni too had drooped on her lumpy mattress, one hand around the handle of a suitcase, in the other a bouquet of white underthings. I tried to wake her, but Toni had never been one to hear me.

I'd read all kinds of stories by then, I knew how this would end. Their father would find them draped across their own luggage, he would find the money in Frankie's purse. He would put on the biggest show he could—cops and sirens, orphanages and asylums, towers and keys. Such things would make him feel real. Such things turned a shoemaker into a movie star, some kind of king.

He'd keep the money.

The door to the apartment rattled. "Damn hot," Dewey said, almost tumbling into one of the armchairs when he tried to take off his jacket. Change dropped out of the pockets and rolled across the floor. He swore again, and dropped to his knees to find it. Feeling along the ground with his hands, he crawled over to the couch.

I let go of myself, unraveling, spiraling out. Wake up, I said in Frankie's ear as loud as I could. He's coming.

Frankie scrabbled backward, rubbed the side of her face, her arms where my tendrils had chilled her. But she could also smell the whiskey or whatever bootleg swill Dewey drank mixed with his terrible Dewey stink. She fished under the pillow for the fork Loretta had given her so long ago.

His hand went up her leg. "Hey! Look what I found." He grabbed the handle of her purse, yanked it.

She plunged the fork into the meat of his arm. Dewey howled. Wolf howled back.

"What the hell was that? What the hell?" Dewey said, clutching his bloody forearm.

Frankie didn't know if he was talking about his wounded arm or the howling of the wolf—a wolf?—but she didn't wait to find out. She ran for her sister's room, slapped Toni awake. She grabbed their bags and hauled Toni back into the living room, slamming right into her father.

"What are you doing?" he said. "It's the middle of the night!"

Ada stepped into the room, Bernice and Cora piling up behind her. Ada's face blanched when she saw Dewey's bloody arm. "Oh my lord, what happened!"

"She stabbed me!" Dewey yelled, pointing at Frankie. "She's crazy!"

"You grabbed me!" Frankie shot back.

"What is this?" Frankie's father said, snatching Toni's suitcase out of her hand. "Where you think you go?"

"Away from here," said Frankie.

"You stabbed him," Ada shrieked. "You stabbed my son!"

Bernice wrapped a towel around Dewey's arm. "Maybe she should go to the nuthouse with her mother."

For a moment Frankie was so angry she stopped breathing. To the others, it looked as if she was frozen solid, still and unmoving as a statue. But they couldn't see the sparks coming off her, the tendrils of herself, spiraling out. Not golden like Marguerite's, not silver like mine, but coppery red, living and pulsing. The ribbons of her spirit entangled with my ribbons, teasing and braiding. I felt a jolt, a blast of heat. Everyone in the room stared—as if I were there, real and solid as anyone.

"Who the hell is *that*?" said Bernice. "*What* the hell is that?"

"Get out of my house!" Ada shrieked.

I felt heavy and light at the same time, the air weighing upon my skin that was suddenly, briefly, skin, the breath that filled my lungs, the blood that sped through my veins, the breath that whistled through my teeth. Every nerve that was now a nerve twitched, every cell throbbed in gratitude.

"Who are you?" Frankie whispered.

"Sono qui. Io sono qui per te," I said, my own voice vibrating in my own throat, humming in my own ears. "I am here, I am here for you."

I didn't know which of us did it, or maybe Frankie and I did it together. The couch flipped over. The coffee tables spun and crashed into the wall. Dishes flew from the cabinets in the kitchen, soaring through the apartment like warplanes. Glasses smashed. The bulbs in the lamps whined, illuminating the whole room and the people who cowered there, arms over their heads, in a white-hot light. Then the bulbs burst, plunging the room once again into darkness.

Then all was quiet.

The twitching of my nerves faded, my breath leaked away. I cried not-tears as my brief life ebbed. Wolf sniffed at my not-fingers, the ribbons of dimming silvery light.

"Hello?" Frankie said. She blinked at the space where I had been, blinked at the returning shadows, stunned for just a moment.

"What is going on?" Dewey moaned.

Cora pasted herself to the back wall. "Stay away!"

"I call the police," said Frankie's father.

Frankie remembered them, her not-family, remembered herself. She swiped at her tears, squared her shoulders. She turned toward the door. If she put her nose against it, she would have smelled the pencil smell of the wood, and the other smells that had sunk into it—leather, garlic, salt, blood. All the things she hoped for could be on the other side of it. Vito could be there, walking tall, and Loretta too, her nose in a book, her hand in Beatriz's. Nancy and Harvey laughing together, maybe even Ray of Sunshine with his twinkly eyes. There could be a room with two beds and two dressers and a window that opened to the street, a hot plate for soup that a person could eat at night, every night, so she never went to bed hungry.

But pain could be on the other side, too. Failure. Ruin. She couldn't be sure what was waiting behind it, wing or tooth or claw.

But she was sure of one thing: she was going to live. She was going to live.

Frankie grabbed their bags and her sister's hand. She opened the door. We raced into the night, Frankie, Toni, and me, the fox loping after—all of us wolves, all of us angels.

AUTHOR'S NOTE

My late mother-in-law, Frances Ponzo Metro, was many things: a self-taught pianist, a painter, a cook, a waitress, a cardsharp. But like the best poker players, she kept her cards close to the vest. I remember chatting over dinner at one of our early meetings, when she suddenly said something like "At the orphanage, we would sneak into the kitchens when the nuns weren't looking, steal an egg, and suck out the insides." I said, "Orphanage? Nuns? Eggs? What?" And she said, "Want another meatball?"

I had to ask an awful lot of questions to find out about the years she had spent at Angel Guardian, a German Catholic orphanage in Chicago, during the Depression and World War II. The stories emerged out of order, little snippets here and there, about how her father took her and her brother and sister to the orphanage after the death of their mother, about the abuse some of the orphans endured, about the fact that her father soon took her brother and the children of his second wife out of the orphanage but left Fran and her sister there till Fran was seventeen.

Fran endured my endless questions about her early life with bemused good cheer and characteristic generosity. She didn't understand why I was so fascinated by her upbringing—"What's the big deal?" she wanted to know. But when I told her I wished to write a novel based on her teen years, she did the best she could to help me. She didn't consider her own story to be worth much, but if I wanted to write about it, well, then, that was okay with her. "Ask whatever you want," she'd say while beating me at rummy.

Writing a historical novel obviously means tons of research. So I read everything from books about World Wars I and II to transcripts of interviews with young women who worked in the meat-packing districts of Chicago during the '30s. I pored over family photographs, as well as photos and videos of other children at the Angel Guardian Orphanage available in library archives and on the web. And I combed through numerous folk and fairy tales, including those gathered and/or retold by Zora Neale Hurston, Julius Lester, Virginia Hamilton, John Steptoe, Ashley Bryan, and the Grimms, among many others.

But because I was primarily interested in the stories that families tell themselves *about* themselves, my main source of information was always Fran, along with her brother, Vito; sister, Toni; and friend and fellow orphan, Loretta. I relied heavily on their recollections of the meals, jobs, church services, nuns, celebrations, school, family visits, and general day-to-day life at a Catholic orphanage in the 1930s and '40s, as well as the city of Chicago itself. As you'd expect, some of their recollections conflicted, especially as it concerned Fran's family, so I did my best to weave these recollections into a coherent narrative.

Some personal stories—likely apocryphal—didn't make it into the book, such as rumors that Fran's father was being chased by the Italian mob or that Fran's stepmother and stepsiblings were wanted by the feds (!!!). No one ever implied that the nuns at the orphanage took babies from young mothers and offered them for adoption, but since that has happened elsewhere, I admit I took quite a few liberties (and added a whole battalion of ghosts, something that delighted Fran when I told her that I was going to do it).

And then I wrote. And wrote. And wrote.

For more than ten years, I worked on this story, but I kept getting it wrong.

I couldn't get it right until I realized that the orphanage, though a difficult place to grow up, was also a safe place in many ways. That the most painful betrayals were not those committed by nuns or priests, but rather the family that was supposed to cherish and protect you. That making your way in a world that thinks so little of you takes a particular kind of courage, a kind not always obvious from the outside.

This is a story about Fran's teen years. But it is also a story about girls. Girls with ambitions, brains, desires, talents, hungers. It is a story about how the world likes to punish girls for their appetites, even for their love.

Fran read and approved an earlier version of this novel, and I kept her up-to-date on my progress until her death last year. My only regret is that she never got a chance to hold the book in her hands.

Every word is fiction. And every word is true.
I hope it honors her the way the way she deserves.

Laura Ruby
2019

ACKNOWLEDGMENTS

Thirteen Doorways is about many things, the nature of memory among them. Since I first conceived of this story back in 2002, it's difficult to remember every angel who helped and challenged me along the way. But I owe it to all of them to try.

Thanks to my brilliant agent, Tina Dubois, and my equally brilliant editor, Jordan Brown, for their continued faith in me, and their endless patience with me. Thanks also to everyone at Balzer + Bray and HarperCollins, including Alessandra Balzer, Donna Bray, Tiara Kittrell, Patty Rosati, Nellie Kurtzman, Bess Braswell, Michael D'Angelo, Olivia Russo, Andrea Pappenheimer, Kerry Moynagh, Kathy Faber, Jen Wygand, Heather Doss, Jenny Sheridan, Allison Brown, Josh Weiss, Mark Rifkin, and Renée Cafiero. And thanks to Alison Donalty, Molly Fehr, and artist Sean Freeman for the moody and mysterious cover art.

Thanks to my dear friend Gretchen Moran Laskas, who read one of the earliest iterations of the book and, in the kindest and most generous way possible, told me not to show it to anyone else before I figured out what the heck I was doing (and then helped me figure out what the heck I was doing). Thanks also to Gina Frangello, Cecelia Downs, Zoe Zolbrod, and Karen Halvorsen Schreck, who wrestled with various (dreadful) drafts of the novel. Thanks to Miriam Busch, Christine Heppermann, Annika Cioffi, Linda Rasmussen, Tracey George, Esther Hershenhorn, Esmé Raji Codell, Franny Billingsley, Myra Sanderman, Carolyn Crimi, Brenda Ferber, Jenny Meyerhoff, Sarah Aronson, Katie Davis, Tanya Lee Stone, Melissa Ruby, Joan Ruby, Richard and JoAnn Ruby, Melissa Metro, Jessica Metro, Joe Metro, Tony DeYoung, Greg Metro and family, and all the various Ponzos, who patiently listened to me talk and talk and talk about this story over the years (and probably assumed that I would never, ever finish).

Eternal gratitude to my friends and colleagues at Hamline University's MFAC program, the fabulous ladies of the LSG, Harpies, and the Shade for their endless support. I love you all. Special thanks to Swati Avasthi, Tessa Gratton, Heidi Heilig, Justina Ireland, Kelly Barnhill, Laurel Snyder, Kate Messner, and Martha Brockenbrough for their thoughtful reads of later drafts. And thanks to Olugbemisola Rhuday-Perkovich and Tracey Baptiste for the discussions and for pointing me in the right direction with regard to folk tales. Thanks to the wonderful people at the Butler Center at Dominican University for letting me spend some lovely days sifting through their special collections, including their folk and fairy tale reference collection, as well as their Effie Lee Morris Collection of African American–focused books. And thanks to Renée Cafiero and Nita Tyndall for translating the German (and to NT for the joke about squirrels=oak croissants), and to Claudio Bertelli and Max Cantarelli for translating the Italian. Any errors of fact or representation are mine.

Of course, this book would not exist at all if it weren't for my late mother-in-law, Frances Ponzo Metro, who graciously allowed me to write about her life, particularly her experiences as a teenager growing up in an orphanage during the Depression and World War II. Though many names and dates are changed to suit the narrative or to preserve privacy, the main trajectory of Fran's early life is reflected in Frankie's story.

My friend Claire Rudolf Murphy has said that a single book has several story arcs, including the arc of the book itself, the arc of the author's life during the writing of the book, and the arc of the world during the writing of that book. When I began this project long ago, I didn't know I'd be writing through my own bout with cancer, my father's struggle with dementia and his eventual death, and then Fran's death. And I never could have imagined that I would be working on this book during a time of rising attacks on immigrants and the poor in our country, as well as a horrifying resurgence of anti-Semitism around the globe. All of this informed my thoughts about memory and legacy, American dreams and American nightmares, whiteness and darkness, war and resistance, justice and love. So I must thank two people who have been with me through all this reckoning: Anne Ursu, for everything she is and everything she does, and Stephen Metro, who inherited his mother's eyes, her spirit, and her heart.

Everyone knows
Bone Gap is full of gaps . . .

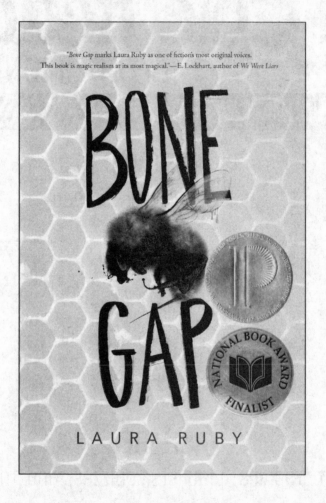

Read Laura Ruby's Printz Award–winning novel.

An Imprint of HarperCollins*Publishers*

epicreads.com